WE'LL ALWAYS HAVE MURDER

WE'LL ALWAYS HAVE MURDER

A HUMPHREY BOGART MYSTERY

BILL CRIDER

new york
www.ibooks.net

DISTRIBUTED BY SIMON & SCHUSTER, INC.

CHAPTER

1

J ack Warner's plan had been to make Buck Sterling (real name, Seymour Grape) the new Gary Cooper. Buck had the look of a westerner, even though he'd been born in Pittsburgh and lived there most of his life, but when he made his first oater, a little problem cropped up: Buck developed an unfortunate interest in horses, especially palominos. Maybe it was that golden color, or maybe it wasn't. Whatever it was, the attraction was real.

It's dandy, of course, for a cowboy to love his horse, but he shouldn't carry it to the lengths that Buck did. There was just something about a palomino he couldn't resist, and it wouldn't do for the public to find out the whole sordid tale.

"And God help us if the son of a bitch ever gets near a big star like Trigger," Jack Warner told me. "Roy Rogers will gun him down."

"I think Trigger's a male," I said.

"What difference does that make? You'll have to do something about Sterling, Scott, and do it quick."

Terry Scott, that's me, and my job when I'm working for Warner is to make sure that the studio's dirty little secrets, of which there are plenty, remain secret. Which explains why I went to Arizona and fetched Buck from the Cactus Valley Dude Ranch where he'd gone for what he told Mr. Warner was "a little vacation." The ranch owner had cabled Mr. Warner that Buck was making a nuisance of himself in the stables.

There was a little trouble when I got to the dude ranch, as there often is when I try to interfere with the course of true love, but it wasn't too bad. I got out of it with nothing more than a set of scraped knuckles. Buck, on the other hand, got his nose rearranged in such a way that gave his face a bit of character that had been lacking before, not that he thanked me for it.

I managed to settle up with the owner of the Cactus Valley and with his foreman. They were the only two people who'd found out about Buck's unsettling tendencies, and I got Buck back to the studio without a single reporter finding out. I left him to Mr. Warner, but I had a feeling that Buck had made his last western, though probably not his last picture. After all, *Song of the Cimarron* had made a couple million bucks, and that was the kind of thing that warmed the cockles of Mr. Warner's heart. That's assuming he had cockles. And assuming he had a heart. At any rate, the studio would find something for Buck to do. Maybe they'd put him in one of those gangster movies that Warner Brothers did so well. There wasn't much danger of Buck falling for a Chevrolet. If they decided not to fix his nose, Buck could easily play a tough guy.

After I left the studio, I went to my office to make out the bill for services rendered, plus expenses. Mr. Warner pays me fairly well for the little jobs I do for him. At least he pays me more than the forty bucks a day I get from my other clients. That doesn't mean I have an office in Beverly Hills, though. It's in L.A., and not the best part of town at that.

The studio has its own security force to handle its ordinary problems with the law, naturally, but some problems require more finesse and intelligence than the ordinary studio cop can muster. That's why Mr. Warner keeps me on retainer. I'm no Einstein for brains or Cary Grant for suave, but I'm willing to go to Arizona at a moment's notice, and I have a talent for keeping my mouth shut. Louella has never been able to claim me for a source. Hedda thinks I'm a granite statue. You'll never hear about me on the Jimmy Fiddler show. The silents may be dead, but in some cases silence is still golden in Hollywoodland.

I brushed some of the dust off my desk, went through the mail that had accumulated in the floor beneath the door slot, and sat back to wait for the phone to ring. I knew it would, sooner or later. There's always work for a private investigator in California: a missing daughter, a cheating husband, a thieving employee. I take whatever comes along. A guy has to make a living, after all.

CHAPTER
2

I was dreaming about something that involved me, Rita Hayworth, and a tube of Burma-Shave when the ringing phone jarred me awake. I'd fallen asleep tipped back in the desk chair, and I nearly toppled over before I fumbled the phone off the hook. I have no idea exactly what was going on in the dream, which was too bad. You can never recapture a moment like that.

"Scott Detective Agency," I said muzzily into the phone. "We never sleep."

"Have you been drinking, Scott?" Mr. Warner asked.

My tongue felt as if it had been dipped in a hotel ashtray. I said, "No, sir. I don't drink."

Which was more or less the truth.

"I'll have to take your word for it," Warner said. "I need you at the studio."

I took a bleary look at my wristwatch. It was five-thirty, which meant that I'd been asleep for quite a while and that Mr. Warner was working very late. And that there was obviously some kind of emergency that needed my unique talents, such as they were.

"I'll be right there," I said.

I could hear Mr. Warner hang up as soon as the words were out of my mouth. He wasn't one for wasting time, yours or his. I rubbed my eyes, thinking that the trip to Arizona had taken more out of me than I thought. Or maybe Rita Hayworth had.

I left the chair, closed the office, and went down to my pre-War Chevrolet, the 1940 model, which was all I could afford when I got discharged. It was still running like a sewing machine, though not getting quite the mileage that a well tuned Singer would.

It was a warm day, and the late-afternoon sky was full of exhaust fumes and a smoke-colored haze. I turned the wing-vents in to let a little of the hot, hazy air blow into the car, sneezing a couple of times as it tickled my nose.

All around me were cars full of men going home to kick off their shoes, have a drink, and read the paper or listen to *One Man's Family*. The war was over, and life was good. They'd managed to find housing, and there was no more gas rationing. Their wives would have cooked them a nourishing meal with real butter, also no longer rationed. Their kids would show them report cards with all A's on them.

The burger joints weren't busy yet, but before long the neon lights would come on, the jalopies would pull in, and the bobbysoxers would be there with their fellas, drinking malts and eating french fries.

Meanwhile I was on my way to hear some sordid story about the asinine antics of some moronic movie star and figure out how to keep everything on the q.t. Well, it was a living.

In any other city in the world, the huge soundstages of the Warner Brothers Studio would make it look like part of the warehouse district. Judging from the outside, it's hard to believe that dreams are being captured on film in those buildings.

I drove up to the main gate and the man on duty waved me on through. I don't have a pass stuck on the windshield, but all the gatekeepers know me on sight. Maybe it's just the car they recognize. At any rate, I never have any trouble getting in.

Security is a little tighter in the executive building, but I knew the studio cop on duty at the desk.

"Hey, Joe," I said. "I'm here to see Mr. Warner."

Joe had been a stuntman in the silent days, and he still had the limp to prove it. He gave me a tired smile and said, "He told me, Scotty. Go ahead."

Mr. Warner's secretary wasn't in the outer office, so I went on past her desk and tapped on the Big Guy's door. A muffled voice told me to come in.

I opened the door and stepped inside. Far away on the opposite side of the room, Mr. Warner sat at his desk, on which a skilled pilot could probably have landed a P-38. Take-off might have been a little tricky, though.

Mr. Warner was a dapper guy, slim, trim, and tanned. Since he was around the studio so much, I don't know when he got out in the sun. He was always so well dressed that you wondered if he had a tailor stationed in the next room.

Sitting beside the desk in one of the big brown leather visitors' chairs was a man smoking a cigarette. He looked vaguely familiar, but he was so far away that I needed to get closer to see who he was.

I stuck my hat on the rack by the door and trekked across a carpet so thick that it was almost like walking in deep sand. Rumor had it that one contract player who'd been called to a meeting with Mr. Warner sank down into the carpet about halfway to the desk and was never seen again.

I arrived at one of the big chairs only slightly weak in the knees and saw that the man sitting in the other one was Humphrey Bogart. That was odd, since of all the Warner Brothers crew, he was one actor I'd never been called about.

It wasn't that he led an especially quiet life. In fact, when he was married to Mayo Methot, he was in more fights than Dempsey in his prime. Sluggy, as Bogart called Mayo—and with good reason—won her share of fights, according to all reports. Once she even stabbed him. All in good fun, of course.

Normally that kind of behavior was frowned on by the studios, but the Battling Bogarts could get away with it. For whatever reason, maybe because they never tried to cover things up or maybe because they just didn't give a damn, they didn't attract the disapproval of the gossip columnists or the public. That marriage hadn't lasted, and now he was married to Betty Bacall, living the quiet life.

Warner didn't bother to stand up when I reached his desk. He said, "Have you met Humphrey Bogart?"

I said that I hadn't. Bogart did stand. He stuck his cigarette in his mouth, squinting as the smoke curled up into his face, and offered me his hand. I shook it and said, "Terry Scott. Pleased to meet you."

7

"Charmed, I'm sure," Bogart said without removing the cigarette and with only a hint of the sarcasm for which he was famous. He had the almost-but-not-quite lisp that his fans loved, caused, I supposed by the fact that when he spoke his upper lip hardly moved. It had been frozen by the injury that caused the small scar visible on it.

He was about the same height I am, which is to say of noble stature, at least in Hollywood, where five-feet, seven inches passes for tall. He was thin, almost frail-looking, but when he spoke, his voice was so commanding that he seemed bigger and tougher. He wasn't wearing his hairpiece. That was a little surprising since most actors I'd become acquainted with never took theirs off. I think they even slept in them.

He had luggage under his eyes and looked as if he needed a shave, but there was nothing new in that. He appeared that way sometimes in the movies, too. He was wearing a dark suit and tie that looked like what he'd worn in *The Big Sleep*, right down to the white pocket hanky. Since actors (though not actresses) had to provide their own wardrobes, it might well have been the same clothing. On the third finger of his right hand he wore a gold ring set with a large ruby. He was about twenty years older than I am, forty-seven or -eight, and he looked it. I liked to think I wouldn't show my age when I got that old, assuming that I would, but I knew I was only kidding myself.

We sat down and Bogart picked up an ashtray from the floor by his chair and tapped his cigarette on the edge.

I looked away from him to Mr. Warner and said, "What's the problem?"

"It's blackmail, Scott."

Well, now I knew why I'd been called.

B lackmail isn't uncommon in Hollywood. If someone found out about Buck Sterling, for example, he'd be a prime target. That's why the studios had guys like me.

"Who's involved?" I asked.

Mr. Warner steepled his fingers. "Do you know Frank Burleson?"

"Sure, I know Frank." I didn't add that he was a louse, though that would have been true. "He works for Superior."

Superior was an up-and-coming studio that had produced a number of moneymaking movies in the last couple of years. Their secret was to find a picture that was a hit and make one just like it. Not an outright steal, of course, but a picture with enough similarities to the original hit to rake in some box-office dough before people figured out that they were being conned. Nobody at the established studios liked Superior's way of doing business. They didn't like Thomas Wayne, its owner, either, but they had to admit he had a knack for making money. And if you made money, nobody in Hollywood really cared if the movies were good or original or either one.

Except maybe for the man sitting next to me. Bogart was well known for turning down scripts he thought stunk and then being suspended by Mr. Warner. Nearly everyone who worked for Mr. Warner had been suspended at one time or another. Still, I suspected that Bogart might have held the record.

"Burleson has threatened Mr. Bogart with blackmail," Mr. Warner said, which didn't surprise me. That's the kind of guy Frank was.

"You want me to put a stop to it?" I said.

"That's right. Quietly. No publicity."

"There's never a guarantee that I can do that."

Bogart snuffed out his cigarette, stuck his hand inside his jacket, and fished a pack of Chesterfields from his shirt pocket. He found a folder of matches in another pocket and lit the cigarette. He took a puff, waved the match out, and dropped it in the ashtray. He let some smoke trickle out of his mouth and coughed. When he'd finished coughing, he said, "If this gets out, it will hurt somebody I care about. But I don't believe in paying blackmail."

"Neither do I," I told him.

I've never understood why people pay blackmailers. It never works out. The blackmailer is never satisfied and keeps coming back, asking for more and more. The payments never end. The studio chiefs know that, but some of the actors don't. And some of them aren't smart enough to go to the studio chief and tell him what's happening. Bogart was smart.

"I'm turning it all over to you, Scott," Mr. Warner said. "You and Bogart can sort it out between you. I don't want any more to do with it."

That was usually the way it went. I was on my own from here on in, and Mr. Warner would be kept strictly out of it. The studio was my client, but nobody would help me out if I got in trouble.

Mr. Warner stood up, a clear sign that we were dismissed. Bogart squashed his coffin nail in the ashtray and said, "Come on, Scott. Let's go have a drink."

We trudged through the carpet, our shoes sinking in so deep that we couldn't see the tops, and retrieved out hats from the rack before leaving the office.

"We'll go to the Formosa," Bogart said, meaning the Formosa Café, which was on Formosa Avenue, right across from the studio.

"My car or yours?" I said.

"Which one is yours?"

I pointed to the black Chevy. "That one."

"Looks sturdy enough," Bogart said. "Let's go."

He got in on the passenger side, lit up another Chesterfield, and offered me the pack.

"No thanks," I said. "I don't smoke. I don't drink, either."

"Jesus Christ, what are you? A Mormon?"

"No. I gave up all my bad habits a few years ago."

Some people would have asked why. Bogart wasn't one of those people. He said, "All of them?"

"Not really. I hung onto a couple for old time's sake."

"Good. I don't trust a man with no bad habits. Let's go."

I cranked the Chevy and drove the short distance to the Formosa Café. It had once been a trolley car, and in its new incarnation was frequented by movie stars who wouldn't have ridden on a trolley car at gunpoint. It wouldn't have been frequented by movie stars, either, if it hadn't had the advantage of proximity. Actors usually preferred the tonier places like Chasen's and Romanoff's.

I parked in front of the café. We walked under the striped awning that covered the sidewalk and went inside. I'd heard that the Formosa's Chinese food wasn't bad, and it also had a pretty good bar, which is where Bogart headed as soon as we were inside. He didn't seem to have much interest in food.

The bar was dark, but there was enough light for me to see that there were no other movie people around, not at that time of evening. They were probably somewhere in the high-rent district, getting ready for an evening out at someplace swanky.

Bogart got himself a martini, and I got a Coke. We found an unoccupied booth and scooted in across the red leather seats.

Bogart took a sip of his drink and said, "I needed that." He lit another Chesterfield, which he held cupped in his left hand. He slid the pack across the table toward me. "You sure you don't want one?"

"Wanting doesn't have anything to do with it," I said.

"I see."

He pulled the pack back and left it on the table beside the book of matches. He tugged at his earlobe with his free hand and looked me over.

"You don't look like a detective," he said after a moment. "You're young, you're bald, you're ugly, you're short, and you're a little chubby."

"You played Philip Marlowe and Sam Spade. They're detectives. But at least you're not chubby. Or young."

Bogart laughed and took another sip of his martini.

"You don't mind the needle," he said. "That's a rare quality. I usually get under people's skins pretty quickly."

"There's something you didn't notice about my skin. It's very thick."

"Good. So's mine. Maybe we'll get along."

I leaned back in the booth and said, "I don't get it. Why should we get along?"

"Because of what you heard in Mr. Warner's office. Frank Burleson is trying to blackmail me, and I'm not going to pay. I'm going to tell him that. I'd like you to be there when I do."

I usually work alone. The last thing I needed was some actor, even if it was Bogart, tagging along with me, much less trying to take over.

"Why would you want to do the telling?" I asked.

"Do you want the long version or the short one?"

"The short one will do."

"All right, but I need another drink. The world is always supposed to be three drinks behind me, and I think it's gaining."

CHAPTER

4

B ogart waved to the bartender, and with fresh martini and another cigarette in hand, he said, "I met your friend Burleson for the first time a few years ago."

"Frank wasn't my friend," I said. "He was a first-class louse, and I'm surprised Wayne hired him at Superior. If he'd asked me for a recommendation, he wouldn't have."

"He was a louse, all right, and a snooper." He looked at me through cigarette smoke. "No offense."

"None taken. It's what I do. It's what Frank does, too."

"I know. I just happen to think it's a poor way to make a living."

I shrugged. Most people I meet felt the same way.

"It's different in the movies," Bogart said. "Private eyes, at least the ones I play, may be a little on the shady side, but they have scruples, a code of their own."

"Frank doesn't," I said. I didn't bother to defend myself. "Or very few. Tell me about meeting him."

"It happened when I was courting Betty. I was still married to Sluggy at the time, and she was insanely jealous. She knew as well as I did the marriage was over, and had been for some time. But she couldn't admit it, not even to herself. So she hired a private dick to check up on me. The dick was Burleson."

"Your wife knew about you and Miss Bacall?"

"She didn't know, but she suspected. Betty and I were filming *To Have and Have Not*. Sluggy kept calling the set after I'd left to find out where I'd gone. She was always told that I was 'out with the cast.' Before long, everybody was calling Betty *The Cast*. Naturally Sluggy was suspicious."

"And that's where Frank comes in."

"That's right. He wasn't very good at his job, and I spotted him pretty quickly. Spade and Marlowe would have laughed at him."

"I thought this was the short version," I said. "All this was three or four years ago."

"That's not when he tried to blackmail me."

"Ah. And when did that happen?"

"Today," Bogart said. "At Romanoff's, not in the restaurant itself, but just outside. When I'm not working I go there for breakfast nearly every day around noon. Everybody knows that, and that's where Burleson met me. He said he had some 'information' I might be interested in. It was about Sluggy, not me, but she doesn't have a great deal of money these days because she's not getting any work. Burleson couldn't expect to get any money out of her, but he thought I'd pay to keep what he had to tell out of the papers. I told him I wasn't paying and that I'd kill him if any hint of what he'd said ever saw print or if he ever bothered me or Sluggy again."

That's the kind of good-for-nothing Frank was, all right. The kind who'd try blackmailing his former clients or their husbands if he needed the money, which he often did because of another one of his lousy habits: he played the ponies. That's fine if you win, or if you have plenty of dough, like Mr. Warner. But Frank had never been a winner, and he didn't have any more dough than I did.

"What did he say when you threatened him?" I asked.

"He got a good laugh out of it. He said he knew I wasn't as tough as I liked people to think and that he'd be in touch."

"And you didn't believe him."

"No. I thought he was just testing me to see how I'd react. But he called, all right, later this afternoon."

I had finished my Coke, and I rattled the ice that was left in the glass. Bogart was still working on his second martini. He didn't seem to be drinking as much as I'd heard he did. But I'd lost count of the cigarettes.

"What does he have on Mayo?" I asked, not quite able to call her Sluggy.

"You don't need to know that. If Sluggy has problems, maybe she has an excuse. Let's just say it's the kind of thing that could hurt her, and she's having enough trouble these days as it is."

Hollywood gossip, of which there is never a shortage, said that Mayo had pretty much gone to hell in a handbasket after the divorce, losing her battle with the bottle as well as her looks. It made no difference whether any of that was true. What mattered was that it was being said. So it was no wonder that Mayo couldn't get work, and a genuine scandal of any kind would most likely finish her off as far as ever making another movie was concerned.

"All right, let's say I don't need to know about the blackmail except for the threat itself. We still haven't gotten to why you want to be the one who does the talking."

"Because I'm Bogart. Nobody does my talking for me. But I wouldn't mind if you just stood there and looked menacing."

"Like Bob Steele," I said. "Eddie Mars's best boy."

"That sounds right. I'll be Bogart, you'll be Bob Steele."

"And you think we can convince Frank not to do anything with his information?"

Bogart looked at me the way he'd looked countless times at Jimmy Cagney and Edward G. Robinson.

"Two tough guys like us?" he said. "Why not?"

"Frank knows me. He knows whether I'm really tough or not."

"How tough are you?"

"Tough enough for me to worry Frank," I said. "All right, I'll be your right-hand man."

I didn't like it, but Mr. Warner liked to humor his stars when he could, especially one as big as Bogart. If Bogart wanted to be Bogart for one night, I supposed that was OK.

"The way I see it," Bogart said, "is that your pal has to be stopped now. He might get the idea that he can run his con on other people if I let him get away with it."

Frank still wasn't my pal, but Bogart had a point. Frank was in a position to hurt a lot of people, or to make a lot of money from them. He knew plenty of secrets, if his job was anything like mine. And it was.

"All right," I said. "We'll pay Frank a little visit."

"'Pay him a little visit,' huh?" Bogart said, running the backs of his fingers down his jawline, letting the tip of his thumb trail along. "I like the sound of that. Maybe I'll use it in a movie."

I didn't even feel the needle. I said, "Feel free. But before we go, there's one other thing I want to ask you."

"What about?"

"It's a question about a movie."

"Forget it. I don't know who killed Sternwood's chauffeur, and neither did Raymond Chandler when we asked him about it. William Faulkner was on the set, and he's the one who was stumped in the first place. If he and Chandler couldn't figure it out, nobody could."

"I guess it doesn't matter in the long run, then."

"Not when you're sleeping the Big Sleep, Junior. Now are we going to make that visit or not?"

I wondered how long it had been since anybody had called me *junior*. A lot of years.

"Let's go," I said, sliding toward the edge of the booth.

"Hold on just a second," Bogart said. "When you're working for the studio, you're on an expense account. Isn't that right?"

I told him that was right.

"I thought so. You can get the check."

5

There was a pay phone in the Formosa, so I looked up Burleson's address before we left. I expected his place to be some fleabag apartment, but it wasn't that at all. It was a little bungalow on North Harper, one of several in a unit just off Santa Monica, and it was practically new. There was even an open court with a swimming pool and palm trees.

"Not bad," Bogart said when I pulled up. "You have a place like this?"

"No," I said. "I couldn't afford it. Your pal Frank might already have talked to some other people. And they might have paid off."

"He's not my pal," Bogart said.

"He's not mine, either," I told him.

I stopped the car and we got out in front of Burleson's place. The slamming doors seemed to echo in the still air. The day had been warm, but an evening chill had started moving in from the west just as night had moved over the mountains from the east. If you looked toward L.A., you could see the miles of neon that lit up the night.

A dog barked somewhere down the street, and another dog, farther away, answered. They sounded lonely.

"Maybe you should have used that pay phone to call ahead," Bogart said.

"Lesson Number One in the Detective's Handbook," I said. "Never let them know you're coming. You want to catch them off-guard. Sam Spade would have known that."

"But if Burleson's not home, we've wasted our time driving out here."

"True, but Lesson Number Two says that we're paid by the hour, so we don't mind if we have to come back. Anyway, he's home. The light's on."

A window that I assumed opened into the living room glowed in the night, and a faint yellow light shone through the thin curtains and onto the grass in the tiny yard.

"Come on," I said.

I walked to the door and thumbed the bell-button. A muted chime sounded somewhere inside.

I waited for Burleson to respond. Bogart stood behind me, smoking a cigarette. We stood like that for fifteen or twenty seconds. No one came to the door. I rang the bell again, leaning on it a bit longer than necessary. It didn't make any difference. Nobody came that time, either.

Bogart coughed and said, "I don't like this, Junior. In the movies, we'd go in and find a body on the floor."

"This isn't a movie, and we're not going in. I don't do breaking and entering."

That wasn't strictly true. I'd done it a time or two, but not when there was a witness around.

"In the movies the door's always unlocked," Bogart said. "Give it a try."

I'd tried doors before, and they'd never been unlocked. Hardly anyone in California trusted his neighbors, and with good reason.

"I'm sure it's locked," I said. "He's probably in there, waiting us out. He must have seen you get out of the car."

Bogart edged past me and put his hand on the doorknob. It must have turned easily because the door swung open.

"If he's hiding in there," Bogart said, "we'll find him." He held the door open and turned sideways. "After you, Alphonse."

"*Non, non.* After you, Gaston."

"No, no. I insist," Bogart said, waving me in with his hand.

I went past him into the living room. It was decorated about the way you'd expect, which is to say it wasn't decorated at all. The walls were bare of pictures and bookshelves. There was a couch with a sprung cushion, an overstuffed chair that looked almost new, and a big cabinet radio. There was a coffee table in front of the couch, and the ashtray was full of butts. But there was no sign of Burleson.

Bogart came into the room and went over to the coffee table to put his own cigarette butt in the ashtray. When he did, he said, "There's a spark in here. Burleson hasn't been gone long. Maybe he's hiding in the bedroom."

There were only two other rooms in the small bungalow, a kitchen and a bedroom. I looked into the kitchen, flipping the light switch by the door. There were dirty dishes in the sink and even on the table. They had once been white, but now they had food residue crusted on them in various colors: brown, yellow, green. Frank wasn't just a louse. He was a slob, too.

"Is he having a sandwich in there?" Bogart asked.

"No, but I wish I was. Having a sandwich, I mean, but not in there. It's Ptomaine Tavern. We should have eaten at the Formosa."

"I wasn't hungry, but I could have stood a bite. Why didn't you say something? We could have had a meal on Mr. Warner."

"I can eat later," I said, moving to the bedroom.

I flipped the light switch and looked in. I wished I hadn't because what I saw ruined my appetite. It was just like one of those movies Bogart had mentioned. Frank Burleson lay on the floor at the foot of the bed. He was wearing brown slacks, brown shoes, and a white shirt.

Frank looked a little surprised, as if he couldn't believe what had happened to him. The front of he shirt was stained a dark, wet red by the blood that had leaked out of him. There wasn't a lot of it because whoever had shot him knew pretty well where the heart was, or had gotten lucky. And after the heart had stopped, so had the blood. There was a .45 automatic lying not far from the body.

I must have said something, or made some sound, because Bogart came over to stand behind me.

"What is it?" he said.

"You don't want to see it," I told him.

"Why not?"

"Because it's Frank Burleson, and he's dead. Really dead. It might look like some movie set, but it's not. Frank's not some movie corpse that's got chocolate sauce poured on it to look like blood. The director's not going to say *cut* and have everybody get ready for the next scene. Frank's not going to get up and read a book or start a chess game with his stand-in."

Bogart looked past my shoulder into the room.

"Christ," he said, which I thought was a lot better than "I told you so."

"If you're going to be sick," I said, "do it outside. We don't want the cops to find any sign of us."

Bogart pulled out his display hanky and wiped his face.

"There might be one already," he said, putting the handkerchief back in its place.

"Don't worry. I'll wipe down the light switches and the doorknob. Don't touch anything else."

"It may be too late for that," Bogart said.

He turned away and walked back into the living room. I went with him.

"What are you talking about?" I asked.

"Did you see that .45?"

"I saw it, all right. Why?"

Bogart's face was as gray as an unwashed ghost, and I thought for sure it was the sight of Frank's body that had sickened him. But after what he said next, I wasn't so sure.

"Why?" he said. "Because I think that's my pistol, that's why."

CHAPTER

6

A lot of things went through my mind right at that moment, none of them good. I said, "There are a million of those things around. Why do you think it's yours?"

"Maybe it's not," Bogart said. "Let's have a look."

It had been only a couple of seconds since he'd moved out of sight of the body, but he was already recovering. He was a lot better at being Bogart than I was at being Bob Steele. My stomach was still twitching a little.

We went back to the bedroom. Frank was still lying there on his back, staring up at nothing in particular. The room was more or less a mess, which might have been because Frank was a slob or because someone had searched it.

The pistol was still lying right where it had been. Bogart walked into the room and looked down at it.

"It's mine, all right," he said. He knelt down and pointed to the grips. "See that big scratch right there? That happened one night when Sluggy threw the pistol at me."

"You should have taught her a little about firearms safety."

Bogart stood up. "She didn't care about safety or anything else when she was mad. She just threw whatever came to hand. I'm damned lucky she didn't shoot me with it instead."

I was curious, so I said, "Why didn't she?"

"The safety was on. She didn't know how to take it off. I never showed her."

A wise move, I thought. I said, "Where was the pistol? Not out in plain sight, surely."

"It was in the drawer of a bedside table. She'd already thrown the table lamp at me, and she pulled the drawer to throw it next. But the pistol was in there, so she grabbed it."

He said it in a flat, unemotional voice, as if it were just one more unremarkable incident in the life of the Battling Bogarts. Which it probably was.

"There are a couple of possibilities here," I said, "but we really don't have time to talk them over."

"Why not? Your pal Frank isn't going anywhere?"

"No, but you are. If that little spark in the ashes out there was live, that means the killer hasn't been gone long. Someone probably heard the shot that killed Frank, and that somebody might have called the cops. And if the cops were called..."

"Then they should be on the way here," Bogart said.

"Give the man a silver dollar."

"And we shouldn't be here when they arrive."

"You shouldn't."

"What about the pistol?"

I'd thought about that. I said, "Where did you get it?"

"I served in the Navy. Don't you read the papers?"

"I also read that you and some writer had opened a rattlesnake farm in Arizona."

"You shouldn't believe everything you read. Only the true things."

"About the pistol," I said.

"I brought it home with me after the war. Lots of guys did the same."

"It probably can't be traced to you, then. We can leave it for the cops."

"It might be traceable. I'm not sure."

"It's no different from a thousand others. Don't worry about it."

"I'm worried. I don't want the cops to get it."

I was going to argue with him, but that's when we heard the sirens.

"Time for you to get out of here," I told Bogart. "Do you think you can get out of the neighborhood and catch a cab?"

"I've done things like that often enough," he said. He twisted the ruby ring. "What happens after I catch the cab?"

"Go back to the studio, get your car, and go home. Garden of Allah, right?"

"That's right, but I don't think Allah's visited it lately."

"I'll come by later."

I took out my wallet and located a card, checked to be sure it was the right one, and handed it to Bogart.

He looked at it and said, "This your shyster?"

"That's right. If I'm not at your place by midnight, call him and have him come bail me out of jail."

"You think they'll take you in?"

"They'll take us both if you don't get out of here."

"And the pistol?"

"Leave it. I'm not going to withhold evidence of a murder. We'll just have to hope they don't trace it to you."

He looked at the pistol and shook his head sadly.

"Don't worry about it," I said. "Maybe it has the killer's fingerprints all over it."

I didn't believe that, and neither did he, but he gave me a half smile.

"You know what happens in the movies, don't you?" he said.

"Sure. They always arrest the wrong guy, which is what's going to happen if you don't get out of here."

He thought that over for a second and then nodded.

"See you later, Junior," he said, and walked out of the bedroom.

I heard the front door close when he left. I hoped the cops didn't spot him. Mr. Warner would surely fire me if Bogart was jailed for murder. There was a story about one of Mr. Warner's assistants, a man who'd been with him for nearly twenty years. One day, Mr. Warner fired him outright. When Darryl Zanuck asked him why, Mr. Warner said, "It just wasn't working out." So you couldn't call him a sentimental guy. At any rate, while I wouldn't withhold evidence, I didn't see any need to have Bogart there for questioning. And I might even lie a little if the need arose. Which it probably would.

I looked out the window until Bogart disappeared into the night. After that it was only a couple of seconds until the cops arrived.

I went to the door to let them in. While I was standing there, I smeared the fingerprints. I didn't think Bogart had touched anything else. Except maybe that pistol. I didn't smear those prints, though. I wasn't going to withhold evidence, and I wasn't going to taint it, either.

The cops didn't come to Frank's place first. There were two of them, and they stopped by my car to look it over. I saw one of them put his hand on the hood for a second as if he were resting. He didn't rest long. The two of them went to another one of the small units and knocked on the door. I figured that whoever called them lived there. They'd ask where the shot had come from, and then they'd come to Frank's place. I sat down on the couch, avoiding the sprung cushion, and waited for them.

While I sat there, I thought about Frank, and about Bogart's pistol. Mostly about the pistol.

It was a cinch that it had been used to kill Frank, and there were only a couple of ways it could have gotten there. One was that Bogart could have brought it earlier and used it.

I didn't much like that idea, but it could be true. I hadn't seen the spark in the ashtray, and it sure wasn't there now.

What if Bogart had told me about it just so I'd think there'd been someone there earlier?

What if this whole thing was just a set-up to use me as his witness when the cops found out that Frank was dead?

There were a couple of things wrong with those questions. The cops, for one. They wouldn't have come unless someone had called them, but Bogart could have set that up, too, with the person who'd done the calling. Of course the coroner would establish a time of death, and that might let Bogart off the hook. I hoped so. I'd gotten to like him.

The other thing was the pistol. It didn't seem likely that Bogart would have left it behind had he done the shooting. He wasn't that careless.

But it didn't have to be Bogart who'd done Frank in. There was always Mayo, who was known to be violent and who couldn't afford to have Frank spreading any scandal about her. She'd known where the pistol was kept, and Bogart was still living where he'd lived when they were married. It wouldn't have been hard for her to get her hands on the .45.

Mayo couldn't afford to pay Frank's blackmail, but she could afford a bullet. Hell, Bogart probably kept the pistol loaded, and she could have figured out the safety. It wasn't very tricky.

She might have panicked and dropped the pistol after killing Frank, or she might even have left the pistol there deliberately, depending on how she was feeling about Bogart at the time. She might have wanted him to take the fall for her.

Mayo or Bogart, I wondered. Had one of them pulled the trigger or not? Well, I'd find out sooner or later. People had tried to keep secrets from me before, but it hadn't worked out for them. It never did.

7

I t didn't take the cops long to find their way to Frank's place. They knocked on the door, more or less politely, but I could tell it wasn't Emily Post out there.

I opened the door and got out of the way. They didn't come in like Emily Post, either.

The first one through the door said, "You Frank Burleson?"

He was in a plainclothes unit, probably homicide, and he wore a dark double-breasted suit with a light stripe in it. He was big, with wide shoulders, long arms, and thick, clumsy-looking fingers that could twist your ear off in about half a second. He had big white teeth that could chew up the ear in even less time than that. He looked about as excitable as a fireplug.

But he wasn't bad looking, for a cop, with sort of a square face, with bushy eyebrows and dark eyes. The thing that would keep him out of pictures was the wart just to the right of his nose. It was the size of a pencil eraser, and there were a couple of short black hairs growing in it.

The other man was in uniform. He was smaller, but he looked plenty tough. His face was seamed, and his nose was crooked, as if it had been broken more than once.

"I'm not Burleson," I said. "And who aren't you?"

The big one took off his hat and ran his hands through his hair, which was black and shiny, as if he'd used one dab of Brylcreem too many. I could see that the leather liner was stained dark.

He put his hat back on his rumpled hair and said to the uniform, "Tell me something, Garton. Is this guy Lou Costello, or not? He looks like Costello. He's funny like Costello. So he must be Costello. Tell me it's Costello."

Garton smiled, and his face got even more seamed. He looked a little like a chimp that had escaped from a Tarzan movie.

"It ain't Costello, Lieutenant Congreve," he said.

"Damn. I always wanted to get that guy's autograph." He turned back to me. "Now we know you're not Burleson, and we know you're not Costello, so you can cut the comedy. Who the hell are you?"

I told him. He didn't seem impressed. I almost wished I were Costello.

"And what are you doing in Frank Burleson's house?" he asked.

"Frank and I are old friends," I said. As long as everybody thought I was Frank's pal, I might as well take advantage of it. "I dropped by to see how he was doing."

"I see. And how is he doing?"

"Not so hot," I said. "Cold, in fact." "How cold?"

"Getting colder all the time," I said.

Lieutenant Congreve sighed and turned back to Garton.

"He's funnier than Costello, don't you think?"

Garton didn't smile this time. He was edging around Congreve toward the open door of the bedroom, fumbling to release the thong that held the pistol in the holster he wore on his belt.

"Ah-ah," Congreve said, putting a hand on his arm. "Don't get in such a rush, Garton. We'll take a look in there in just a minute. Maybe Mr. Scott would like to tell us what we'll find."

"Frank," I said. "You'll find Frank."

"Sleeping, is he? And at this hour of the night. You'd think he'd be out here talking to his old friend Scott, maybe having a little drink. Is he feeling ill?"

"He's not feeling much of anything," I said.

"Feeling no pain, is he? Been drinking a little too much? Carousing a bit with his old friend?"

"Look," I said. "I'm no Costello, and you're no Bob Hope. Frank's lying in there on the floor, and he's dead as a hammer."

Congreve sighed. "I was afraid you were going to say something like that, I really was. I wish you hadn't, though. Cuff him, Garton."

"Wait a minute," I said. "I didn't kill him. What's the matter with you. You think I killed him and then sat on the couch waiting for you to get here? I haven't been here more than five minutes, myself."

"That may very well be, and we'll find it out for sure in time. In the meanwhile, put your hands behind your back so Garton can slip the cuffs on you, gently and politely. Or we'll do it the hard way. Garton would like that."

On the last sentence, his voice changed. It had been almost pleasant, as if we were having a conversation about the weather. But now it was so hard you could crack glass with it.

I put my hands behind my back. Garton cuffed me, but there was nothing gentle or polite about it. I hadn't really expected that there would be.

When he had the cuffs on tight enough to satisfy him, Garton gave me a quick frisk. He didn't find anything. I never carry a pistol. My theory is that if you carry one, you might have to use it, and I don't plan to shoot anybody.

Garton shoved me in the back, and I stumbled across the room toward Congreve, who was standing in the bedroom doorway, looking down at the body.

"So this is Frank," he said.

"It *was* Frank," I said. "At least it was the last time I looked."

Congreve knelt down by the body and felt for a pulse in Frank's neck. He didn't find one.

"He's stone cold, all right," Congreve said when he'd stood back up. He wiped his hands on his pocket handkerchief. "Why did you kill him?"

"I didn't kill anybody," I said evenly. "I came by to see how he was doing, talk over old times. I found him there, and then you knocked on the door. That's all I know."

Congreve wasn't listening. He went into the bedroom and looked things over. Then he turned to face me.

"I told you to cut the comedy. We come in here, we find you with the body. You killed him, all right."

"Why don't I just shoot him," Garton said behind me. "We could say he was trying to escape."

Congreve shook his head. "We're cops, Garton. Cops don't do that kind of thing, not in L.A. We don't want to ruin our reputation. Let's have a look around and see what else we can find."

They searched the bedroom and the little bathroom beside it. They did a quick but thorough job, and of course they didn't find anything much. If Frank had kept a file on his work for the studio and used it for blackmail, he wouldn't have been stupid enough to keep it at home. Or maybe whoever had killed Frank had already found it. The only interesting thing they found was a pistol, which was in the top drawer of the dresser.

Garton sniffed it. "Hasn't been fired in a long time. Hasn't been cleaned lately, either."

"We're not here to worry about anyone's firearms hygiene," Congreve told him, and they kept on looking.

They searched the living room and even the kitchen, neither of which the killer had searched. Finally Congreve said, "All right, Scott. We give up. Where did you hide it."

"What?" I asked, with big innocent eyes that Bambi would have envied.

"Whatever you killed Burleson for. I can tell when a room's been tossed."

"I didn't toss it. If there was anything in there, the killer probably took it with him."

"Maybe, or maybe you had help."

"Think about it, Lieutenant," I said. "If I'd killed him, would I have waited here and opened the door for you, or would I have lammed out of here long ago? Which one makes more sense to you?"

Congreve ignored my questions. He said, "You never told me how you and Burleson got to be friends. You told me your name, but you didn't tell me anything about who you are."

"I have a card," I said. "In my wallet. Garton knows where it is. If he'd gotten any friendlier, we'd have to get married."

"Get the wallet," Congreve said, and Garton reached inside my jacket and pulled it out of the pocket. He handed it to Congreve, who went through it carefully.

"You have a lot of cards here," he said when he was done.

"Yeah, but only a couple of my own."

"So I see. And they say you're a private eye, just like on the radio."

"I don't get hit on the head as often as they do, but I'm a private eye, all right. So is Frank. We've never worked together, but I've met him a few times over the years. We keep in touch."

That last bit wasn't true, naturally, but Congreve didn't need to know that, not now. Maybe not ever.

"Just a pair of old buddies," Congreve said. "So I guess you'd know who'd want to kill Burleson, you being such a great pal of his, wouldn't you."

"Just about everybody who knew him would want to kill him," I said, "except me. Listen, Congreve, Frank worked for Thomas Wayne at Superior Studios. He did a lot of jobs that the studio wanted to keep quiet. That's where I'd start if I were you."

"But, thank God, you aren't me," Congreve said. He looked down at Frank's body with distaste. "And neither was this poor bastard. Spending his life trying to cover things up like a sick cat covering crap. What a hell of a way to make a living. Don't you agree, Scott?"

"Absolutely," I said. "A terrible thing."

"Not that you'd know anything about it."

"That's right. I do mostly divorces, runaway daughters, that sort of thing."

"Good clean jobs," Congreve said. "Isn't that right, Garton."

"I wouldn't know, Lieutenant. I'm just a cop. I get mostly the dirty jobs. Like this one."

"You don't have to worry about this one," Congreve said. "This one's mine, all the way."

"Yes, sir. That's the way it should be, Lieutenant."

"Is that your car out front, Scott?" Congreve asked. "The old beat-up Chevy?"

I resented his description of my car, but I didn't think it would be a good idea to let Congreve know it. So I just said, "That's right."

"You really haven't been here long, then. The hood was still warm when we got here."

I nodded. Whatever else Congreve was, he wasn't stupid.

"And your friend's been dead for a while. Probably longer than you've been here."

"That's what I was trying to tell you."

Congreve looked at me as if I were something he'd found on the bottom of his shoe.

"I'd have liked it a whole lot better if you'd been Lou Costello."

"So would I," I said. "He's a funny guy. And he makes a lot more money than I do."

"Uncuff him, Garton," Congreve said, ignoring my remark. "We're not going to keep him."

"Damn," Garton said. "I really did want to shoot him, Lieutenant."

"Maybe next time."

Garton unlocked the cuffs, and I rubbed my wrists, trying to restore a little of the circulation. It was a good thing I didn't want to hit anyone. I wasn't sure I could even make a fist.

"I don't suppose you work for Superior," Congreve said. "You didn't mention it if you do."

"I don't. Divorces, remember? Runaways. Like I said."

"I remember. And you don't have any ideas about getting revenge on whoever killed Burleson here, do you? You know. Like Sam Spade when somebody killed his partner. What was his name?"

"Archer," I said. I wished he hadn't mentioned Sam Spade. "Frank wasn't my partner, though, just a guy I knew."

"Just enough to drop by, see how he was doing."

"That's right. Just enough. But no more."

"That's swell," Congreve said. "Isn't that swell, Garton?"

"Yeah," Garton said. "Swell."

Congreve clapped me on the shoulder with one meaty hand, nearly knocking me into the wall.

"You can go on home now, Scott," he said. "I don't suppose I'll run into you again. Certainly not because of anything related to Frank here."

"Certainly not," I said.

"I'd better not," Congreve said. "Now get out of here."

He didn't have to tell me twice.

CHAPTER

8

The Garden of Allah wasn't exactly the earthly paradise the name might lead you to expect. Not that the builders hadn't tried.

Its official address was 8152 Sunset Boulevard, but it actually covered most of a city block, bordered by Havenhurst, Crescent, and Fountain as well as Sunset. It had started out as a private estate in the '20s, but a Russian actress named Nazimova had converted it into a hotel of about twenty-five bungalows sometime before the '30s. Nazimova had also added the swimming pool that Marlene Dietrich went skinny-dipping in and Errol Flynn chased women around.

There was a big curved wall that gave the illusion of privacy, though the bungalows were so cheap that you could supposedly hear your next-door neighbor snoring.

The grounds were planted with tall evergreens, and bamboo grew everywhere. I guess the trees were supposed to add to the "garden" motif.

The architecture was more Spanish than anything else. Maybe with a Moorish influence, which I suppose would explain the "Allah" part of the name. Not that it mattered. I didn't think any of the residents spent much time in worship.

I parked on the street and walked through the wrought-iron gate into the garden. There was a flagstone path that wandered among the bungalows. I was hoping to see Marlene Dietrich naked in the pool, but she didn't live there any longer. Neither did Errol Flynn. The place was going downhill, and I figured Bogart would move to a bigger and better place before too long.

Part of my job is to know where all Mr. Warner's stars live, and I located Bogart's place with no trouble. I knocked on the door, and he let me in. He had a drink in one hand and a cigarette dangled from his lips.

"You look as if you could use a Scotch," he said. "Have a seat, and I'll get you one."

"I don't drink," I reminded him, looking around the room.

It didn't look like a room in the home of a movie star. It was filled with battered furniture that might have been in anybody's house anywhere, and the place was a mess. Glasses sat on the coffee table along with a couple of empty liquor bottles, the ashtrays were full, the couch was covered with newspaper, and one chair was overturned. The only classy thing in the room was the picture of Lauren Bacall on the mantel.

Bogart saw where I was looking. "Beautiful, isn't she?"

I nodded.

"Best thing that ever happened to me. I know people say that all the time about their wives, but most of them don't really mean it. I do."

"Does she know about Frank?" I asked.

Bogart took a drag on his cigarette and followed it with a sip of Scotch.

"No," he said. "She's not here at the moment."

"Where is she?"

"In New York, doing a short publicity tour and visiting her mother. In a few weeks, we're going to be shooting a picture together. It's called *Dark Passage*. Betty wanted to see her mother before we got started, and the studio wanted to get her picture in the New York papers. *Dark Passage* is going to be a good picture, and a popular one, too, if people can get over the idea that a man would actually have plastic surgery and choose to wind up looking like me."

"Half the guys in America would like to look like you," I said.

He stroked his chin. "I can't imagine why."

I pointed to the picture of Bacall. "There's one good reason."

He laughed. "Well, I can't blame them then." He looked around the room. "I'd offer you a seat, but there doesn't seem to be one. The maid didn't come in today."

I righted the chair and sat down.

"What happened here?" I asked.

Bogart swept newspapers off the couch and settled on it. The papers settled on the floor.

"There was a little party last night," Bogart said by way of explanation for the way the room looked. "Nothing formal, as you can tell. Just one of those things that happens every so often." He stuck his cigarette into one of the ashtrays, where it was smothered in a heap of ash. "People drop by. You know how it is."

I didn't know how it was. Nobody ever dropped by my place. Not even my old pal Frank Burleson. Mostly I listened to the radio if I wasn't working. *Amos and Andy, Fibber McGee and Molly, The Shadow.* I knew them all, but we didn't meet socially.

"Did Marlene Dietrich get naked and go for a swim?" I asked.

Bogart laughed. "She wasn't around. Neither was Benchley."

I remembered the Benchley story. A while back it had gone all over Hollywood in less than a day. Someone had been pushing him in a wheelbarrow and dumped in him the Garden's pool.

"Get me out of this wet suit and into a dry martini," Benchley was supposed to have said, and probably did.

"Too bad he wasn't here," I said. "He sounds like a barrel of laughs. Did you kill Burleson?"

Bogart lit another Chesterfield and waved smoke away from his face.

"That was a pretty quick change of subject. Were you hoping to catch me off guard?"

"Right out of the Detective's Handbook," I said. "But you're too smart for me."

"I doubt it. What makes you ask that, anyway?"

"It was your pistol lying there by Frank," I pointed out.

"I've been thinking about that."

"So have I. Did you kill him?"

"No. I was hoping that you trusted me enough not to ask."

"I have to ask," I told him. "It's part of the job. In the Detective's Handbook, too."

"So you asked, and I answered. Do you believe me?"

"Sure. Why not? I've heard a lot of things about you since I've been working for Mr. Warner, some of them not so good. You might find this hard to believe, but there are actually people in this town who think you're a son of a bitch."

Bogart grinned. "And they're absolutely correct. But I earned the right to be one. Let me tell you something, Junior. When I came to this town, I took every role they offered me and never complained. Even after I started to make a name for myself, I still took whatever they told me to. 'Just give me the script,' that was all I ever said. But it's not that way any longer. I have a little power now, and I'm finally using it. There are some people who don't like it. Fuck 'em."

He took a deep drag on his cigarette. The coal glowed brightly.

"If that's true," I said, "why did you make *The Two Mrs. Carrolls?*"

"Jesus," Bogart said, and laughed again. "Your needle is almost as sharp as mine. I made that thing two years ago for that bastard Harry Cohn, and I should have known better. Harry Cohn was reason enough to avoid it, and playing an English painter was another. Even Harry didn't want to release it, which tells you a lot. But he finally did, the greedy son of a bitch. What else have you heard about me?"

"Even the people who say you're as much a son of a bitch as Harry Cohn admit that you're a man of your word. You never lie, and you never back down. I'd like to think they're absolutely correct about that, too."

"So would I."

"We'll take it as a given, then. Which means you didn't kill Burleson. So who did?"

Bogart got rid of his cigarette and lit another. Instead of answering my question, he said, "How did you get away from the cops?"

"They weren't stupid. That's both good and bad, but at least they were smart enough to realize I hadn't killed Frank. Maybe they'll find out for us, though we can't count on it. And there's another problem."

"I know," Bogart said.

"I'm not talking about who killed Frank. I'm talking about what might have been missing from his house."

"I thought the room looked as if the killer might have searched it. Do you think he took anything?"

"It's possible. Frank might have been stupid enough to keep something in his house, but that's doubtful. If it was blackmail information, it was probably at his office, or even in a safe deposit box. If it was in either of those two places, the cops will find it. They didn't find it at Frank's, at least not while I was there."

"So someone else might have."

"That's right, and that brings us back to my earlier question. Who killed him?"

"Why would I have any idea about that?"

"We're back to that pistol again. Your wife is out of town, so you know she didn't do it. Who does that leave?"

"As I said, I've been thinking about that."

"And what did you decide?"

"It could have been anyone," Bogart said evasively.

He took a sip of his Scotch. It was only the second one I'd seen him take. Again I got the impression that he didn't drink nearly as much as people said.

"Was Mayo at that party you told me about?" I asked. If he wasn't going to get to the point, I was.

He nodded but didn't look in my direction.

"So were a lot of other people," he said.

"But Mayo knew where the pistol was."

"You're wrong if you think Sluggy had anything to do with killing that skunk. She's crazy, sure, but she's not that crazy. Besides, she never picked on anyone except me."

We both knew that wasn't true, and there were plenty of newspaper stories to prove it wasn't. For example, once when Bogart had been accosted by a man who wanted to show how tough he was, it had been Mayo who decked the guy.

Bogart noticed that I looked skeptical. "All right, she might have a violent streak, but she wouldn't shoot a man. You can believe me. I know her better than anyone."

"But she was here last night, and she knew where the pistol was."

"Sure, she knew. And she was telling people about it last night. She was a little drunk, or maybe she was a lot drunk, and she started talking about some of the fights we used to have. People were laughing, and that encouraged her. She told them that if we'd ever really gotten angry, one of us would have shot the other, and then she showed them the pistol."

"She showed it to them?"

"That's what I said. She went into the bedroom and got it."

This was getting more complicated than I'd thought. And it was worrying me besides. Maybe I should have made Bogart stick around and have a few words with Congreve.

"Did any of them touch it?"

"I don't remember. I don't think so."

"Did you touch it?"

"No. What difference does it make?"

"Think about it," I said. "You've made enough crime movies to figure it out."

He did, and he came to the same conclusion that I had.

"Sluggy's prints could be on that pistol," he said. "Even if she didn't do it."

"If the killer was careful enough," I said.

"That's rough. I wouldn't want to see Sluggy get in trouble for something she didn't do. And she didn't do it."

"We don't know that for sure."

"I know it."

"All right. But we're going to have to talk to her just the same."

"'We'?"

"That's right. I think having you along will make things a lot easier for me. If she's as feisty as I've heard she is."

"There's no question about it. She's as feisty as they come."

W e went out to get my car and I looked over at Schwab's drugstore across the street. I asked Bogart if Lana Turner had really been "discovered" there.

"You know about publicity departments," he said, lighting a Chesterfield.

"Yeah. You and the rattlesnake farm."

"Don't forget the time I put on the false beard and played the bull fiddle in an orchestra."

We got in the car and I asked where we were going.

"I knew you needed me for more than an introduction," Bogart said, and he gave me the name of the hotel where Mayo was living.

It was on Sunset, but Sunset is a long street, and some parts of it are better than others. The hotel he named was in one of the others.

We wound through the traffic, which is always heavy on Sunset, no matter the time of day or night. The difference is that it's more dangerous late at night, when drivers were likely to be a little more careless than usual, having fortified themselves with a martini or three, or perhaps a few glasses of good (or not-so-good) Scotch.

"How long have you been working for Jack Warner?" Bogart asked me.

"A couple of years," I said.

"A man your age must have been in the service."

"That's right. Marines. I got out a few years ago."

"I notice that you have a little limp. Did you pick that up in the service?"

"Yeah. Saipan."

"Purple Heart?"

"Yeah, and a ticket home."

"You're lucky you didn't get killed," Bogart said. "But you probably didn't think about that. I know I never did. Hell, when you're a kid, you don't worry about dying, not even when it's happening all around you. You don't start to think about it until you get to be my age and start reading the obituaries of people whose accomplishments you read about when you were growing up, or of people your own age. Those are the worst."

He opened the ashtray and tapped his cigarette on the edge.

"I shot a man once," he said. "When I was in the service."

I'd heard the story, or thought I had. I didn't say anything, just waited to see if he'd tell the rest of it.

"I didn't kill him," Bogart went on. "I know that story is going around, and, hell, I don't care. It's good for my reputation. But I didn't kill him."

"It's like the rattlesnake farm all over again," I said.

Bogart flicked his cigarette out the car window, and it trailed a sparkling tail like a comet.

"Yeah," he said, "except this time it's almost true. I was escorting a prisoner to Portsmouth, where he was going to spend the rest of his time in the brig. We went on the train. He was handcuffed, and he didn't give any trouble. We even started talking, and he didn't seem like such a bad sort. There were plenty of men in the brig who probably didn't belong there, or so I thought at the time."

"If that's the case, why did you shoot him?"

"I'm coming to that. We were changing trains in South Boston, and he asked me for a cigarette. I stuck one in his mouth, and when I started to light it for him, he slugged me in the face with both hands. It wasn't his hands that hit me, though. It was the handcuffs. They nearly cut my lip off. So I shot the son of a bitch."

"But you didn't kill him."

"No. There was a lot of blood, but most of it was mine. You'd be surprised how much you can bleed from a cut in your lip. I just winged the guy, and he hardly bled at all. I got him on down to Portsmouth, and a doctor sewed me up without benefit of anesthetic. Unless you count Scotch. There was some of that as I remember."

"I hadn't heard that part of the story."

Bogart ran his index finger over his upper lip and grinned.

"Not many people have. I guess you could say I owe that guy a lot. He's the reason for this stiff upper lip, and for that little lisp I sometimes have."

"I thought you got the wound in the lip from shrapnel."

Bogart lit another Chesterfield and exhaled smoke.

"That's another one of those rattlesnake farm stories. Someone must have thought that getting a shrapnel wound in battle sounded more glamorous than getting hit in the face with handcuffs."

Shrapnel wounds weren't glamorous at all. I could vouch for that. I said, "The gun you shot the man with. Is that the one you kept?"

"Yeah. The one I brought home from the service. The same one you saw tonight."

"I don't think they bothered with ballistics tests on the bullet they dug out of your prisoner."

"No. They didn't bother much with him. The doc sewed me up first, in fact." He looked out the window and gave a jerk of his head. "That's the place where Sluggy's staying."

It was called The Palms, and it wasn't the most prepossessing place on the Sunset Strip. A couple of tall, ratty-looking palms grew out front. The canopy over the walk had a couple of fair-sized holes in it. They looked as if they'd been there a while. I pulled the Chevy to the curb and we got out.

A black Packard Clipper drove past us. It was a pre-War model. I could tell because of the fender-shells that covered most of the back wheel-wells.

"Do you think we were tailed?" Bogart asked.

"Tailed?" It hadn't entered my head. "By that car?"

"Yeah. It's been behind us since we left my place."

"How do you know?"

"I saw it pull out behind us," Bogart said, "and I glanced in the mirror a couple of times. I think you're supposed to do that, according to the Detective's Handbook."

"Just a coincidence," I said. "Nobody has any reason to follow us."

Bogart shrugged. "If you say so. I think you should check that Detective's Handbook, though."

He looked toward the hotel entrance and tossed his cigarette to the sidewalk, then crushed it under his shoe.

"Sluggy might not be glad to see us," he said.

"Not if she killed Burleson, she won't," I said. "And I wouldn't blame her."

"That's not the reason. She might be a little angry with me."

"Should I ask why?"

"She thought that with Betty out of town, we might be able to have some fun last night. I told her I was a married man. She was a little upset."

"At least she didn't shoot you."

"No," Bogart said. "She didn't shoot me. Shall we go in?"

I could think of several reasons why we shouldn't but I said, "We might as well."

T he lobby of The Palms was no more impressive than the outside. The ashtrays hadn't been emptied in a week or so, and there were pieces of newspaper lying in the chairs, except for the chair the house dick was asleep in. He'd been reading the news, and the paper he'd been holding had dropped from his hand onto the floor. There was a potted palm in a dark corner. It was dying. The night desk clerk didn't look especially healthy, either.

"Can I help you gentlemen?" he asked when we approached the desk.

He had a face like a weasel and small yellow teeth with a toothpick clamped between them. His eyes also had a yellowish cast, too, as if he might have had jaundice at some time or another. His thin black hair was slicked down close to his head. He looked closely at Bogart, and his eyes narrowed.

"Hey," he said, "aren't you..."

"Reilly," Bogart said. "Doghouse Reilly."

The clerk nodded. "Yeah. I thought I reckanized you."

The toothpick wagged when he talked.

"And I'm Bob Steele," I said. "We're here to see Miss Methot."

The toothpick wagged again. "You don't look like Bob Steele."

I got a dollar out of my wallet and slid it over the counter toward him. He glanced over at the house dick, who was still in dreamland.

Knowing that nobody was going to report him, he slipped the buck from under my fingertips and made it disappear.

"Room two-sixteen, Mr. Steele," he said.

"Thanks," I said.

Bogart and I didn't bother to take the elevator, which probably wasn't working anyway. The stairway had the odor of stale smoke and dirty laundry. The rug was worn thin as a miser's dime. Things weren't any better in the hallway. I could hear a radio playing dance music behind one of the thin doors, but I didn't think anyone would be dancing in there. It just wasn't that kind of place.

Room number 216 was at the end of the hall. The door was slightly ajar. I said, "Don't give me that line again about what happens in the movies when the door is open."

"If something's happened to Sluggy, there'll be hell to pay," Bogart said.

I tapped on the door. It swung farther open, but there was no other response. I knocked on the jamb, and the sound echoed up and down the hall. There was no sound from the room, however.

Bogart put a hand on my shoulder and moved me out of the way. He seemed to want to take charge in these situations, and I have to admit I didn't make it much trouble for him. He pushed the door all the way open and went into the room, with me right behind him. I was supposed to be protecting him, after all.

The place was dark, and it smelled like the den of an unhealthy animal. It also smelled like cigarette smoke and booze. Lots of booze.

"Sluggy?" Bogart said. "Are you in here, Sluggy?"

I thought she was probably around somewhere, all right, but I wasn't at all sure about her condition, not considering the way the room smelled. I was reaching for the light switch when I heard a movement, but I couldn't tell where it came from.

Bogart heard it, too. "Sluggy?"

I flipped the switch. The light came on, but it didn't help much. It must have been a twenty-watt bulb. The Palms was that kind of place, but I was grateful for the dimness. The room was a mess. A slip hung over a chair back, and there was an overturned ashtray on the floor by the coffee table, which had cigarette burns on the edges. An empty Dewar's bottle lay on the floor near the couch. There were dark stains on the couch cushions where someone had spilled something wet.

I heard another movement. This time I thought might have come from the bedroom, which was still dark except for the light that got inside though the half-open door.

"Sluggy?" Bogart said again.

"Ain't nobody here but us chickens," said the voice from the direction of the door.

Us sounded more like *ush*, and *chickens* came out something like *shickensh*.

"That's her," Bogart said. "I think she's a little under the weather."

I'd figured that part out for myself.

"I'll see about her," Bogart said.

He started toward the bedroom, having made the same mistake I had, though I didn't know it was a mistake until he walked passed the couch. When he did, a wild-eyed, wild-haired woman jumped up from behind it.

It must have been Mayo, but I didn't recognize her. Maybe that was because I wasn't looking at her face. I was looking at the scissors in her hand. She was gripping them like a knife, and the point was heading right for Bogart's face.

Bogart saw her out of the corner of his eye. He turned, and with his right arm he swept the scissors aside.

Mayo screamed an obscenity and kicked him in the shin. He bent over, and when he did, she swung the scissors up in order to bring them down between his shoulder blades.

By that time I had crossed the room. I grabbed her wrist and twisted, hard. The scissors went flying.

Mayo didn't even seem to notice. She crossed over with her left hand, and her open palm slammed into the side of my face with the velocity of a V-2 rocket. When it connected, it popped like a pistol shot.

The blow rattled my brain. I let go of her wrist and took a step back. Mayo dropped down on all fours and scooted around the couch, quick as a large cat. Bogart made a jump for her, but he missed and landed flat, nearly hitting his head on the edge of the couch as he fell.

The right side of my face felt as if it was on fire, but I didn't have time to worry about it. I went after Mayo.

She scuttled over to the scissors and grabbed them. I went after her and as I reached her, she sat up and whirled around, holding the scissors like a dagger again. She jabbed at my knee with them. The

45

point ripped through the leg of my slacks and slashed a red-hot line just above my knee. I backed away.

Still brandishing the scissors, Mayo slid on the floor until her back was against the wall. She pushed herself up it and stood facing me with a feral grin that bared her teeth. She might have been a beautiful woman at one time. For that matter, maybe she still was. But not at that moment in that situation. She was wild drunk and crazy, and I didn't have any trouble at all imagining her as the person who had killed Frank Burleson.

"I think you'd better calm down, Sluggy," Bogart said at my back. Mayo looked over my shoulder at him.

"Straighten up and fly right, you son of a bitch," she said. "That's what you mean, isn't it?"

The words were a little slurred, but I understood them well enough. So did Bogart.

"That's right," he said. "You need to straighten up and fly right. Now give me those scissors."

She shifted the scissors to her left hand, then took hold of the point with her right. When she drew her arm back to throw them, I ducked and rushed her.

The scissors went over my shoulder, and then I had her around the waist. It was like grabbing a wildcat that was having a seizure. She jerked and twisted, kicked and spit, clawed and shouted, "Bastard, bastard, bastard."

It sounded more like *bassard*, but I got the point.

I couldn't turn around or let go to see if Bogart had gotten the other point, the one on the end of the scissors, but it turned out that he hadn't. He walked around behind Mayo and said, "You can let her go now, Scott."

In my position, bent over with my arms around Mayo, I could see only Bogart's shoes and the cuffs of his pants. Mayo was still writhing like a python.

"I'm not sure I should do that," I said.

"Go ahead. It's me she wants, not you."

"All right. If that's the way you want it."

I released Mayo and jumped back, turning aside just in time to avoid getting kicked in the family jewels. Her foot connected with my hip, and that was painful enough, considering that there was still some shrapnel in there that they hadn't been able to dig out of me.

46

I stumbled into Bogart, who grabbed me by the shoulders and moved me aside.

"That's about enough," he said to Mayo.

"Enough for you, maybe, you bastard. You still have a career."

"You can have one, too."

Mayo pushed her hair away from her face. It didn't help her appearance any, and it didn't say where she moved it, anyway.

"The hell you say. Some son of a bitch called me today. He said he was going to tell the papers about something if I didn't pay him."

"He came to me, too," Bogart said. "I don't pay blackmailers."

"You don't pay anybody if you can help it, you cheap bastard. That's why he called me, because you wouldn't pay him."

"There's nothing he can do to hurt you."

"You don't know. You don't know anything."

"I know about the men, Sluggy," Bogart said. "I know they didn't mean anything to you. People don't care about things like that."

Mayo glared at him for a second or two and the started blubbering. Big tears ran out of her eyes and down her cheeks. Bogart went to her and put his arms around her, much more gently than I had.

"All I wanted was to be happy," Mayo said between sobs. "But none of those could match up to you, Bogie."

He patted her on the back, and her tears soaked into the shoulder of his jacket. It was a very touching scene, and I might have been more affected by it if I hadn't turned to look for the scissors and seen them sticking in the wall

Bogart took Mayo's hands and led her to the couch. They sat side by side, and I tried not to hear too much of what they were saying to each other. I gathered that there had been a lot of men in Mayo's life in recent weeks, and that Bogart was telling her that no one was going to find out about them because Frank Burleson was dead.

"Dead?" Mayo said. "I'm glad. It's bad to say that, but I mean it, Bogie. He was a nasty man, and I'm glad."

Bogart said he didn't blame her, and I didn't think anybody else would either. Except, of course, for the police.

I walked over to them and said, "Did you kill him?"

Mayo looked up at me. Her eyes were red, and her face was streaked. She looked even worse than she had before.

"I wouldn't do a thing like that," she said.

I looked over at the scissors. Mayo and Bogart followed my gaze.

"She didn't mean to hurt us," Bogart said.

"Yeah, I could tell," I said, reaching down and sticking a couple of fingers into the tear on my pants leg. When I brought the fingers out again, they were tipped with red.

"That was an accident," Bogart said. "Besides, she didn't get like in just a few hours of drinking. She got drunk last night, and she's been drunk ever since."

Judging by the smell of the room and of Mayo herself, I believed him.

"She couldn't have killed Burleson, not in this condition," Bogart said.

He was right. Oh, she might have killed Burleson if he'd come to the room. She was angry enough to do it. But she'd said he called her, not come to see her. She was too drunk to make that up.

"I tell you what, Junior," Bogart continued, "why don't you go on home, and I'll stay here with Mayo for a while, until she's feeling a little better about everything."

I didn't like the idea of leaving him there. I liked the brush-off even less. But there didn't seem to be a lot I could do about it.

"We have a lot to talk about," I said.

"I'll talk to you tomorrow," Bogart said. "Romanoff's, around noon. We can have breakfast."

There was no use in telling him that most people had breakfast before noon. He knew that. So I just said, "I'll be there."

I walked over and pulled the scissors out of the wall. It wasn't as easy as I'd thought it would be. They were stuck in there pretty well, and I had to jiggle them around a little. I slipped them into my jacket pocket.

"I'll just take these with me," I said. "You never know when you'll need to make some paper dolls."

By the time I got back to my apartment, there was nothing on the radio I wanted to listen too, but that was OK. I had plenty to worry about.

I didn't worry about any of it until the next day, however. It had been a long day, and as soon as I undressed and put some merthiolate on the cut the scissors had made, I lay down on the bed. The merthiolate stung a little, but I hardly noticed. I was asleep before I knew it.

CHAPTER

11

I dreamed about Rita Hayworth again, but this time the dream wasn't pleasant at all. She was chasing me with a pair of scissors, and she was yelling something about which part of my body she was doing to cut off with them. It was one of my favorite parts, even if I didn't get to use it often, at least not for recreational purposes. When I woke up, the sheets were clammy with my sweat. I got up and worried for a while. Then I took a shower, and of course the phone rang before I'd finished. I managed to get to it before the caller hung up. It was Mr. Warner.

"What are you doing, Scott?" he asked.

"Taking a shower," I said.

"You're supposed to be protecting the studio, not wasting your time on personal hygiene. Get over to Bogart's place now."

"Why? What's the matter?"

"The police are on their way already. They said they wanted to have a little talk with him. He thinks it must be about Burleson, and I think he's right. Should I have Smithson meet you?"

Smithson was one of the best lawyers on the studio payroll. I said I was sure I could handle things and that we wouldn't need Smithson.

"You'd better be right," Mr. Warner told me. "Now stop wasting time and get on over there."

I stopped wasting time and got over there.

The cops don't read the Detective's Handbook, so they'd called Bogart to ask him if they could stop by. He'd said yes, of course, but he'd given them a little stall. That was fine with me, as it gave me time to get to him first, although I was only minutes ahead of Congreve and his minion, Garton. The way my luck was running, I should have known it would be them.

Before they arrived, Bogart had time to fill me in.

"They called early," he said, flicking cigarette ashes carelessly on the rug. "It was barely nine o'clock, the uncivilized bastards."

He was wearing a ratty old robe and leather slippers, and he had on his ruby ring. He hadn't shaved, and I was sure he hadn't eaten. The circles under his eyes were a lot darker than they'd been the previous day.

"'Early to bed, early to rise,'" I said.

Bogart grimaced. "Yeah. They're both a pain in the ass. Do you know why the cops are coming here? Is it the gun?"

It could have been the pistol, but I didn't think that was it. I thought it might be one of the other things I was worried about.

"You told Burleson you'd kill him," I said. "Outside Romanoff's. Did anybody hear you?"

"I imagine so. There were several people hanging around outside the restaurant. Any of them might have heard what I said. at the time. The one closest to me was Peter Lorre. He was with me, in fact. He heard every word."

"Would he have told the cops?"

"No way in hell. He and I are old pals."

"Who else was there?"

"I don't really remember. John Wayne was there, I think. He might turn me in. We aren't exactly pals. Joey Gallindo, maybe. Jimmy Stewart. I was too upset with Burleson to look around and make notes about the people who happened to be standing nearby."

I'd picked up a paper on the way to his house, and I showed him the headline: HOLLYWOOD DETECTIVE FOUND DEAD.

"Somebody read that and called the cops," Bogart said. "I don't mind a reasonable amount of trouble, but this is beginning to look as if it's going to be a *lot* of trouble."

"I'm not sure that anybody had to read it before making that call,"

I said. "You're forgetting the gun. This could all be part of a frame-up."

"The cops will tell us how they found out, won't they?" Bogart asked.

I was still laughing about that one when the doorbell rang.

Congreve and Garton were no happier to see me than I was to see them. In fact, you might say they were downright cantankerous if your vocabulary inclined toward fancy words.

"What the hell are you doing here, Scott?" Congreve said. He looked a bit more rumpled than he had the night before. "I told you I didn't want to see you again and that I especially didn't want you mucking around in this Burleson business."

That wasn't exactly what he'd said, but it didn't matter. It was what he'd meant.

"You shoulda let me shoot him," Garton told Congreve. "It woulda worked out a lot better."

"You'll have to pardon Officer Garton, Mr. Bogart," Congreve said. "He prefers the crude approach to crime solving."

"I can see that," Bogart said. "Would you gentlemen like to have a seat?"

Congreve looked around. The room didn't look any better than it had the day before.

"We can stand," he said. "This won't take long. But we need to get rid of Scott first."

"He stays," Bogart said. "I like having him around."

"I don't," Garton said, fingering the grips of his revolver.

Congreve looked at me and said, "You never told us why you were here in the first place."

I hoped he wouldn't notice the morning paper I'd tossed on the floor. It had landed with the headline face down, and there were plenty of other papers around to camouflage it.

"I might not have told you everything about me last night," I said.

Congreve widened his eyes and said, "I'm shocked—shocked!—to discover that you might have lied to me."

Bogart grinned at Garton, who just stared at him as if he didn't know what was going on. He probably didn't.

"I didn't know you gambled in Rick's place," I said to Congreve.

"There's a lot you don't know about me, and a lot more that I don't know about me. You'd better tell me or I might consider other alternatives. Such as Officer Garton's solution. And I wouldn't want that. Neither would you."

He was right about the last part, at least. So I told him that I worked for Warner Brothers on retainer, doing pretty much the same kind of work that Burleson had done.

"You asked me if I worked for Superior, and I told you I didn't. That was the truth. But since I do work for Warner's and know Mr. Bogart, he asked me to come over. Just in case. He's not accustomed to dealing with the police."

Congreve sighed and rubbed the back of his neck with one big hand. I figured he hadn't gotten as much sleep last night as I had.

"All right, Scott. Maybe that's the truth, and maybe it's not."

"I'll bet it's not," Garton said.

"No matter," Congreve said. "We're here to ask you a few questions, Mr. Bogart. If you want Scott to hear them, that's all right with us."

It wasn't all right with Garton, I thought, but Garton didn't have much of a say.

"I'd offer you some coffee," Bogart said, "but I didn't have time to make any."

"Thank you for the offer," Congreve said. He was being polite, but I could see it was a strain for him. "Do you know a man named Frank Burleson?"

"I don't believe so," Bogart said.

I just stood there and kept a straight face.

"Scott does," Congreve said. "Isn't that right, Scott?"

I nodded. Garton glared at me. I tipped him a wink.

"He was shot to death last night," Congreve said. "Mr. Scott could tell you about it."

"No need for that," I said. "They didn't know each other."

"We hear different," Garton said. "We hear..."

Congreve shot him a look, and Garton shut up. His face was getting red, and I worried about his blood pressure. But not much, and not for long.

"What Officer Garton means," Congreve said, "is that the two of you—you and Burleson, that is—were seen talking yesterday outside a restaurant. It seemed to be a somewhat acrimonious conversation."

Acrimonious. I liked that. I looked at Garton to see if he knew what it meant. He looked puzzled, which didn't surprise me.

"I see a lot of people," Bogart said, twisting his ring. "And some of them don't like me. We have acrimonious conversations. But I don't know any Burleson."

"The restaurant was Romanoff's," Congreve said. "A number of people overheard you and Mr. Burleson."

Bogart pretended to think about it. He did a pretty good job, but then he was practically the highest-paid actor in town. He should have done even better. But he was good enough to fool Garton, and maybe even Congreve.

"I remember a man with offensive manners," Bogart said. "He waylaid me yesterday and made some nasty remarks about my ex-wife. I told him what I thought about him."

"Did you say you were going to kill him?"

"I might have."

Bogart got a pack of Chesterfields and a book of matches out of a pocket on the side of his robe. He offered the pack, but no one took him up on it. He lit a cigarette for himself and waved the match out.

"You don't remember?" Congreve said. "It seems to me you'd remember a thing like that."

Smoke drifted in front of Bogart's face. He made no effort to wave it away, and when he answered, the cigarette was still in his mouth.

"I say a great many things, and I don't remember all of them. I know that the man who confronted me yesterday was very disagreeable, and I may have said I'd so something like that. Of course I didn't mean it. It's just a way of talking. You know what I mean."

Congreve nodded, as if he'd expected something like that.

"But you say you didn't know Burleson."

Bogart removed the cigarette from his mouth and picked a speck of tobacco from his lip. He put the cigarette back.

"You don't suppose he introduced himself, do you? He was making remarks about my wife, not trying to get to know me."

That was only partially true, as I well knew. He'd introduced himself, all right, but I was willing to bet there was nobody to say so. The anonymous caller probably hadn't mentioned it, and the cops wouldn't be able to call back to check.

"Peter Lorre was with me," Bogart went on, after taking a drag from his cigarette. "You could ask him. I'm sure he'll tell you that the man didn't introduce himself."

I was sure, too, because Bogart would be on the phone to him as soon as Congreve got out the door.

"What about the time of death on Burleson?" I asked. "Do you have one yet?"

Congreve took a few seconds to decide if he wanted to tell me. Finally he said, "Around 8:00 last night."

I was glad to hear it. That meant that Bogart hadn't killed Burleson, not that I'd ever really thought he had.

"That lets us both out," I said. "Mr. Bogart and I were in the Formosa Club at that time. It should be easy enough for you to check that out."

"I will," Congreve said, but he knew he was licked.

He asked a few more meaningless questions, told me again that I'd better not get involved in his case, and then he and Garton left. Garton turned back before they went out the door and gave me another glare. I resisted the urge to wink at him again.

Bogart closed the door and said, "Should I call Lorre?"

"It might not be a bad idea. We haven't see the last of those two."

"Why not? You saw that he'd given up."

"That's what you think. You've played enough tough guys to know the cops better than that."

"Those are movie cops," Bogart said.

"And real cops are just the same, only worse. Where do you think the writers get their ideas?"

Bogart looked around for a clean ashtray. He couldn't find one, so he just stuck the butt into a pile of ashes in a dirty one.

"I thought they made all that up," he said.

"You could be right. Maybe the movies don't learn from the cops. Maybe the cops learn from the movies. Either way it works out the same: they don't quit. Once they get hold of an idea, they keep after it. No matter how it looked to you just now, you're still their number one suspect."

I could see he didn't think much of that idea.

"And they don't like it that I was here," I added. "It just makes them more suspicious."

"Then we'd better find out who killed Burleson," Bogart said, "before they arrest me. Getting arrested for murder would pretty much be the end of my career."

"What do you mean *we?*" I asked.

"You're going to need help. How can you turn down Sam Spade and Philip Marlowe all rolled into one?"

I looked him over as he stood there in his rumpled robe, smoking a cigarette. He wasn't wearing his hairpiece, and he hadn't combed the hair he had.

"You won't like it," I said. "The pay's too small."

"I'll like it fine. And you're going to need my help if you want to know who was at the party when Mayo showed them the pistol. Any one of them could have gone in that room and taken the pistol at some point. People were drinking. No one would have noticed."

"Not even you?"

"Not even me. And certainly not Mayo."

"How is Mayo today?"

"I haven't heard from her this morning. I doubt I'll ever hear from her again. She blames me for all her troubles, and she might even have a point." He looked a bit sheepish. "I'm the one who ran out on her, after all."

"You didn't run," I said. "At least not very fast."

"I guess I hoped it would work out for us. But after I met Betty, there wasn't a chance in hell that it would."

"That wasn't your fault, either. It just happened. Of all the movie sets in all the world, she just happened to walk onto yours."

"Not a bad line," Bogart said with a grin. "Sounds familiar, though."

"Never mind that. What about Mayo?"

"She calmed down some after you left. I stayed and had a couple of drinks with her, and then she went to sleep. She didn't kill anybody. You know that."

I hoped he was right.

"So how about it? Am I helping you with this or not?"

"I guess you'll do," I said.

12

W hile Bogart was getting dressed, I gave Mr. Warner a call to tell him what had happened. He wasn't too pleased with me.

"Bogart's an actor," he said, "and a pretty good one, though you don't have to tell him I said so. At any rate, he's not a detective. This is going to get into the papers if you're not very careful."

"Nobody has to know the cops have questioned him. He's not going to tell, and neither am I."

"You're going gallivanting all over town with him at your heels, though. What about that getting into the papers?"

"The way I figure it," I said, "I'll be the one at his heels. He knows everyone involved, and he can perform the introductions. I promise that's all he'll do."

"All right, but if you get him hurt, or if his name gets in the papers as a suspect, you'll never work in this town again."

I had a feeling it wasn't the first time he'd said those words, and maybe he could even make them stick. I wasn't worried about it, however.

"Nobody's going to get hurt," I said.

"Besides, you're not a real detective. You're just a guy who cleans up messes. What do you know about murder?"

"I saw *The Big Sleep*," I said.

"That won't help you much. Nobody knows what the hell happened in that picture."

"But everybody lived happily ever after. That's what you want, isn't it?"

"You'd better not make any mistakes, Scott."

I said I wouldn't, and he hung up. It was nice to know how much confidence he had in me.

The first place Bogart and I went was Romanoff's. It was nearly twelve-thirty, and Bogart said he had to have breakfast before we did any detective work.

If Mayo's hotel had catered to the low-income crowd, Romanoff's was at the opposite end of the scale. It was on North Rodeo Drive, surrounded by stores that sold jewelry fit for royalty, including movie-star royalty, of course, and clothes that were so expensive I couldn't even afford to window shop there. Which is why I insisted that we go in Bogart's car, a spiffy blue Cadillac convertible. It would fit into the neighborhood, whereas my Chevy might have been hauled off by the junk man.

We drove with the top down, and it was one of those California days that made the tourists want to stay right there and never go back to Texas or New York or Iowa or wherever it was that they'd come from. The sky was a brilliant blue, the haze was gone, and the air was actually fresh. It was almost enough to make me want a convertible myself.

The streets of Los Angeles were filled with the usual assortment of people, the hustlers and the hopeful, the tourists and the touts, the dynamic and the down-and-out, the dazzling and the damned. I promised myself, as I often did, that someday I'd actually walk somewhere just to have a closer look at all of them, but I knew I was lying.

We got to Rodeo Drive without incident. If the shops there sold things fit for royalty, then Romanoff's fit right in. It was Michael Romanoff's conceit that he was descended from nobility and that he was, in fact, a prince. In between two big pillars was the big door that opened into his restaurant, and the middle of the door was the Romanoff coat of arms. It was a pair of golden Rs on a shield. For all I knew it might even have been authentic. But I didn't think so, any more than I thought Romanoff was a real prince.

We went inside and walked through the waiting room. When we got into the restaurant proper, Bogart was immediately greeted by the maitre d', who looked at me with something between distaste and suspicion.

"Your usual table?" he asked Bogart.

"That's correct, Reinhardt," Bogart said, and we were ushered to the second booth from the entrance.

When we were seated, I looked the place over. The wallpaper was bright enough to keep a dead man awake. It looked as if someone had stirred three or four cans of bright green, yellow, and orange paint together and spilled the result on it. Or that some parrots had exploded in the room.

Over to one side was the bar, and there were already a couple of drinkers there, though it was only barely after noon. There were some caricatures over the bar, but I didn't recognize any of them. On the wall was a large portrait, clearly the prince himself in a tux and top hat, smoking a pipe, carrying a cane, and wearing a monocle.

"How do you like the picture?" Bogart asked.

"The monocle is a nice touch," I said.

"Right. His real name's Harry Gerguson. He started this place with dough he borrowed from Cary Grant and Benchley, among others, but don't let him know I told you that."

"There's not much chance of that. We don't move in the same circles."

"You do now. Here he comes."

I looked toward the bar and saw a man heading in the direction of the table. He was shorter than I was, but he was dressed much better, in a dark blue suit that might have come from one of the nearby shops. His tie had a knot in it as big as an egg from a healthy hen. He had a thin moustache and a big nose. And, so help me, he was wearing spats. At his heels were two bulldogs.

"Good morning," Romanoff said when he reached the table.

He looked at me the same way the headwaiter had, except with more distaste and less suspicion.

"Hey, your Royal Fraudulence," Bogart said. "How are the dogs?"

"Confucius and Socrates are fine," Romanoff said, looking down at the animals. "They'll be dining with me shortly." He looked back up and turned his eyes on me again. "Who is your friend?"

"This is Mr. Terry Scott. Scott, meet Prince Michael Alexandrovich Dimitri Obolensky Romanoff, educated at Harvard and descended from Rasputin."

"From the man who *killed* Rasputin, my dear Bogie," Romanoff said, drawing himself up a little straighter. "Not from Rasputin himself, thank God."

He sounded more British than Russian, but then I suppose he knew that.

"I keep forgetting just who it is you're descended from," Bogart said, "because it keeps changing. Didn't you once tell me you were the morganatic son of the Czar?"

Romanoff allowed himself a small smile. "I may have. I don't remember. One tells so many stories."

"I suppose it depends on who one is," Bogart said. "But who cares? It was in another country, and besides, the wench is dead. Would you be interested in a little game today?"

Romanoff looked at me. "I don't know how long you've known dear Bogie, but he fancies himself a chess player. Notice that I say *fancies*. He has lost vast sums of money to me by betting on games. He never beats me."

"You know better than that, your Phoniness," Bogart said. "I don't do too badly for a guy who doesn't have the benefit of a Harvard education like you do."

I knew about Bogart's chess playing. The story was that he'd once picked up money by taking on all comers for twenty-five cents a game. Some of the stories said it was fifty cents, but the point was that he was supposed to be pretty good.

"Your playing got you in trouble during the war, my dear Bogie," Romanoff said. He looked at me. "Secret codes and all that, you know."

I said I didn't know, and Bogart explained that he liked to play chess any way he could.

"Sometimes I even played by mail. Somebody got hold of the letters and thought I was a spy."

During this conversation, a waiter had been hovering nearby. Like the dogs, he was too well-trained to interrupt. Bogart noticed him and said, "Bring me the usual, and the same for my friend."

The waiter nodded and turned to go. I had no idea what I'd be getting, but I had a feeling I knew who'd be paying for it.

"Mr. Lorre will be joining us," Bogart said before the waiter could get away. He'd made a call of his own before we'd left his place. "You know what he wants."

The waiter turned back, nodded, and left.

"I really must see to the dogs," Romanoff said. "Good day to you, my dear Bogie, and to you, too, Mr. Scott."

I said good day, and he walked toward a small table, the dogs following dutifully.

"He'll feed them their lunch there," Bogart said. "They eat better than most people in this town."

"He's quite a guy," I said.

"He's a fraud, but I like him. He entertains me. He's had more aliases than I've played parts."

"He's good at his own role," I said. "He's very good."

"You couldn't ask for better," Bogart said.

"Class. He seems to have it."

"He doesn't, though," Bogart said. "I do, and I know what it is. He's a good actor, but he doesn't have real class."

I didn't say anything to that because he was probably right. One thing I knew for sure was that whatever class was, I didn't have it. So maybe I couldn't recognize it, either.

The waiter came back with a martini for Bogart and one for me.

"I can't use mine," I said.

"Don't worry," Bogart said. "I can."

I pushed it over to him just as Peter Lorre joined us. I thought maybe Bogart would offer him my drink, but the waiter appeared with a bourbon and water and set it in front of Lorre, who at least waited until after Bogart performed the introductions to have a sip of it.

He was round and short, sad-faced and soft. Even his voice was soft. Just like in the movies. He had large dark eyes and thinning hair.

"So, Mr. Scott," Lorre said after sipping his drink, "you're a detective. What has our Bogie gotten himself into now?"

"He said you knew all about it. It happened yesterday outside this restaurant."

"You mean that most unpleasant man who wanted to sell what he called *information*? I told Bogie he should have called for the police."

"He didn't call for the police, though, did he."

It wasn't a question, but Lorre was going to answer me anyway. He clammed up, however, when the waiter arrived with a plate of bacon and eggs for Bogart and one for me. He set them down in front of us and moved off.

"Sometimes I like a lamb chop or a hamburger," Bogart said. "This week, it's bacon and eggs."

"There's nothing like bacon and eggs to set off a martini," I said.

"You got it, Junior. Dig in."

I wasn't ready to dig in. I wanted to finish my conversation with Lorre. I said, "You were just about to tell me what happened when Mr. Bogart didn't call the cops."

"None of that *Mr. Bogart* crap," Bogart said. "Call me Bogie. Everybody else does."

That was fine with me, but what I wanted was an answer to my question. Lorre gave it.

"He told the unpleasant man that he'd kill him if he ever bothered him again."

As if telling me had made him thirsty, Lorre ducked his head and took a drink of his bourbon.

"And what did Mr.—Bogie—tell you on the phone this morning?"

"Only that he wanted me to meet him here because there was a little problem to discuss. He mentioned a detective, but I didn't know why he needed one. I still don't."

"Did you read the paper this morning?"

"No. I seldom read the papers."

"Well, that's all right. I just happen to have one with me."

I'd torn the front page off the paper and brought it along. I took it out of my inner jacket pocket and unfolded it. Then I smoothed it on the table and handed it to Lorre.

"Your eggs are getting cold," Bogart told me. "They're not very good even when they're hot. When they're cold, you won't be able to eat them."

I thought he might have a point, so I shook on some salt and pepper and started eating while Lorre read the article. The eggs weren't all that bad, but the bacon was a bit limp.

"There is no picture of the victim," Lorre said when he'd finished reading. "Am I to assume that the dead man is the one who accosted Bogie yesterday?"

"You can assume whatever you please," Bogart said. "But it's the same guy, all right. I can guarantee it."

He didn't say why he could give such a guarantee, and Lorre didn't ask. He knocked back the rest of his bourbon and looked around for the waiter, who seemed to appear out of thin air with a fresh drink already in his hand. He set it on the table, and Lorre took a deep swallow.

"There's no mention of you in the article," Lorre said when he'd fortified himself.

"The cops don't have any reason to give his name to the papers," I said.

"Yet."

The police were always willing to play along with the studios up to a certain point. The point wasn't always the same, but we hadn't reached it in this case.

Bogart had finished with his breakfast, and he'd started on the second martini and a Chesterfield for dessert.

"And did you kill him, Bogie?" Lorre asked. "This Burleson, I mean."

Bogart blew out a stream of smoke and said in the same lousy British accent he'd tried in *The Two Mrs. Carrolls*, "I did, old boy. Hit him squarely between the eyes with a stale crumpet. It was either him or me, you see."

"You shouldn't tease me, Bogie." Lorre's voice turned sinister. It was still soft, but it had an edge like a steak knife. His sad face became sinister. "You know I don't like it."

Bogart laughed. "You never could take the needle. You need to stick around Junior here. He doesn't let things like that bother him. Right, Junior?"

"Don't call me *Junior*," I said, trying to sound as much like Lorre as I could.

I wasn't even close, but both Lorre and Bogart got a laugh out of it. Bogart was quick to tell me I'd never make a living doing impressions.

"That's why I'm a shamus," I said. "Now let's get down to business. Who else was there when you told Burleson you'd kill him?"

"As I said, I don't remember. That's why I called Peter."

Lorre lit a cigarette of his own, breathed smoke, and said, "I don't remember much about who was there. Nobody we know, I'm sure, or I would recall."

"Nobody who'd have any reason to hurt Bogie for any reason? Frame him for murder, maybe?"

"Who would want to do that? He's such an amusing fellow."

"Not to everyone," Bogart said.

"Mr. Warner, for example," Lorre said. "You don't amuse him most of the time."

"But he wouldn't frame me for murder," Bogart said. "At least I don't think he would. All right, Shamus, since my lead didn't pan out, what does the Detective's Handbook say we should do next?"

"We talk to someone else," I said.

"Who?"

"We might as well start at the top," I said.

13

When Thomas Wayne built Superior Studios, he was widely regarded as a snotty upstart who wouldn't last long.

One reason was that nobody was exactly sure where he'd gotten his financing. The most popular rumor was that it came from the mob. For all I knew, that was the truth.

Another reason people didn't like Wayne was that he wasn't part of the old-time crowd. Most of the studio owners had been in Hollywood since the Keystone Kops if not before. Hollywood was a lot like a little town anywhere else. Everybody knew everybody else, knew where they'd come from and what they'd done. But nobody knew where Thomas Wayne had come from, and he made it a point not to tell them.

He built his studio near Paramount, a little to the south of Warner Brothers, and started cranking out movies. At first he didn't have a lot of success, but then he hit on the idea of making the same movies that everyone else made except different. After that, the money started rolling in.

Before long he had stars and people to protect and secrets to conceal from the press and the public. Because in Hollywood, as in a lot of other places, a sin well hidden is half forgiven, people like me and Burleson had jobs with the studios, although considering his reputation, I couldn't figure out why Wayne had hired Burleson. So I was going to ask.

While we drove through town, I asked Bogart to tell me who'd been at his party on the night that Mayo brought out the pistol. We'd have to talk to them, too.

It's not easy to talk in a convertible, not with the hum of traffic, the horns, and the grinding gears, but Bogart hardly had to raise his voice, which had the remarkable clarity that it always had in the movies.

"I was wondering when you'd get around to that party," Bogart said, flipping a cigarette butt over the side of the convertible. "I'm not sure I can remember all of them."

"Give it a try," I suggested. I had to talk a lot louder than Bogart did or he'd never have heard me.

"Well, there was Joey Gallindo, for one. Ever heard of him?"

I'd heard of him, all right. Bogart had mentioned him earlier. Like Thomas Wayne, he was rumored to be tied in with the mob. They said that about George Raft, too, but the stories about Gallindo were much more detailed. And the mob connection was supposedly one reason he was working at Superior.

"I heard he killed a couple of men back East," I said. "Did he?"

"Joey doesn't confide in me," Bogart said. "He just comes by now and then and has a drink or two. Or three."

It wasn't hard to believe Joey had killed Burleson. His hot temper wasn't a rumor. It was a fact. He'd been in several nightclub brawls and had put one man in the hospital. I couldn't imagine what Burleson could have used to blackmail him. His reputation couldn't get much worse, though it was possible Burleson had uncovered another murder, maybe even one that Joey could actually be proved to have committed.

"All right," I said. "That's one. Who else?"

"Carl Babson was there, the son of a bitch. I don't know why he showed up. He hates me because I refused to do one of his scripts. Mr. Warner suspended me, but it was a rotten script. Most of his are, and he's sold only one since. It's probably rotten, too. He and Gallindo might have been together. He wouldn't mind seeing me take a deep breath in the death house, that's for sure. He blames me for his troubles."

"You make friends wherever you go."

Bogart gave me a wry grin.

"You might say that. Which reminds me that Robert Carroll and Stella Gordon were there, too."

Carroll and Gordon had been married a year or so ago, one of the biggest weddings the town had seen in years, since it was between two of Superior Studios' up-and-coming young stars. I'd seen the pictures in the papers. It was hard to tell who was the more beautiful, Carroll or his new wife.

"A pair of lovebirds if ever there was one," I said.

"I'm not so sure," Bogart said. "There's something funny going on there, but I don't know quite what it is."

"You think Burleson had something on them?"

"I wouldn't know about that. You're the detective. I'm just a movie star."

"Philip Marlowe," I reminded him. "Sam Spade."

"Just roles I played. I don't know a damned thing about being a detective."

"Then what good are you to me?"

"I can get you in places you'd have trouble getting in by yourself, remember?"

He had a point, so I asked who else was on the guest list.

"There was no guest list. I told you that. People just dropped by."

"Fine. Who else dropped by?"

"'The funniest man in Hollywood.'"

"Slappy Coville," I said.

"You must not have seen his act."

I'd seen his act, all right. His jokes were so old that they had dust in their wrinkles.

"He's a hit on television," I said. "Somebody must like him."

"Morons," Bogart said. "Slappy and television were made for morons. They're perfect for each other."

"They're going to show the World Series on television this year, or so I've heard."

"Free entertainment right there in your living room. Who's going to pay for a movie ticket if they can get free entertainment?"

"Radio's free," I said. "And it's in my living room. You've been on radio yourself. I've heard you in those movie adaptations you do. People listen to those programs and still go to movies."

"Television has pictures that move. It's not like radio. It's different."

"Maybe," I said. "It's made Slappy Coville a star. It must have something."

"Yeah, but nobody knows what it is. Stoney Randall was there last night, too. You know who he is?"

I had to admit that I didn't. I thought I knew all the stars and near-stars, but Stoney Randall was a new name to me.

"He's a stuntman," Bogart said. "He's doubled for me in a couple of pictures, like *The Oklahoma Kid*."

No wonder I hadn't heard of him, even though he'd worked at Warner Brothers. The studios didn't worry about stunt workers because the public didn't care about them. They didn't get into the fan magazines. Nobody outside the industry even knew their names. If Buck Sterling had been a stuntman, nobody would have cared about him and his feeling for his horse.

"I saw *The Oklahoma Kid*," I said. "You didn't look much like a cowboy."

"Neither did Cagney, and he didn't have to wear a moustache. I look like hell with a moustache, but they insisted. After all, I was the bad guy."

"The man who shot Cagney's paw."

"I didn't shoot him. I got him hanged, though, so you were close. Do you know Barbara Malone?"

That was a quick change of subject, but I figured there was a reason for it. I did know Malone, who'd been around town for a while, doing mostly walk-ons and bit parts until Thomas Wayne saw something in her and signed her at Superior. She'd done a turn in some moonlight and magnolias historical epic reminiscent of *Gone with the Wind* that had come out a couple of months back, and she was good, so good that there was already talk of an Academy Award nomination.

"Her, I've heard of," I said.

"She's Stoney's girlfriend. They've been going together for a couple of years, and I don't think either one of them thought there was a chance of getting any closer to the top than they already were."

"It's not easy to do," I said.

"I did it," Bogart said. He wasn't bragging, just making a comment. "I told Barbara how I did it. It worked for me, and now maybe it's worked for her."

"And what advice was that?"

"You take whatever parts they give you, and you don't complain. I did *The Oklahoma Kid*, I did Dr. X, I did *The Amazing Dr. Clitterhouse*. I never complained. All I ever said was, 'Hand me the script.'"

"You're not quite as easy to get along with now. If you were, Babson wouldn't hate you."

"Babson's a moron. He should write for television. He and Coville would make a lovely pair. Anyway, I earned the right to be choosey, and Barbara's on the way to earning it, too. I don't think she'd have a reason to frame me."

I couldn't think of a reason either, but I told Bogart we'd have to talk to her just the same.

"That's all right with me." He turned the Caddy into the Superior Studio gate. "Here we are." The man in the booth didn't want to let us in.

"Look, buddy," he said to Bogart, "I know who you are, but I don't care. My job is to keep people out unless they have an appointment."

"You haven't read the Detective's Handbook," Bogart told him.

"Huh?"

"You never let the person you're going to interview know you're coming," I said.

The guard shook his head. "I don't get it."

"Never mind," Bogart told him. "Just call Mr. Wayne and tell him Humphrey Bogart wants to talk to him. He'll tell you to let us through."

The guard was a big, broad-shouldered guy who looked as if he might have played a little football somewhere along the way. But the football had been a long time ago, and he'd seen and done a lot since those days. He wasn't impressed by movie stars.

"I know you're a big star and all, Mr. Bogart," he said. "But I still can't let you past."

"I'm not asking you to, Junior," Bogart said. "I'm asking you to make a phone call."

His tone made it clear that he wasn't going to take no for an answer, and to emphasize the point he lit a cigarette and leaned back against the car seat to wait.

The guard looked at him for a second, then looked at me. Then he shrugged and made the call. It didn't take long. Bogart was Bogart, after all.

The guard stuck a piece of stiff red paper under the windshield wiper and said, "Go three blocks and turn right. It's a big red building at the end of the street. If you run into the jungle, you've gone too far."

Bogart thanked him and we took off, slowly, because the street was busy. We passed a couple of crusaders, a passel of cowboys, three Indians, a chorus line, and a guy in a gorilla suit. We passed a feudal castle, an old English village, and a bombed-out battlefield before we came to the turn. We went right and saw the back-lot jungle at the end of the street. The red building was on the left.

Bogart parked his car in a reserved space and we got out.

"Aren't you afraid you'll make somebody mad if you take his space?" I asked.

"Who cares?" Bogart said, flipping his cigarette away. "I don't work here. And if I did, I'd have my own spot. Did you happen to see anybody following us today?"

"No, but then I wasn't looking."

"Some detective you are. It was that Packard again."

"I don't want to hurt your feelings," I said, "but there are a lot of black Packards in Hollywood."

"That's right. But this one was on our tail. I might not be a detective, but I could tell."

"It's gone now," I said. "So let's not worry about it."

Bogart shrugged. "You're the detective. Shall we go see Mr. Wayne?"

We entered the building, where the security was at least as good as at Warner Brothers. But they were expecting us, and before long, and after only a minimum of trouble, we were entering Thomas Wayne's office.

The carpet was just as luxurious as Mr. Warner's and probably cost twenty dollars a yard, but the office wasn't quite as large, and the desk wasn't nearly as clean.

Thomas Wayne was behind it, and he stood up as we came through the door. He was tall and thin, with a pinched face and ears that stuck out like Gable's. He wasn't as handsome as Gable, though, and he didn't have that winning smile. He didn't have any smile at all.

He came around the desk, shook hands with Bogart, and told him how much he admired his pictures and how he hoped there was a chance that someday Bogart might do a picture for Superior.

"I worked for Harry Cohn," Bogart said. "And if I'll work for him, I'll work for anybody. Just come up with the right script, and we'll see."

I didn't know if he meant it or not, but it seemed to make Wayne feel good. He almost seemed to smile. Or maybe I just imagined that.

Bogart introduced me. He explained that I worked for Warner Brothers and was a friend of Frank Burleson's. Wayne asked us to sit down and went back behind his desk to his own leather chair. There was no hat rack in the office for some reason. Bogart and I had to sit with our hats in our laps.

"In fact," I said, "Burleson's the reason we're here. I wasn't really his friend. It was more that we're in the same business, but he didn't have the same ethics I do. Yesterday he threatened Mr. Bogart with blackmail."

Wayne didn't look happy to hear that, but he didn't look surprised, either.

"He's dead now," Wayne said. "So he won't be blackmailing anyone. You don't have to worry about him any more."

He obviously didn't know the whole story.

"He's still a problem," I said, though I had no intention of saying what the problem was. "Maybe even more of one."

Wayne didn't seem to care. He said, "So what are you planning to do about it?"

"I'm going to find out who killed him," I said.

If Wayne was pleased by my announcement, he didn't show it. He said, "What business is it of yours?"

"I don't like blackmail. And while we're talking about things that aren't my business, why did you hire a man like Burleson in the first place? He had the morals of an alley cat."

"I don't have to explain my hiring practices to people like you," Wayne said.

Well, I hadn't really expected him to tell me.

Bogart tugged an earlobe.

"He must have had something on you," he said, sounding exactly like Sam Spade.

Wayne's left eyelid twitched, but that was all the emotion he showed.

"I think it's time for the two of you to leave," he said. "And as for you, Bogart, I don't think I want you to make a picture here, after all."

"Gee, and here I was hoping to do something like *Stan Shovel in the Case of the Baltic Eagle.*"

I thought it was funny. Wayne didn't. He stood up and pushed a button on a console on his desk. His ears were getting red.

The door behind us opened. Neither Bogart nor I looked around to see who was there. Tough guys never do.

"Mr. Bogart and his friend were just leaving," Wayne said.

"We were?" Bogart said.

"We might as well," I said. "We got what we came for."

"I guess we did, at that."

Bogart stood up, and so did I. I put my hat on, smiled at Wayne, and said, "Burleson had something on you, all right, and we're going to find out what it was."

"He's dead. Just leave it at that."

"He might be dead," I said, "but that doesn't mean the information he gathered is gone. Somebody searched his place after he was killed. It's possible, it's even likely, that whoever killed him got hold of his notes or his pictures or whatever it was that he had."

Wayne's mouth tightened, and I thought I'd scared him a little. If I had, he wasn't going to tell us. He looked past me and Bogart and said, "If they don't leave, throw them out the front door."

I nodded to Bogart, and we turned to leave. Just inside the door stood a couple of men, each of whom would have made two of either me or Bogart. The shoulders of their unpadded jackets were strained tight, and I thought that if either of them made a sudden move, the jackets would split right down the back. They weren't carrying pistols, but then they didn't need them. They were big enough to hunt hippos with a tack hammer. They probably had to turn sideways to get through the door.

"We were just leaving, gentlemen," Bogart said, with a mock bow.

They stepped aside to let us out of the room, then followed us until we were outside. They stood watching as we got into Bogart's Caddy and drove away from the building.

Bogart pulled the car around the corner and stopped.

"That went rather well, I thought," he said. "You're a really smooth operator. Did you learn subtlety by reading the Detective's Handbook?"

"I must have skipped that part. Anyway, we know Wayne has something to hide. We just don't know what it is."

"But somebody does, at least if your guess about Burleson's information being taken is right."

"It's not a guess. It's a supposition.

"Which amounts to the same thing."

"Whatever you say. Anyhow, it could be that somebody will use that information the same way Burleson was doing."

"Or maybe the information was destroyed," Bogart said.

"If there was any information there to be found. As you say, I'm just guessing."

"I thought it was supposing."

"It doesn't matter, since we really don't know. I think we'd better assume that someone has access to whatever it was that Burleson had."

"All right. Let's assume that. What's our next step?"

"Why don't you take a guess. It's your turn."

"We round up the usual suspects," he said.

"Absolutely right, and you didn't even need the Detective's Handbook."

"Maybe I have a feel for this kind of thing. Who do we start with?"

"Whoever's closest," I said.

Bogart started the car, but we hadn't gone far before he stopped it again.

"Hey, Charlie!" he said.

Across the street a man looked in our direction. He was dressed in a safari outfit. He wore a pith helmet, a light-colored jacket with a lot of pockets. His pants were tucked into brown boots, and there was a machete at his belt.

"Is that you, Bogie?" the man asked. He started across the street toward the car. "What the hell are you doing down here in the slums?"

"I thought I might make a picture here."

"Hell, you might as well. If you don't, they'll find somebody who looks like you and hire him."

"Nobody looks like me," Bogart said as the man reached the side of the car. "Charlie Dawson, this is Terry Scott."

Dawson was nearly six feet tall, and he was lean where I was round. He had a weathered face and sharp black eyes.

"Glad to meet you, Scott," Dawson said.

I told him the pleasure was mine, and Bogart said, "Charlie's a stunt man. He's worked on every lot in Hollywood."

"And plenty of damn' locations, too," Charlie said. "You an actor, Mr. Scott?"

There was a certain amount of skepticism in his tone, for which I didn't blame him. If I looked like anything at all, it wasn't an actor.

"I'm a detective," I said.

His skeptical look didn't change. I didn't look like a detective any more than I looked like an actor.

"You're a good friend of Stoney Randall's, aren't you?" Bogart said.

"We've done some pictures together."

"You know where he's working now?"

"Sure. Same place I am, back there in the jungle. You looking for him?"

"We wanted to talk to him about Frank Burleson," I said.

"That son of a bitch," Dawson said. "I guess Stoney's the only person here who'll miss him."

"Stoney knew him?" Bogart said.

"Nobody knew him, but he was always hanging around. Nobody liked him, unless it was Stoney. They weren't pals or anything, but he loaned Stoney a hundred bucks once, and Stoney's never forgotten it."

"I remember that. He and Barbara took a vacation or something with the money. Nobody ever talks bad about Burleson when Stoney's around."

"That's the truth. What's your interest in Burleson, anyhow?"

"Scott's looking into something for me. I'm just along for the ride."

"Speaking of which," I said, "Hop in the back. We'll give you a ride to the jungle."

"I'd get the car dirty. I've been wrestling with a lion this morning. Poor old toothless thing." Dawson scratched his chest. "I think he had fleas, too. I'd better walk."

"What kind of scene are they filming now?" I asked.

"Some action scene in the water, with a big rubber crocodile. Or alligator. I get those things confused. Anyway, Stoney will be doing the fighting because Robert Carroll doesn't like getting his hair wet."

"So Carroll is in the jungle picture?" I said.

"Yeah. It's sort of ersatz Tarzan stuff. *Jan of the Jungle*, it's called. It's a remake of a serial based on some stories by a guy named Kline. Maybe he's an ersatz Edgar Rice Burroughs."

The movie sounded perfect for Carroll, who was a handsome muscle boy with long hair, rippling thews, and a chest that the village smithy would envy. He would look right at home running around the jungle in a breechclout. I asked Dawson if Stella Gordon was in the movie, too.

"You bet. She's the princess of the Lost Kingdom of Mu. She gets to run around in some skimpy outfits that the kids are gonna love. At least the boys are. The men, too. Thomas Wayne's a shrewd bird. He's getting plenty of free publicity for the picture from the big wedding, so he's hoping it'll take off at the box office."

"Sounds like we've hit the jackpot," I said. "If we can get on the set, maybe we can talk to all of them."

"We can get on the set," Bogart said. "Isn't that right, Dawson."

"Sure. Nobody pays much attention if you look like you know what you're doing."

"I know what I'm doing," Bogart said.

I didn't, but I figured I could fake it by watching him. So far no matter where we'd been or what we'd done, he'd moved with the confidence of a born actor. Or a born con man. Whether he was dealing with the cops or a corpse, his voice was crisp and his movements were precise, as if he were perfectly at home in the world, whatever it might be like at the moment.

He turned the convertible around and steered it toward the back lot, which didn't look much like a jungle at all, at least not from where we were. He parked the car, and we waited until Dawson caught up with us before we got out.

"Follow me," Dawson said, and started into the trees along a well-worn path. He wasn't going to need his machete.

We followed him. The trees got thicker. They were hung with vines that had never grown naturally in California. In fact, neither had some of these trees. Before long we could hear noises up ahead. We came to a place that was clear of trees but full of just about everything else. A couple of huge fans produced a jungle breeze, and carpenters and electricians were bustling around. There were Klieg lights and thick cables and cameras and booms. A script girl was reading over the script. A make-up man was touching up Stella Gordon's beautiful face.

I would have enjoyed touching up the rest of her, of which there was quite a bit exposed. She wore a short skirt that barely covered the subject and a brassiere that appeared to be made of gold coils. It showed nearly as much as it concealed, which I'm sure was its purpose. She was tugging on the skirt as if she'd just pulled it on and was uncomfortable with the way it fit.

Off to the side a man was sitting with a chimp, and both of them were smoking cigarettes. That might be an unusual sight in a lot of places, but not on a movie set. Hell, in Hollywood you might even see it on the street.

You wouldn't see many tarantulas on the street, though, not even in the part of town I live in, but here there was a small wire cage full of them. I was sure they'd come in handy in a jungle movie, where there were usually more tarantulas per square inch than there ever were in a real jungle. I wasn't fond of spiders, even little ones, of which there was an ample supply in the part of town I lived in, and the ones in the cage were as big as a cake plate. I wasn't going anywhere near them.

Robert Carroll was down by a big pool. A man was showing him a crocodile that was surely made of rubber. The man worked the croc's jaws up and down and grabbed its tail to wiggle it from side to side.

Carroll looked the way Johnny Weismuller wished he could look, all muscles and hair and teeth, though he was shorter than Weismuller. He was as tan as Cary Grant, and his stomach was ridged with muscle, unlike my own stomach, which was as soft as cookie dough. The breechcloth covered just enough to keep him modest.

There was another man beside Carroll, also wearing a breechcloth, and he was paying a lot more attention to the manipulation of the croc than Carroll was. I figured he must be Stoney Randall, and Bogart confirmed that I was right.

"That's Harvey Elledge, the director," Bogart said, pointing out a tall, cadaverous man walking in the direction of the pool.

"Most of the fight will be on top of the water," Dawson said. "They don't have any underwater cameras."

Elledge spoke briefly to Randall, who nodded. Then Carroll, Elledge, and the man who'd been explaining the croc all walked away from the pool.

"They don't have to show the crocodile going into the water," Dawson said. "They have stock footage for that."

I knew what he meant. Sometimes I thought all the studios used the same footage of crocodiles slithering off a mudbank and into a river.

Randall got into the water and dragged the rubber reptile in with him.

"Quiet on the set," someone called out.

Someone else slapped together a clapper with the scene number on it.

There were a few seconds of silence and then Elledge said, "All right. Lights. Camera. Action."

Klieg lights came on to improve the daylight, and a couple of cameras ground away. Down in the pool, Randall and the alligator started whipping the water to a froth.

From where I stood, the action looked pretty good. If I hadn't known better, I'd have thought the alligator was real. It seemed to me to be thrashing around and trying its best to eat Randall, who was slashing at it with a knife. It defied his efforts, and they rolled over and over in the water. Then Randall got on its back. It took him awhile, but he finally clamped its jaws together, pulled its head up out of the water, and "killed" it by slicing its throat.

Elledge said, "Cut! Print it." and Randall rolled off the croc and came out on the bank of the pool with water running off him. Someone ran up to him with a towel.

"One take," Bogart said. "Randall's good."

"Sure he is," Dawson said, "but Elledge never does more than a couple of takes, no matter what. Producers love him. So does Wayne."

I was about to comment on the likely quality of Elledge's movies, but I didn't get a chance. I was interrupted by a woman's screams.

15

I thought at first that the screaming might be part of a new scene, but then I realized there'd been no set-up and no one had called for quiet. And after all, it was far too soon for another scene to begin. Moviemaking didn't move at that pace. The change from one scene to another usually took quite a while.

I looked around for the source of the screams and saw a beautiful woman, not Stella Gordon, covered with big, black, ugly spiders.

She screamed again. I can't say that I blamed her. If I had hairy, sticky-legged spiders crawling all over me, I'd scream too, and I was wearing a lot more clothing than she was. When I say *a lot*, I mean that I had on a jacket, pants, shirt, and shoes, not to mention a hat and tie, whereas she was wearing an outfit that might have fit a first-grader, if the first-grader had been of below-average size. I guess that in the jungle, skimpy clothing was the order of the day. Maybe that was even why jungle pictures did well at the box office.

If I'd been as heroic as I sometimes liked to think I was, I'd have rushed over and knocked the spiders off the screaming woman. She stood there, rigid as a lamppost, as if she were waiting for someone to do just that, and kept up the yelling. I hoped someone would do something, because I knew it wasn't going to be me. If it had been anything else crawling on her, snakes, for example, I'd have been right on the case. Snakes don't bother me. Spiders do.

Anyway, I thought it was Robert Carroll's job to take care of them. He was the hero of the picture. Let him handle it.

He didn't want to handle it. He was huddled behind Harvey Elledge, and he was screaming, too.

No surprise there. Nearly everyone was screaming or yelling by now. I couldn't make out any words, but that wasn't my fault. Everyone was pretty much incoherent. Even the chimp, which had fled up a tree, was chattering.

I looked around for Dawson, but he wasn't anywhere that I could see. He'd run away, I supposed, which is exactly what I would have done if only my knees had worked.

Meanwhile the woman stood there her arms held out slightly from her sides, her legs a bit spread, as the spiders crawled over her and even into her long black hair.

Just about the time I decided that no one was going to make a move, Bogart walked over to the screaming woman. He was as calm as he'd been when we were walking into Romanoff's for some eggs and bacon. He said something to the woman, and then he started brushing the spiders off her and onto the ground. He was so casual about it that you might think he dealt with vicious flesh-eating spiders every day.

It didn't take him but a couple of seconds to get all the spiders off the woman. The trouble with that was that the spiders were running in all directions, and people were scattering like scared rabbits. I didn't go anywhere. It wasn't because I was too afraid to move. At least I told myself that.

Stella Gordon didn't go anywhere, either. She went over to the woman, who was sobbing now, and put her arms around her to comfort her. The woman's shoulders shook, and Stella held her gently. People started drifting back, and Stella led the woman into the trees so she could cry in private.

I forced my locked knees to flex again and walked to where Bogart stood. I said, "You saved her life."

"Saved her life, my ass. Those spiders wouldn't hurt anybody."

"Don't tell me," I said. "Let me guess. You're going to say that they're as afraid of us as we are of them. You'd be wrong, though, at least in my case."

"I wasn't going to tell you that," Bogart said, pointing. "Look at them."

I looked around. Most of the spiders were gone, and a rotund little man was scampering around trying to gather up the ones he could find. Each time he caught one, he picked it up as if it were no more dangerous than a doughnut and put it back in the cage before going to look for another.

"I don't see anything special about them," I said. "They're tarantulas."

"Yeah, the kind you could find in the desert, not in the jungle, not that anybody who sees this crummy picture will know that."

"I don't care where they're from. I don't like them."

"You have a phobia?"

"Maybe. I know I don't like spiders."

"They won't hurt you much. If they did bite you, which isn't likely, it wouldn't be any worse than a little wasp sting."

"I'm not all that fond of wasp stings if you want to know the truth about it."

"What kind of shamus are you, Scott? You're supposed to be a tough guy. Tough guys aren't afraid of spiders."

"I never said I was a tough guy."

"You're a detective, though. I do have that part right, don't I?"

"I'd like to think so."

"Good. Why don't you start detecting and find out who dumped those spiders on Wendy."

"Wendy?" I said.

"Wendy Felsen. She's been around my place a few times with Robert and Stella. She looks pretty good in that jungle suit, doesn't she?"

I admitted that she did, but I didn't see what the spider episode had to do with anything we were interested in.

"Maybe nothing," Bogart said. "But you never can tell. It's the little things you have to watch for. They're always what trips up the crooks. That's in all the movies. Did they leave it out of the Detective's Handbook."

"I probably skipped over that part."

"You shouldn't do that." He ran the ball of his thumb along his jawline.

"Let's ask the little guy who's catching the spiders if he noticed anything."

I didn't see anything wrong with that as long as I didn't have to deal with spiders. As we walked in his direction another man appeared on the scene and started yelling about how it was costing him five thousand dollars an hour to film the movie and what the hell was going on around there anyway?

"Producer," Bogart said out of the side of his mouth in the same tone he might have used to discuss dog droppings on his rug. "Just ignore him."

I did. Elledge was the one who went to him and started speaking to him in soft tones so that I couldn't overhear. Carroll trailed along behind Elledge, standing so close to him that they might almost have been Siamese twins. I guess Carroll liked spiders even less than I did, if that was possible.

But the spiders were pretty much taken care of now. The man who had been gathering them up had closed the cage and seemed to be satisfied that either he had all of them or that the ones he didn't have weren't ever going to be found. The skin on my arms prickled at the thought of any of them running around loose. It was funny in a way because I'd withstood enemy fire on Saipan without turning a hair, and I had the scars to prove it.

The man looked up when he saw us coming and said, "Oh, my. Can it be Humphrey Bogart in person? I loved your work in *High Sierra*."

"I was pretty fond of that, myself," Bogart said. "Especially since I almost didn't get the part."

"It would have been unthinkable to use anyone else. No one would have been right for it."

"Leslie Howard was the only one who thought so at the time. Are those your spiders?"

The man looked at the cage. "Oh, yes. Yes, indeed. Do you like spiders?"

"I don't," I said. "My name's Terry Scott, by the way."

"Oh, I didn't introduce myself, did I? I'm Lane. Lane Trueblood." He extended a soft, limp, and slightly damp hand. "I do a lot of work with animals for the studio."

"You have to be careful with animals," Bogart said with a glance at the spider cage. "They might get loose."

"Oh, the spiders didn't get loose. And they're not animals. They're arachnids."

I wasn't interested in a biology lesson, but one thing he said did get my attention.

"If they didn't get loose," I said, "how did they get all over Miss Felsen?"

Trueblood clasped his pudgy little hands together and looked around.

"It could be construed that it was my fault," he said.

"We wouldn't construe that," Bogart assured him, but Trueblood didn't seem to care. He wasn't worried about us. He was thinking about the producer.

"You see," he said, "I'm supposed to be with the spiders at all times, for safety's sake, but I had to go...relieve myself. There are times when it's absolutely necessary, and the spiders were secure, or so I thought."

"They didn't open that cage by themselves," Bogart said.

"No. Indeed they didn't. Let me show you."

He walked over to the cage, picked it up, and brought it back to where we were standing.

When he got close, I moved away. I knew the spiders couldn't get out, or part of me knew it. The other part of me wasn't so sure.

"Look," Trueblood said, and he pointed out the latch on the cage. There was a hasp that slipped over a U-bolt, and a piece of metal was run through the bolt to hold the hasp in place. "I know it was secure before I left. I checked."

"So somebody let the spiders out," Bogart said. He looked at me. "Now all you have to do is find out who it was."

"Oh, I know who it was," Trueblood said. "I saw it happen."

We waited for him to tell us the name of the guilty party, but he didn't. He returned the cage to its place and then came back over to where we stood.

"Well," I said, "are you going to tell us who it was or are you planning to make us give you the third degree?"

"That sounds rather exciting," Trueblood said. "Would you both be involved?"

"Look, cutie," Bogart said. "We like you, but you're not really our type. Just tell us who let the spiders out."

"Oh, all right, if that's the way you want it."

"That's the way we want it," I said. "Tell us who it was."

"It was Wendy," he said. "Miss Felsen, I mean. She let them out herself."

I must have looked surprised because Trueblood said, "I *did* see her. I don't make up stories just to get attention."

"He doesn't like spiders," Bogart said. "Naturally he was a bit shocked."

Trueblood was disappointed in me. The corners of his soft mouth turned down.

"You don't like spiders? But they won't hurt you. They're far kinder than most human beings I know."

I didn't want to get into a philosophical discussion. I said, "Why would someone do a thing like that?"

"Just for fun?" Bogart said, but I knew he was only needling me.

Trueblood, however took him seriously. He got a sly look in his eyes.

"It just depends on what you mean by *fun*."

I didn't know what he meant, but Bogart seemed to. He gave a wry grin and said, "So that's it."

I was going to ask him to explain it to me, but before I could say anything someone yelled out, "What's that son of a bitch doing on this set? I want him out of here right now!"

We turned around to see who was causing the commotion. A man in a light-colored suit and hat was staring in our direction and pointing a skinny finger.

"I don't think he likes you much," Trueblood said.

"You're right," Bogart said. "Is he the writer on this picture?"

"Yes, indeed. I'm surprised he's here, though. He's always complaining about the way the actors play the scenes. Mr. Elledge has had him removed from the set several times already."

"It figures," Bogart said. "I knew he'd sold a script. I didn't know it was this cheap jungle epic. That figures, too."

It was beginning to look as if nearly everyone who'd been at Bogart's place for the party was working on *Jan of the Jungle*.

"I mean it," Babson said. "I want him off this set. He has no business here. He's trying to steal our ideas for some Goddamned Warner Brothers picture."

Trueblood giggled. "As if Warner Brothers needed to steal from Superior."

A man wearing a white hunter's outfit walked over and took Babson's arm. I'd seen enough jungle movies to know that the white hunter was invariably the villain. And I happened to recognize this one.

"Joey Gallindo," I said. "Let me guess who's playing the comic relief."

"The chimp," Bogart said. "It's always the chimp."

"Not this time," Trueblood said. "Where *is* Timbo, I wonder."

Timbo had to be the chimp.

"He's up a tree," I said. "You could probably get him down if you offered him a cigarette."

"Oh, I'd never do that. Smoking isn't good for him." He looked disapprovingly at Bogart, who'd lit up a Chesterfield. "It's not good for you, either."

Bogart grinned at him and then blew out a plume of smoke, which Trueblood waved away with fluttering hands.

"If Timbo's not the comic relief," I said, "who is?"

"Timbo's a serious actor," Trueblood said. "He wouldn't stoop to the cheap humor in this picture. So they had to hire someone who would."

"Slappy Coville," I said.

"How did you ever guess?"

"It was easy," I said.

16

W hat *wasn't* easy was figuring out where to start. Everyone from the party was working on the same Superior picture, which meant that Burleson could have had something on all of them. And maybe that each of them knew about the others. It was getting complicated, and I didn't like complications. I preferred cowboys who fell in love with their horses. Odd, maybe. Even perverse. But not complicated.

Joey Gallindo had pulled Babson off to the side and was talking earnestly to him. It didn't really matter. No one had paid Babson any attention in the first place, so Babson was calming down. He didn't want us to notice how little influence he had.

"I must coax Timbo down from that tree," Trueblood said. "He's supposed to be in the next scene. It's been a pleasure to meet you."

He meant Bogart, but I said, "It's been a pleasure to meet you, too" before the walked off to see about his chimp.

When he was gone, I said to Bogart, "You neglected to mention that everyone who came to your party was in the same picture."

"I told you I didn't invite them. They just showed up. If I'd invited them, Babson wouldn't have been there."

"Let me see if I have this right. He'll drink your whiskey, but he doesn't want you on his set."

"*His set*. I like that. You're always good for a laugh, Junior."

"You know what I mean."

"Yeah. I do. So let me tell you the way it was. He showed up at my house with a bunch of other people. They'd all had a drink or two by the time they got there. I don't know why they came, but they did, and I wasn't going to turn them away. I like most of them, except for Babson."

"One of them probably framed you for murder."

"And I know which one would be the most likely suspect. Babson. Too bad there's a problem with that."

I didn't see the problem, and I said so.

"You need to go to more movies, Junior. The most likely suspect is never the guilty party."

"It's not that way in real life," I said. "Usually the most likely suspect is the one who did it. That's why he's the likely suspect."

"Good. Let's call your friend Congreve and have Babson hauled off to the pokey."

It wasn't that easy, and Bogart knew it. He was giving me the needle again. I would have called him on it, but just then Dawson came sauntering up as if he'd just stepped away for a refreshing drink or maybe to have a smoke with the chimp. But I suspected that he'd been hiding behind a tree somewhere.

"Never a dull moment," Dawson said.

He took off his pith helmet and wiped the leather sweatband with a handkerchief that he produced from one of the many pockets of his jacket. The outfit was similar to the one being worn by Joey Gallindo.

"Are you doubling for Gallindo?" I asked.

He returned the handkerchief to his pocket and put the helmet back on his head.

"How did you guess?" he asked.

"He's a professional detective," Bogart said. "He sees things other men don't notice."

The needle again, but I ignored it. I said, "Why weren't you at the party last night?"

"Did I miss a party? How unlike me."

"At Bogie's house," I said. "Half the cast was there."

"I didn't know about it. But then I'm not so friendly with most of these people." He looked over to where Babson and Gallindo were still deep in conversation. "Frankly, they make my skin crawl."

CHAPTER

"I'm not all that fond of them myself," Bogart said. "So why did they end up at my place?"

That's what I was wondering. Whose idea had it been to go to Bogart's place? Was there someone in the group who had known about the pistol even before Mayo had brought it out? And if so, which one of the partygoers had it been?

Dawson told us that he had no idea how the group had gotten to Bogart's house. He said that several of them got together every evening after filming and went somewhere. It didn't seem to matter where.

"Maybe they all talked about Burleson," Bogart said.

I didn't think that was the case. If they had secrets they wanted to keep hidden, they wouldn't have discussed them openly. On the other hand, I knew that on a set there were sometimes very few secrets. Things had a way of coming out whether they were discussed openly or not. Whatever Burleson had known might have been known to others as well.

"We'd like to talk to Stella Gordon," Bogart said. "But she seems to have disappeared."

"It happens now and again," Dawson said. "You know what stars are like."

"Present company excepted," Bogart said.

Dawson nodded. "Goes without saying."

"Thanks."

"At any rate, there won't be any talking here for a while," Dawson said. "Everyone's leaving for a break because they're upset about the spiders. So we'll be setting up for the another scene, and it won't be filmed until after dark."

"It's a night scene, huh?" I said.

Dawson and Bogart just looked at me. I suppose it wasn't the brightest thing I'd ever said, but I tried to defend myself.

"Sometimes they do night scenes during the day," I said.

"They always look shoddy and faked," Dawson said, "and they never, so far as I know, do the reverse."

"Never mind," Bogart said. "What time will they be finishing up?"

"Probably around ten," Dawson said. "Or even sooner if things go well. Gallindo and Carroll have a fight on a precipice overlooking a waterfall, which of course means that Stoney and I have a fight."

I looked around. I didn't see either a precipice or a waterfall, but I knew that didn't make much difference. The fight would be on a something that looked like a flat rock, and the rest would appear in the final film with back projection or some other trick. It seemed to me they could do that on a soundstage.

"We'll be moving to the soundstage as soon as we film the chase," Dawson said, as if he knew what I'd been thinking. "Everything's already set up there."

"And when they finish the filming, they'll go somewhere else for a party," I said.

"That's the general idea."

"Maybe we can join them tonight," I said.

"Count me in," Bogart said. "But we're not going to my house."

"I don't blame you," I told him.

Bogart wanted to have an early dinner, no doubt looking forward to another chance to stick Mr. Warner with the check, but I begged off, saying that I needed to stop by the office and check the mail. He didn't ask to go with me.

He dropped me off at my car, and I told him I'd meet him at the set that evening around nine-thirty. He said I'd better take the pass from under his wiper, and I did, knowing that he wouldn't have any trouble getting in, whereas I'd never pass the gate without it. So I took the pass and stuck it under the worn-out wiper on the Chevy before I got in and drove away.

My office always looked shabby, but when I opened the door and saw the dust and the grimy window, I thought it looked even worse than usual. It didn't, of course. It was just that I'd been riding in a Cadillac, associating with one of the biggest stars in Hollywood, and visiting a movie set as if I belonged there. A fella could get used to that sort of thing if he didn't watch out. He might forget his place in the big scheme of things, and that would be too bad. Some people were meant to be stars, and some people were meant to clean up their messes. It was best that I keep that in mind.

I limped over to my desk and sat down. My hip was hurting, either because Mayo had kicked it even harder than I thought the previous evening or because I was feeling sorry for myself. Probably the latter.

If there had been a bottle of bourbon in the bottom drawer of the desk, I might have been tempted to drown my sorrows. I knew it wouldn't work. I'd tried it once upon a time, and I'd wound up in a hospital ward with pink zebras and stripped elephants dancing across the bridge of my nose. Which was why didn't drink any more. One experience like that was enough for me.

Somewhere on top of the desk there was a little notebook with telephone numbers in it. I located it under a copy of *True Detective* that someone had handed me as a joke. I flipped through the notebook until I found a number for Leon Jones.

Leon was either at home or at Santa Anita. If he was at the track, he was betting. If he was at home, he was handicapping the races. He knew most of the gossip, and he'd heard all the rumors, so I had a question for him.

He answered on the third ring, sounding if he had a sock stuffed in his mouth.

"What the hell, Leon?" I said.

There was the sound of chewing and then some swallowing.

"Is that you, Scotty?" Leon said in a more normal voice.

I told him it was.

"I was eating an egg sandwich," he said.

As far as I knew, sandwiches were all Leon ever ate. He never seemed to have time for anything else

"I need some information," I said. "I think you're the man to give it to me."

"If it's about the third race tomorrow, forget it. My lips are sealed. Sure, I have it nailed, but I can't let just anybody in on it. I stand to make a bundle."

If he'd ever made a bundle, I didn't know about it. Maybe he had, but if so, he'd invested it all in other bets that hadn't panned out. Anyway, he was only saying he had it nailed because he hoped I'd offer him some money for the tip.

"I hope you break the bank," I said. "But I'm not asking for a horse. I'm asking about Frank Burleson."

"Dead as a mackerel," Leon said. "Which is lucky for him. If he was alive, Charlie O. would have him knee-capped."

Dead, or knee-capped? For me it wouldn't have been a hard choice, but maybe Leon didn't see it that way.

"He owed Charlie O.?" I said.

Charlie O. was Charles Orsini. He owned a nightclub and was a big-time bookie, among other pursuits.

"Everybody owes Charlie O.," Leon said. "That's just the way it is."

I was sure Leon spoke from experience. It was much easier to believe in his losses than in his supposed winnings.

"But not everybody gets knee-capped," I said.

"True, and it's a good thing for me that it is. But then I never lost ten Gs in one afternoon."

"Ten thousand dollars?"

"Give or take. Close enough."

"Give or take, that's a lot of money," I said.

There was a short laugh from the other end of the line.

"Not to Charlie O. But he can't let anybody who owes him that much for so long off the hook. It wouldn't be good for business. You know Charlie O."

I knew Charlie O., all right, though it wasn't from gambling. My relationship with him had been strictly personal.

I also knew that my hunch about Burleson and the ponies was correct. He needed money, and he needed it fast, so he was putting the squeeze on everybody he could.

"You think Charlie O. had him killed?" I said.

There was another short laugh, more like a snort.

"Dead men can't pay off," Leon said. "What kind of business would that be?"

"Bad business, I suppose."

"Damn right it would be. If Charlie O. went around killing everybody who owed him ten large, there wouldn't be a lot of people left in L. A. or Hollywood, now would there."

"But you said Burleson was desperate."

"Who wouldn't be? It's no fun having your kneecaps broken, but most of Charlie O.'s clients can pay off before it comes to that. Your pal Burleson couldn't."

"He wasn't my pal. Why does everybody keep saying that?"

"I don't know about everybody. You're in the same business, so I thought maybe you were pals."

"No," I said flatly. "We weren't pals."

"So why are you asking about him then? You're not working for the cops these days, are you, Scotty?"

Congreve. The thought of me working for the cops would probably give him a coronary.

"I'm not working for the cops. I just heard Frank had been killed, and I wondered if his losses had anything to do with it."

"You'd better just forget that. Charlie O. would probably like to know who killed him even more than the cops would."

I told Leon I'd forget it. We talked a little longer, or he did, mostly about horses I'd never heard of. When he hung up, I sat there and wondered about Charlie O.

What I wondered was how much the dirt Frank had on the Superior stars and a few others like Mayo Methot would be worth to a guy like Charlie O.

Ten thousand dollars, give or take?

And how far would he go to collect it? If he had the information and wanted to use it, Frank's being dead wouldn't make much difference to him.

It was something to think about.

17

Bogart seemed to like the idea of pinning the murder on Charlie O.

"I never played the ponies," he said. "Some people would tell you it's because I'm too close with a dollar. Maybe it is. But I know who Charlie O. is, and I've heard he's tied into the mob. If he is, couldn't there be a connection with Thomas Wayne or Joey Gallindo? It would be pretty handy to either one of them to have Burleson out of the way if he was blackmailing them."

"You think Charlie O. did them a favor?" I said. "Some sort of honor–among–thieves deal?"

"Something like that. He might not collect his money, but it would be good advertising. Nobody would ever hold out on him again. Do we have time to talk to him before we go to the studio?"

Of course we had time. It was only seven o'clock, and I'd called to say I'd be by for him around nine-thirty. We could easily get to Charlie O.'s club and back to the studio in time. But seeing Charlie O. wasn't as easy as Bogart thought it was.

"This isn't like the movies," I said. "I can't just drive to Charlie O.'s place and confront him. I'd have to get by two or three guys, and all three of them are likely to be a lot bigger and meaner than I am. Besides, Charlie O. doesn't like me."

Bogart didn't ask why. He just said, "I'll go with you."

"I don't think even Sam Spade will scare those guys. Philip Marlowe, either."

"Not even if he has Canino's best boy with him?"

"I'm not feeling a whole lot like Bob Steele. Maybe I'm worried about my kneecaps."

I wasn't worried about my kneecaps, though. I was worried about other things. Charlie O. and I went back a ways.

"The hell you're worried," Bogart said. "Anyway, we're going. That Congreve has it in for me, and I'm not taking the fall for anybody. We need to find out if Charlie O. had Burleson killed."

"And you think that he'd tell us, even if we could get in to see him?"

"You never know," Bogart said, "until you try."

"And what's your plan for getting past all the muscle?"

"They'll let us in. Trust me."

I was going to say I didn't trust anybody, but it was too late. Bogart had already hung up the phone.

Charlie O.'s club, whether because of an excess of ego or a lack of imagination, or for some other reason entirely, was called *Charlie O.'s*. It was up in the Hollywood hills, and there was a red neon sign that spelled out the name in script letters. There were lots of nice cars in the parking lot, a Lincoln Continental or two, and a Buick convertible, along with a couple of Packards and some Cadillacs. There were Fords and Chevys, too, but I sort of wished we'd come in Bogart's car instead of mine, which could have used a wash and polish.

Unlike my car, the club building had a fresh coat of paint on it, and dance music drifted out the door and into the parking lot. If you liked that kind of place, then Charlie O.'s was the kind of place you'd like.

I parked the car and we got out. I could see the lights of L. A. down below and the oil wells off to the south, though there was a foggy mist in the air.

"I hope we don't have to fight anybody," Bogart said.

I hoped so, too. It was a good thing we hadn't called ahead, or Charlie O. would have had a couple of his goons waiting for us. Not that it really mattered. I was sure they'd be inside, anyway. They always were.

We didn't get inside, however. Leo was still the doorman.

"Hello, Mr. Scott," he said as soon as he saw me. He was a head taller than I was, and twice as wide. "Mr. Orsini ain't here."

"Sure he is, Leo. He's always here."

"Not for you, he ain't. When you're here, he's not. That's just the way it is."

I'd known how it was, though I hadn't tried to explain it to Bogart. And if we somehow managed to talk our way past Leo, which wasn't likely, we'd still have to get past Mike and Tank, not that there was any chance of that. You can guess how Tank got his nickname. He was even bigger than Leo. So was Mike, for that matter.

"What the hell is this guy talking about?" Bogart asked. "Do you know him?"

That distinctive voice caused Leo to notice Bogart for the first time. Leo's mouth twisted into what he probably thought was a smile.

"Jeez, Mr. Scott. I didn't know you had company. It's an honor to have you in the club, Mr. Bogart."

"The pleasure is all mine, Leo. That's your name, isn't it? Leo?"

"That's right, Mr. Bogart. Let me call Felipe over here, and he'll show you to a table. Best one in the house, and the drinks are on Mr. Orsini."

I'd seen the power of stardom before, so I shouldn't have been surprised. But I was. Leo attempting to be affable and gracious was something I never thought I'd witness.

"That's very nice of you, Leo," Bogart said.

He got his pack of Chesterfields out of his pocket, and I thought Leo would break his arm getting to his lighter. He flicked the little wheel and Bogart leaned forward to put the cigarette to the flame. While he inhaled, Leo made the lighter disappear, and he started to wave for Felipe.

"Never mind that," Bogart said. "We'd like to stay around a while, but we really came here to see Mr. Orsini."

"Well, gee, Mr. Bogart." Leo was flustered. Another first. "I'm sure he'd like to see you." Leo looked at me as if I were something he'd found on his shoe after walking through a chicken yard. "But, well, he doesn't want to see Mr. Scott."

"Where I go, Scott goes. Why don't you let Mr. Orsini decide?"

Leo thought it over. You could almost see his lips moving as he considered the various possibilities.

"All right," he said after a minute or so. "I'll let you past. But you'll have to convince Mike and Tank to let you through when you get upstairs. They ain't as soft as I am."

"Thank you, Leo," Bogart said.

He put out his hand, and Leo shook it, plainly impressed. I hoped he didn't ask for an autograph.

He didn't, and we went into the foyer, past the hat-check counter and into the main room. There were tables with white cloths around a small dance floor. A four-piece band was playing "That Chick's too Young to Fry." I figured there were several chicks of that description scattered around the tables, most of them in the company of older gentlemen who should have known better.

Bogart pulled his hat low over his forehead so he wouldn't be recognized, but he needn't have worried. The people in Charlie O.'s weren't interested in anything outside the circle of their own tables.

"Which way?" Bogart asked.

"Follow me," I said, and skirted the tables, heading for a door at the back of the big room. It led to the stairway to the second floor.

When we got there, I opened the door and stepped through. Bogart was right behind me. We stood in a short, empty hallway with doors on either side and stairs at the end.

"I don't see any tough guys here," Bogart said.

"They'll be on the second floor landing," I said. "And they'll be waiting for us."

"Leo called them, huh?"

"That's right."

"Just when I was getting to like him."

"It's his job. Besides, they'd be there anyway."

We went up the stairs with me in the lead. I hadn't closed the door below, and the faint sound of music followed us.

Mike and Tank were standing at the top of the stairs, both of them looking out of place in their dark suits and ties. They looked more like stevedores than nightclub bouncers.

"You shouldn't-a come, Scott" Mike said.

He was the smaller of the two, probably not an inch over six-three, and he had a high, adenoidal voice that would have finished his career in the talkies before it ever got started.

"Yeah," Tank said, which even at that put a strain on his vocabulary. But then talking wasn't his specialty. He had big rough hands, and he could bend a ten-penny nail between his thumb and index finger, though bending nails wasn't his specialty, either.

Bogart didn't seem fazed by either of them. He dropped his cigarette to the floor and mashed it with his shoe.

"Have you asked Mr. Orsini if he wants to see us?" he asked.

"He don't want to see you," Mike said.

Tank didn't say anything. He just nodded.

"I think he does," Bogart said. I didn't interrupt. If he wanted to do the talking, that was fine with me. "Why don't you check with him."

He looked pointedly at the phone on a wooden stand beside the door into Charlie O.'s office.

"You got a message for him?" Mike asked.

"That's right," Bogart said. His voice had roughened, and he sounded a lot more like the racketeer he'd played in *The Roaring Twenties* than usual. "I got a message for him. He'll want to hear it personally."

"The boys sent you here?"

"That's right," Bogart said. "The boys sent me."

"Whaddya think, Tank?" Mike asked his partner.

Tank screwed up his face and concentrated hard. The strain on his thought processes was almost too much.

"Let 'em in," he said finally.

"Sure," Mike said. "You're right, Tank. We'll let 'em in."

This was a new one on me, though I'd heard about it before. There were apparently plenty of people, especially those of the criminal persuasion, who actually believed that Bogart was one of them, that he was a gangster. He was from New York, after all, and he was making big money for doing practically nothing. To some people, that spelled the mob. So Bogart had two things going for him: his star power and the fact that some people confused the fantasy of the screen with reality. And he was smart enough to take advantage of both of them.

Mike opened the door and held it wide. Bogart looked at me, I nodded, and we went through.

CHAPTER

18

Charles Orsini, Charlie O., had as much power as Jack Warner. Maybe more. But you couldn't tell it by his office. The carpet was thin. The desk was cheap veneer. There was only one small window, and there was no view, or at least not one we could see, because it was covered by Venetian blinds that hung at a slight slant.

Charlie O. sat behind the desk. His hair was still black, or maybe he colored it. His cheeks were pink, and he looked freshly shaved. I thought I could smell a faint odor of bay rum in the air. He was big, but not like Mike and Tank. He was built more along the lines of Sidney Greenstreet, though he wasn't nearly as charming.

He might have been more charming if he hadn't been holding a .38 revolver that was pointed at my belt buckle.

"I told you I never wanted to see you in here again, Scott," he said. His voice was hoarse, as if he had a cold, but he didn't. That was just the way he sounded, as if he'd gargled razor blades at some time or other. "For that matter, I don't want to see you anywhere."

"Where's Herbie?" I asked. "He's usually the one with the gun."

Herbie was Orsini's personal bodyguard. He also did some of the dirty work that Mike and Tank didn't get around to.

"Herbie isn't feeling well this evening," Charlie O. said. "But I know how to use a pistol, so I don't need him."

I didn't know whether he could use a pistol or not, but we were only about ten feet from him. It would be hard for him to miss me if he pulled the trigger.

"We're here about Frank Burleson," Bogart said, ignoring the pistol. "The word is that he owed you money."

Charlie O. moved the pistol so that it pointed at Bogart's belt buckle instead of at mine. I confess that I felt a little bit relieved.

"I don't go to the movies, Mr. Bogart," Charlie O. said. "And although I know who you are, I'm not as easily impressed as most of my employees. I must say, however, that I'm flattered you've deigned to visit my little establishment. That's the only reason I haven't shot Scott." He turned the pistol back to me. "That doesn't mean I won't shoot him later, of course."

Charlie O. might have sounded as if he was joking, but I knew better. It wasn't warm in the room, but a drop of sweat slid down from my left sideburn onto my cheek.

I heard the door close softly behind me. The faint notes of "Don't Get Around Much Anymore" were cut off completely. I didn't have to look to know that Mike and Tank were standing by the door, just waiting. Nothing that happened in that room would bother them. They'd seen it all before. I could hear Mike's adenoidal breathing.

"We wanted you to tell us about Frank Burleson," Bogart said. "Not show us how tough you are."

I wondered if he was really as calm and assured as he seemed or if he was just playing a role. It all came down to the same thing in the end, I suppose.

Charlie O. put the pistol down on the light-blue blotter that covered about half his desk. I was tempted to wipe away the sweat that had now trickled down to my jaw, but I didn't do it.

"You don't know about Scott and my daughter, do you," Charlie O. said.

Bogart looked at me and raised his eyebrows. I just shrugged.

"Laura," Charlie O. said. He picked up the pistol and aimed it at me again. "That's her name. She won't come near me. Your fault, Scott."

I decided that if Bogart could be a hard guy, so could I. I said, "It's not my fault that you're a bookie, a shylock, a pimp, and God knows what else."

I thought for a second that he might pull the trigger. I even thought I saw the knuckle of his trigger finger turn white as it tightened, but maybe not. I have a vivid imagination in situations that involve my own personal survival. After a few seconds of silence, he took a deep breath, pursed his lips, and put the pistol down again.

"You are correct, Scott. As much as I hate to admit it, you are correct. I'm all those things, and several more that you neglected to mention. A man has to make a living, after all, and he does what he can. Laura would have found out sooner or later, no doubt. I was just hoping it would be later. Much later. You didn't have to tell her."

I'd been right about him, and he was right about me. I'd told her because I was in love with her and wanted to save her from what I considered the evil influence of her father. You'd think she'd appreciate it, maybe even thank me. That is, you'd think that if you'd had as much experience with women and with being in love as I'd had, which up until I met Laura was no experience at all.

She didn't appreciate what I told her at all, and when I proved it to her, she appreciated it even less. She never wanted to see her father again, which was fine with me, but she never wanted to see me again, which wasn't. That's when I started drinking myself into insensibility and almost beyond. Luckily, there was a spark of consciousness somewhere that didn't flicker out, and I was able to get hold of myself, sober up, join the Army, and go off to get myself shot up on Saipan. Maybe I'd been hoping the Japs would kill me, but that didn't work out, either.

"I'm sorry I told her," I said.

Charlie O. looked at me with understandable skepticism.

"I mean it. I shouldn't have done it. It cost me as much as it did you."

"Oh, no," he said. "Oh, no, it didn't. She was my daughter, Scott. To you, she was just another broad."

If he hadn't had the gun, if the two goons hadn't been standing at my back, maybe I'd have gone for him then.

Or maybe not.

"She was never that," I said evenly.

He shrugged ponderously, which was the only way he'd ever be able to do it.

"It doesn't matter. We've both lost her now. What's this about Frank Burleson?"

Bogart didn't miss a beat. "We want to know if he owed you money. A lot of money."

"He did. Nearly ten thousand dollars. The police have already been here to ask me that. Naturally I lied to them."

"But you wouldn't lie to us," I said.

I don't think he liked my tone.

"I never liked you, Scott," he said. "Not in the least. Even before you cost me my daughter." He picked up the pistol. "Don't make me angry now, not when I have a gun in my hand."

"I have another question," Bogart said, whether to distract him or because he really wanted to know, I wasn't sure. "What's your connection with Thomas Wayne?"

Charlie O. looked interested. "What makes you think there is one?"

"Everybody in Hollywood knows where Wayne got the money to start his studio."

That wasn't true at all, but everyone had heard the rumors, which I suppose amounted to the same thing.

"You and Wayne are bound to know one another," Bogart continued. "You have some friends in common."

"Mere speculation, but I can see where it's leading."

"Where do you think that is?"

"Burleson needed money. He was trying to get it any way he could because he was afraid of what might happen to him if he didn't pay me." Charlie O. looked beyond us at Mike and Tank, who were of course the ones Burleson would have been afraid of. "Frank was right to be afraid. But he wasn't blackmailing Thomas Wayne, and Wayne didn't ask me to kill him."

"You seem to know a lot about it, though," Bogart said.

"Let's just say that I like to keep informed."

"Let's say more than that," I put in, having just had a thought. Or made a guess. "Let's say that Wayne got in touch with you because Burleson was blackmailing his stars. He might have asked you to do something about it."

Charlie O. put the pistol back down and rested his folded hands on it. "You may or may not be correct. I wouldn't tell you if you were. But think about this: if I'd had Burleson killed, who would I have sent?"

He didn't really expect me to answer that, and I didn't. I just stood and listened to Mike breathing.

"Whoever it might have been," Charlie O. continued, "he would never have been a professional, not someone careless enough to leave the murder weapon lying on the floor of Burleson's room. That smacks very much of amateurism, to me. Or of a frame. Don't you think so?"

I did. I'd thought so all along, but Bogart's enthusiasm for putting the blame on Charlie O. had carried me away, though it was my fault for mentioning it in the first place.

"We made a mistake," I said. "I apologize."

"No we didn't," Bogart said. "He knows more than he's telling."

"I always do," Charlie O. said. "I know many things, none of which are any of your business, or Mr. Scott's business. And now I have a question for you, Mr. Bogart?"

Bogart twisted his ring and gave Charlie O. a straight look.

"What makes you think I'll answer you?"

"You don't have to answer me. I'm merely curious. But it would be a courtesy if you did."

"O.K. Let's hear the question."

"What's your stake in this? Why are you associating with a cheap studio peeper? For that matter, why is either of you interested in Frank Burleson?"

Bogart smiled. "He tried to blackmail me. I didn't like it. Now he's dead, and someone's trying to pin it on me."

Charlie O. thought about that for a second. Then he said, "The gun left at the scene. It was yours?"

I started to say *no*, but Bogart was too quick for me.

"Yeah. It was mine. Now you know something the cops don't know."

"I appreciate your trust, and I will respect your confidence."

I knew he would, mainly because he'd never told the truth to the cops in his life.

"And now," he said, "I think our little tête-à-tête is over. There is, however, one bit of unfinished business to take care of."

I didn't like the sound of that. I heard Mike—or Tank—move behind me.

"Mr. Bogart," Charlie O. said, "you and I have nothing more to say to one another. I'm going to ask Mike to escort you back to the club while Tank has a few words with Mr. Scott about my daughter."

I knew what that meant. Orsini hadn't been able to get to me when his daughter departed for parts unknown because I'd joined the Army. When I came back, he'd more or less lost interest. But now that I was right there and handy, he was going to give me what he thought I deserved. Most likely, Tank was going to crush my kidneys or some other essential part of my anatomy that was even more sensitive to pain than my kidneys.

"I think I'll stick around," Bogart said. "I'd like to hear about your daughter."

"I don't think that would be wise," Charlie O. said. "I don't think that would be wise at all.

And then I heard Tank make his move.

CHAPTER

19

If you're going to act at all in a situation like that, you have to act fast.

Bogart did. He turned and punched Mike in the balls. I don't think he meant to hit him there, but Mike was tall and Bogart wasn't, and it just happened. Or maybe it was deliberate.

Either way, it surprised the hell out of Mike, who made a sound like a big cat whose tail has been slammed in a car door and folded in the middle.

I was as surprised as Mike, though not in nearly as much pain and not too surprised to drop to the floor. I wasn't a second too soon because Charlie O. fired his .38 right at the spot where I'd been standing.

Tank, unfortunately for him, had been right behind me, and the bullet intended for me hit him.

He was even more surprised than Mike had been. My ears were ringing from the sound of the shot in the small room, but I thought I heard him say, "Oh, shit."

I didn't worry too much about him. Considering what he'd been planning to do to me, he deserved whatever he got.

I jumped up to go for Charlie O., but Bogart was already there, twisting his arm and trying to get the pistol away.

Mike was still in the same spot where he'd been when Bogart hit him, bent over and clutching his stomach. I wondered why, since it wasn't his stomach that had been hit. He was making retching noises, and probably the smell of gunpowder didn't help him any.

Tank was still standing, too, but he wasn't bent over. There was a wide dark spot on his suit, and when he put his hand to it, it came away wet and red.

Charlie O. might have been fat, but he was strong, and he actually lifted Bogart up off the floor with the arm that Bogart was hanging onto. I put my fingers on a certain spot on Charlie O.'s neck and pressed hard, partially paralyzing him as the pain shot through him. He dropped the pistol, and Bogart let go of his arm to pick it up.

As soon as he got it, he handed it to me. Maybe he didn't want to shoot anybody.

I did. I wanted to shoot Charlie O. and Mike, though that would hardly have been fair. I even wanted to shoot Tank, which also wouldn't have been fair, so of course I didn't. It wouldn't have done any good anyhow, and it would just have made Charlie O. even angrier than he already was.

Which was very, very angry. As the pain faded from his body, his face got mottled and purplish. I thought for a second that he might have a serious stroke, but once again he managed to get himself under control.

It took a while. This time he had to take several deep breaths, and I didn't think he'd be able to do it, but when he finally spoke his voice was steady.

"I should call a doctor for Tank."

I stood beside him with the pistol pointed at his head.

"Go ahead. But be careful."

Tank was very still. Blood dripped off his fingertips to the rug, but he hadn't fallen yet.

Mike tried to straighten up, couldn't, and moaned loudly.

"Be quiet, Mike," Charlie O. said.

He dialed the phone that was on his desk, and after a few seconds he spoke softly into the receiver. He'd know a doctor who'd come quickly and without question and keep his mouth shut about anything he did or saw.

When he was finished giving instructions to the doctor, Charlie O.

hung up the phone. He looked at me, and then he looked at Bogart, who was breathing harshly at my side.

I knew how Bogart felt. I felt a little edgy, myself.

"I underestimated you, Scott," Charlie O. said. "I underestimated both of you. I thought Mr. Bogart would be another Hollywood creampuff, and I thought you'd lost your guts after the war."

"I didn't lose them. I tried to drown them with whiskey. I guess it didn't work."

Bogart lit a cigarette with hands that were just as steady as mine, which wasn't saying much, but at least the pistol didn't waver, and he put the flame to the Chesterfield without having to try twice. He waved the match out and pitched it into a wastebasket by Charlie O.'s desk. He exhaled a thin stream of smoke and said, "I think it's time for us to go."

I thought he was absolutely right. I told Mike to get over beside Tank. He just looked at me, so I didn't worry about him anymore. He wasn't going to try to stop us.

I moved away from Charlie O. Bogart came along, and we went to the door. Before I opened it, I said, "No hard feelings."

"None," Charlie O. said. "If things had turned out differently, I don't suppose you would have complained."

"I probably wouldn't have been in any condition to complain," I said.

His mouth twitched. Maybe it was a smile.

"Possibly not. You'll leave me my pistol?"

"You can get another one," I said.

He nodded and waved a hand dismissively, as if he hadn't really expected to get the .38 back.

I opened the door. The thin strains of "Night and Day" wafted up the stairs.

Mike moaned a little in the wrong key. He was bent so that his knees were almost touching each other.

Tank still hadn't moved. Maybe he couldn't believe what had happened to him. Or maybe his brain had finally locked up for good.

"We're even, Orsini," I said. "Tell your boys that. I don't want to have to look over my shoulder for them."

"I'll tell them, Scott. You stay out of my business, and I'll stay out of yours."

It sounded sincere, or as sincere as Charlie O. ever got.

"Frank Burleson's death is none of your concern," Charlie O. continued. "Forget about it."

First the cops, then the gangsters. Nobody wanted us to find out who killed Frank.

"We'll think it over," I said, and closed the door behind me as Bogart and I left the office.

"I could use a drink," Bogart said when we were in the hall. "Or even two drinks."

"We'd better not stop here for one. I know what Charlie O. said, but I'd just as soon not put him to the test so soon."

Bogart nodded. I slipped the pistol into my jacket pocket. We descended the stairs and went down the hall. The band was playing "Me and my Shadow" now. A few couples were dancing. No one noticed me and Bogart as we walked around the edge of the room.

Leo was still on the door when we went out.

"You have a talk with Mr. Orsini?" he asked.

"We had a wonderful conversation," I said. "Mr. Orsini was very cordial."

"Yeah. He's a nice guy. See you around, Mr. Scott."

Not a chance, Leo, I thought.

We stopped at a drugstore and bought a bottle of Scotch. Bogart paid. He didn't even think to ask about putting it on the expense account.

I didn't have a glass handy, but Bogart didn't care. He took a hefty slug straight from the bottle and wiped his mouth with the back of his hand.

"Are you sure you won't have some?" he asked.

"I'm sure. I tried it, and it didn't work."

"Judging from what you said in Orsini's office, I'd say you overdid it. The trick is to drink steadily but not heavily. That way you always have a little edge, and you stay on an even keel."

"I appreciate the tip." I was just being polite. I didn't intend to drink again. Ever. "And I appreciate what you did back there."

Bogart laughed. He wiped off the top of the bottle with his hand and took another drink. After he'd savored it for a second or two, he said, "I've had a lot of people offer to fight me over the years. They never seem to get tired of testing me, trying to find out if I'm as tough in real life as I am in the movies. So I've worked out a couple of ways to handle them."

"Hitting them in the balls is a good one."

When Bogart stopped laughing, he lit a cigarette. He took a few puffs and went on with what he was going to tell me.

"That's not one of the ways. That just happened."

"We were lucky it did."

"I know. But of the two ways I've used before, one I like best is to tell whoever is challenging me that I'll meet him outside. He always goes out, all hot under the collar, to wait for me. He can wait forever as far as I'm concerned. I never show up."

"What happens then?" I asked.

"Oh, usually the guy cools off and realizes he's made a fool of himself. If he comes back in or ever sees me again to ask why I didn't show up, I just say I didn't want to hurt him."

"And that works?"

"Most of the time. You saw what happened to Mike. I hurt him, didn't I?"

"You hurt him for sure." I didn't mention that he'd admitted it was an accident. "What if the guy won't go outside?"

"I always get in the first punch."

"That's what you did with Mike."

"Yeah, and it worked, but we were just lucky. That's not the way I usually do it. I try not to swing until I'm close to the headwaiter or the manager of the place where we are. I try to wind up as close to one of those guys as I can after I swing. They don't like scenes, and they'll always step in and stop the fight before the other guy can get in a lick."

"Charlie O. wasn't inclined to stop anything."

"No, but I wound up close enough to him to grab his arm before he could take another shot at you."

"So you pretty much had it all planned out from the beginning."

"That's right, Junior. I never get into a fight without a solid plan of action." He tossed his cigarette out the window and had another drink straight from the bottle. "And if you believe that, I have a nice little bridge back in Brooklyn that I'd like to sell you. I have the deed right here in my pocket."

I told him I didn't really need a bridge and asked him what time it was. He held his watch so that he could see the face of it in the light from the street and said, "Too late to catch anyone at the studio, probably."

"Our meeting with Orsini took a little longer than I thought it would. But we can run by the studio just in case they're working late."

"With old One-Shot Elledge on the job, I'd say we don't have a chance."

"We might as well try. We don't have anything to lose."

Bogart lit another Chesterfield and tossed the match out the window.

"Then let's go and see if anyone's around," he said.

There was no one around. The guard was reading a pulp magazine with a gaudy cover, and he simply waved us through without a second glance at the pass stuck under my windshield wiper.

We drove to the sound stage where the night's sceneshooting was to have taken place, and I could see that the red light wasn't on. They'd either finished shooting or there was a lull.

"We're too late," Bogart said. "We might as well go have dinner at Chasen's and see if any of the cast went over there."

"Chasen's is a long way from here. Maybe they're at your place, looking for a party."

Bogart sloshed the whiskey in his bottle.

"The party's right here."

I parked the car and got out, telling Bogart I was going to have a look inside the soundstage and see if anyone was still there. He nodded but stayed inside the car.

The door was locked, as he must have expected it to be. I walked back to the car and was about to agree with his suggestion to have dinner when I thought I heard something, a muffled noise from the jungle set. It might even have been a gunshot.

"Did you hear that?" I asked Bogart. "There's someone down there on the set."

Bogart hadn't heard the noise, and he wasn't interested.

"Couldn't be anyone we care about. Mr. Warner owes us a dinner after what we've been through. Let's go to Chasen's."

Chasen's was a classier place than the Formosa, where we'd eaten the previous evening, and I had a feeling Mr. Warner wouldn't want to pick up the tab. He wasn't known for his generosity any more than Thomas Wayne was.

"Let's have a look down by the jungle anyway," I said.

"Is this something else from the Detective's Handbook?"

"That's right. We professional detectives always check into everything. You never know when you might run across an important clue."

Bogart shrugged. "It's your car. You're driving. If you want to go, go."

I got in and started the old Chevy.

"I don't see anything," Bogart said when we started down the street.

"Maybe it was nothing. We'll have a look, then we'll leave."

I drove down to the jungle and stopped the car. There was nothing moving there. No filming was going on. No one was trysting under the jungle moon.

I stopped the car and looked up at the moon, which was on the wane but still hanging starkly pale in the black sky. I wondered for a second if it was real or just another effect created for the movies. I pushed in the Chevy's clutch and moved the shift lever into reverse.

Bogart smiled as if to say he'd known there'd be no one there, but if that was what he was thinking, he didn't say it.

I started to back up and turn around when a man lurched out of the jungle. His clothing was torn and bloody, and he put his arm in front of his face as if to blot out the car lights. Then he fell faced down in front of us. His hand scrabbled briefly in the dirt and was still.

CHAPTER

20

I opened the door and jumped out of the car, leaving the lights on so I could see who it was. Bogart was right behind me, and as we bent over the fallen man, illuminated by my headlights, we must have looked as if we were posing for a picture by Weegee.

When I turned the man over, Bogart said, "Dawson."

I couldn't really recognize Dawson from what was left of his battered and bloody face, but the safari outfit, ripped and torn as it was, looked familiar.

I felt Dawson's neck, trying to find a pulse. There wasn't one. There was a big red stain on the front of his jacket. There was a small hole in the middle of it.

"He's dead," I said.

"That fight scene with Stoney must have been a lot rougher than he thought it would be," Bogart said. "Either that or he tangled with a rhino."

"The rhino must have been carrying a pistol," I said, and I showed him the bullet hole.

"I guess you did hear something down here, after all," Bogart said.

I was glad his faith in my hearing had been restored, but I didn't say so.

"I heard something, all right. I wonder who shot him."

Bogart didn't have any ideas about that, but he thought it might be a good idea for us to get out of there.

"We can't just leave him here," I said.

"Yes, we can. There's nothing we can do for him, and we don't want to do anything that might disturb any clues. We probably shouldn't even have turned him over."

"Clues?" I said. "What clues?"

Bogart pointed down at the place where I'd seen Dawson's hand moving.

"Oh," I said. "I see what you mean."

There appeared to be some letters scrawled in the dirt, as if Dawson had been trying to write something there before he died. It was hard to make out the letters in the shadowy beams of the car's headlights.

"Can you read it?" Bogart asked.

"It looks like *bob*," I said.

"Do you think Dawson was trying to tell us something before he died?"

"A dying message. Those things are admissible in court."

Bogart's knowledge of the law came from the movies rather than law books, and it wasn't exactly accurate.

"Nothing that vague is admissible," I said. "I wonder what happened to him before he was shot."

"He looks like he might have been in a fight with an animal. Maybe one of the studio's tame lions got out and wasn't as tame as they thought."

"It looks more like somebody worked him over," I said. "With a baseball bat."

"Mob work," Bogart said. "Do you think it had anything to do with us?"

I thought about that. We'd arrived on the movie set with Dawson, and all the people who'd attended Bogart's party had been there, except for Slappy Coville, and he might have heard about it from the others, all of whom had probably seen us with Dawson. Had Dawson mentioned our interest in talking to them? It seemed likely that he had. If so, had he then discovered something, or remembered something, that would have led one of them to kill him?

"It could be related to Burleson's murder," I said. "If Dawson recognized us in the car when we drove up, he might have been trying to let us know his killer's name."

"You mean that somebody named Bob killed him?"

"Maybe. But there's nobody by that name who was at your house."

"You're forgetting Robert Carroll. Everyone who knows him calls him Bob. He just doesn't use that as his professional name."

"Dawson didn't start the word with a capital letter. Maybe it's not a name."

"I thought you were a detective, not an English teacher."

"I'm not so sure that's an *o*, either," I said, peering down at the word.

"Maybe it's an *a*." "*Bab*? What kind of word is *bab*?"

It might not have been a word, but it sounded pretty good when he said it. No wonder the Warner Brothers paid him so much money.

"It's not a word," I said. "Not a complete word, anyway. Dawson might not have finished writing what he wanted to say. See? The last *b* sort of trails off there."

I pointed to where Dawson's finger had made a long mark in the dirt as he tried to close the bottom of the final *b*.

"It was going to be Babson," Bogart said, snapping his fingers. "That son of a bitch. I knew it was him."

I didn't remind him that only a few hours earlier he'd been sure it was Orsini. We'd gotten into plenty of trouble over that particular hunch. The Detective's Handbook says hunches are sometimes all right, but it's best never to trust them too much.

"Maybe it's Babson," I said, "or maybe it's Carroll. We can't be sure. We'll think about it some more after we find a telephone and call Congreve."

"He's not going to be happy when he finds us here," Bogart said.

"Especially you. I don't think he likes you very much."

I knew Congreve didn't like me, and Garton liked me even less, if that was possible. Still, we had to make the call.

"We could always do it anonymously," Bogart said. "Put a handkerchief over the phone or something like that. That's what we do in the movies."

I'd seen that bit many times, the close-up of the man's mouth close to the hanky-covered telephone receiver. For all I knew, it might even work, but I wasn't going to try it. I was about to tell Bogart that, but I didn't get a chance.

Off to our left, a hundred yards or so away, car lights came on. I hadn't looked down that way, and I wondered how long the driver had been sitting there, waiting for us to leave. He must have given up and decided that we were going to stay there all night talking over Dawson's dead body.

"Now who could that be?" Bogart said.

I didn't have an answer for him, but I thought that whoever it was had better have a good excuse for being there, considering what had happened to Dawson.

"Let's find out," I said, and started walking toward the car.

That was a mistake. Or maybe not. Maybe the driver would have done what he did even if I'd stayed right where I was. What he did was gun the engine and aim the car right at me.

For just a second I was frozen in the headlights as the car barreled toward me. Then I managed to scream, "Look out!" just before I threw myself out of its path.

I rolled over a couple of times, but I wasn't too busy to hear a gunshot. Something buzzed by my head and hit the ground beside me, kicking up the dirt.

I scrambled to my feet in time to see Bogart lying at the edge of the jungle. He sat up just as the car's right front tire hit Dawson. The car bounced but didn't slow down. It didn't slow down when the rear tire hit him, either.

Feeling like a stuntman in a Republic serial, I dusted my clothes off and watched the car's small red tail lights fade into the darkness.

Bogart was already running toward the car.

"What are you waiting for?" he yelled. "We have to catch that bastard."

I wasn't sure we had to, but it seemed like a good idea to find out who was trying to kill us. And who had probably already killed Dawson. I had a feeling that whoever had tried to run us down had already done the job on him.

I jumped into the Chevy, slammed the door, and started the engine. The tires spun, then gripped, and we were off.

There was only one problem. I wasn't sure exactly where we were going.

"Follow that car!" Bogart said.

He said it with a straight face, maybe because with Dawson lying dead there wasn't much cause for smiling.

I told him I didn't know where the car had gone.

He pointed through the windshield and said, "It went thataway."

I went thataway, too.

In trying to run over us, the driver had been unable to turn left on the street leading out of the studio, so it had simply gone straight ahead, running along parallel with the back-lot jungle. We passed the jungle quickly and found ourselves in a western town, with false-front stores and a wagon-rutted street. It looked like every other town in western movies, with a mercantile store where the cowardly shopkeeper worked, a saloon where the dancing girls and villains hung out, a watering trough for the hero to duck behind when the bad guys shot at him, a little jail where the lynch mob could gather.

The Chevy bounced in the wagon ruts and tossed Bogart around in the seat beside me. I clung to the wheel and looked for taillights, but I didn't see any.

"Keep going," Bogart said, reaching under the seat and trying to grab the whiskey bottle, which wasn't easy in the pitching Chevy. He finally grabbed it by the neck and put it in the seat beside him.

"I wouldn't want it to get lost," he said.

By that time we were in a small town that Andy Hardy would have been proud to call home, except that Andy Hardy didn't work for Superior Studios. We passed a malt shop, a high school, and houses with picket fences.

And we were running out of road.

"Turn left," Bogart said, which I did since it was about the only option I had.

I turned and then turned left again almost immediately. We found ourselves riding along behind the sets, which were unfinished and skimpy from the rear, nothing like the fronts they showed in the movies. I saw taillights ahead.

"There he is," Bogart said. "You're gaining on him."

I knew that wasn't true. I hadn't been observant enough to notice what kind of car we were chasing, but I knew it was both bigger and more powerful than my Chevy.

I thought it would turn back toward the entrance, which it did, but it turned before we came to the main street. I turned as soon as I got to the corner, and we found ourselves driving past a haunted house that was beside a graveyard. I knew that Slappy Coville had starred in a couple of supposedly humorous horror flicks for Superior. They had involved monsters a lot like the ones that Universal had made so popular. But not so much like them that Universal could sue.

I was actually gaining on the car in front of us now, thanks to the turns, which slowed it down, and now it made another turn. We came to the main street, and it turned once again, this time heading for the entrance.

"It's getting away," Bogart said. "Shoot out the tires."

I'd forgotten all about the pistol that was dragging down the right side of my jacket. I might have been able to claw it out and use it, but I didn't intend to try. I was sure I couldn't hit the tires of the car in front even if it had been standing still. I was more likely to shoot someone by accident, and I didn't want that to happen. I was sure Bogart didn't either, since he was the one I'd be most likely to shoot.

It was too late to do anything, anyway. The car shot past the gatehouse and out into the traffic. We could never overtake it now. Even if we went after it, we could never be sure which car it was unless Bogart had gotten a better look at it than I had.

He hadn't. He suggested that we ask the guard, who was still reading his pulp magazine. *The Shadow*. At least he had pretty good taste.

Taste aside, however, he hadn't seen the car. He hadn't seen anything.

"I was reading," he said. "Besides, my job is to check the cars coming in, not the ones going out."

I didn't bother to remind him that he hadn't really checked me when I came in. I said, "How many cars have been in tonight?"

"I don't keep a count. If they got a pass, they get in."

He was probably supposed to keep a record, but if he was, he wasn't letting on. I thanked him for his help, or lack of it, and left the studio. By the time I'd driven ten feet, he was immersed in his pulp again, one with Lamont Cranston, reveling in the power to cloud men's minds.

21

I called the cops from a phone booth near Chasen's. I didn't ask for Congreve because I wasn't sure that Dawson's death had anything to do with Burleson's and also because by simply calling the station I could do it anonymously. There was no chance anyone was going to recognize my voice. If the guard at Superior tried to tell the cops about me when they showed up, he wouldn't be able to tell them much. He didn't know who I was, and he had no record of my car. Bogart had been over on one side in the shadows, so the guard hadn't had a good look at him. If the cops asked about The Shadow, however, the guard could probably tell them quite a bit.

Chasen's was on Beverly Boulevard, and it wasn't a place where the stars went to be seen by the public or the press. The owner, Dave Chasen, had a strict "no cameras" policy, and the stars went there to be seen mostly by other stars. And, of course, to eat. Chasen's had started out as Chasen's Southern Pit, so named because of a barbecue pit in the back, and while its barbecue hadn't become famous, its chili had. You might not think movie stars would go for chili, but they did, and in a big way.

You could get plenty of other things, too. If you wanted to go kosher, you could have whitefish or lox. Borscht, too. If you preferred something fancier, you could get pheasant under glass. And if you wanted to gain ten pounds in one sitting, you could get the Hobo

Steak, which consisted mainly of strips of beef deep-fried in a pound of melted butter. The waiter would prepare it for you right beside your table on a wheeled cart.

The interior was considerably more tasteful than that at Romanoff's, unless your taste ran to exploding parrots. Chasen's went in for heavy paneling and plush red leather booths.

It was quiet, and the big-name stars could go there without being bothered. I spotted James Stewart and Jack Benny as we walked in, and I thought I saw Alan Ladd in one of the booths.

I hadn't expected any of the *Jan of the Jungle* cast to be in Chasen's, but Slappy Coville was there. He wasn't a big star, but he liked to hang around with them when he could and pretend that he belonged. He was a short, scrawny guy who wore loud ties and had a big mouth. His tie this particular evening looked as if someone had painted a picture of scrambled eggs and ketchup on it. When he saw us headed toward him, he launched into one of the worst Bogart impersonations I'd ever heard.

"Look who's here," he said. "'Play it Sam. If she can stand it, I can. Play it.'"

There was a busty blonde in the circular booth beside him, and she laughed loudly. Either she thought he was wonderful or she'd had far too much to drink.

"Hello, Slappy," Bogart said. "No need to get up."

Slappy hadn't been getting up. He hadn't moved other than to raise his glass to us.

"By gad, sir," he said, not sounding at all like Sidney Greenstreet, "you are a character."

Bogart slid into the both beside him and I slid in beside the blonde. She smelled like Chanel No. 5, and I wondered if Slappy had given her the perfume.

"I didn't know you'd memorized all my movies, Slappy," Bogart said.

"He thinks you're the best," the blonde said. "Isn't that right, Slappy?"

Slappy said it was right, and he introduced the blonde, whose name was Suzie. She was pretty, maybe even pretty enough to make it in the movies. It would all depend on how the camera liked her. Some beautiful women didn't photograph well, and some not so beautiful ones looked great on the screen.

Bogart introduced me to both of them, though Slappy and I had met before. He didn't seem to remember it, and I didn't say anything.

"Lemme tell you a good one," Slappy said.

I doubted that it would be a good one. Every joke I'd ever heard Slappy tell in a movie or on the radio had been around the world at least twice and sometimes more. His jokes were usually so bad that even Milton Berle wouldn't steal them.

"This horse walks into a bar," Slappy said, and Suzie started to laugh.

"I haven't gotten to the funny part yet," Slappy said.

Suzie stopped laughing. She was never going to make it in the movies, not if she was already so desperate that she was with Slappy and, worse, trying to please him.

"I thought it was funny that a horse would walk into a bar," she said.

"That's not it. Wait for the punch line. So, OK, this horse walks into a bar. The bartender looks up at him and says, 'Why the long face?'"

Nobody laughed. Not at first. Then Suzie realized she'd missed her cue and started to cackle. It was too late, but Slappy didn't seem to care. He took a drink from the glass in front of him and set it back on the table.

"Where's everybody else?" Bogart asked.

"Whaddaya mean?"

"I thought the cast of your movie stuck together, but here you are, all by yourself."

I could tell that Slappy liked Bogart's reference to *his* movie. He had been slumped in the booth, and now he sat up a little straighter.

"He's not by himself," Suzie said. "He's with me."

"Yeah," Slappy said. "I'm with her. Who cares where those other lice are."

He and Suzie had obviously been in Chasen's for a while. The drink he was having now wasn't his first, or even his second. So he couldn't have been driving the car we'd chased. But any of the others could have.

"When the cast came to my place the other night," Bogart said, "whose idea was that?"

Suzie turned and hit Slappy on the upper arm.

"You went to Humphrey Bogart's house, and you didn't ask me to go?" she said.

Slappy didn't like it that she'd hit him. I got the impression that if we hadn't been there, or if he hadn't been in a public place, he might have hit her back. I hoped I was wrong about that.

"It wasn't anybody's idea," Slappy said. "We just wound up there."

I saw what Bogart was going for. It was something I should have thought of myself. Whoever suggested going to his place might have known about the pistol in advance.

I hadn't wanted Bogart tagging along with me when all this had started, and now here he was doing my job for me.

"Are you sure about that?" I asked. "Sometimes it seems that way, but if you think it over, you can remember some suggestion that someone made."

"I can't remember today, much less last night," Slappy said. "And that's the way I prefer it."

He drained his glass, banged it on the table, and called for another. When the waiter came over, Bogart ordered a martini. I asked for a Shirley Temple, which seemed appropriate, since the bartender at Chasen's had invented the drink for the little curly-head.

"If you want club soda, why not just get lemonade?" Slappy said.

Just came out *jusht*. Slappy was slurring his words more, and I thought he might soon be in Mayo's condition if he didn't watch himself. And I knew he wouldn't watch himself. I hadn't. I didn't know anyone who ever did, except maybe Bogart. Whether it was because he paced himself, as he'd told me, or because he could control it better than most people, I didn't know.

"I like the cherry," I said.

"It's a sissy drink," Slappy said.

He started shaking his head, and he didn't stop until Suzie put her hand on his face and held it steady.

"We need to go home, Slappy," she said. "You have to be on the set early tomorrow."

I suppose Slappy needed a keeper. Suzie was probably a good choice, as long as she didn't laugh in the wrong places too much.

Surprisingly enough, Slappy didn't argue with her. He called for the check with a certain amount of dignity, and as he was leaving he said to Bogart, in his best Peter Lorre voice, which was none too good, "'You despise me, don't you.'"

"Oh, if I gave you any thought I probably would," Bogart said.

Slappy laughed and allowed Suzie to lead him away.

When they were gone, Bogart ordered another martini, and we both ordered the chili. When the waiter left, Bogart lit a cigarette. Then he asked me what kind of car had nearly killed us. I told him that I didn't know.

"I was too busy getting out of the way to notice."

"I don't suppose you got the license number, either."

"No," I said. "Did you?"

"I was otherwise occupied. And when we were chasing it, we never got close enough for me to see."

"So where does that leave us?"

"It was a big car," he said. "And it was black."

"There are a lot of big black cars in Hollywood."

"Not that have been following us around."

"Are you talking about that Packard?"

"Yes. Didn't you think of that?"

Well, no. I hadn't thought of it because I didn't believe the Packard had been following us. But I could have been wrong about that. It hadn't followed us to the studio, however. The car we'd seen had already been there. Which probably meant that whoever owned it worked there.

"That's what I thought," Bogart said, when I told him. "Now we have to find out who the owner is."

"We don't know it was a Packard."

"We don't know that it wasn't."

He had a point, but I wasn't ready to believe in the phantom Packard. The car could have been a Buick or any other big car for all I knew.

The chili came. I've heard that there are purists who don't like chili with beans. If that's true, they'd better stay away from Chasen's.

I ordered another Shirley Temple to wash down the chili, and Bogart said, "Slappy had a point. It's embarrassing as hell to sit here and eat with a grown man who's drinking Shirley Temples."

"I'm not the one crumbling crackers in his chili," I pointed out.

Bogart looked at his chili bowl. There were soggy cracker parts among the meat and beans.

"Guilty," he said, and took a bite. He didn't look as if he felt very guilty.

"Did we learn anything from Slappy?" he asked when he'd swallowed his chili. And crackers.

"We know he wasn't driving the car that hit Dawson," I said. "Nobody could have gotten as drunk as he is without getting an early start."

"Maybe Suzie was driving."

"She could have been. I didn't see the driver, and I couldn't tell if there was a passenger. I know my passenger had been drinking, though."

Bogart lifted his glass. A martini with chili. And he had the nerve to make fun of my Shirley Temple.

"I'm as sober as Judge Hardy."

He was, too. Or at least he appeared to be. The hand holding the glass was steady as a stone.

"Fine," I said, and wiped chili off my lips with a napkin. "Now what are we going to do about your friend Dawson?"

"Find out who killed him," Bogart said. "When someone kills your friend, you're supposed to do something about it."

It sounded like a good idea to me, but maybe I'd had too many Shirley Temples.

"All right," I said. "Where do we start?"

"Ever meet any Lesbians?"

I thought about some of the things I'd done for Mr. Warner and his stars.

"One or two," I said.

"Good," Bogart said. "Then you might even know where we can go to meet a few more."

CHAPTER

22

C lub Sappho didn't have its name above the door, or anywhere else for that matter. In fact, Club Sappho might not even have been its name, though I'd heard it called that once or twice. It looked pretty much like any other building on that particular block of Vine Street, and it might have been full of the offices of lawyers, dentists, and doctors for all you could tell from the outside. In fact there was a building directory that indicated that offices for people in those professions were indeed to be found inside.

That wasn't the case, however. The directory was just a beard, put there to disguise the building's real use, which was as a meeting place for those of what the scandal rags like to refer to as "the twilight sex."

The inside was quite a bit different from the outer facade. At least it was above the first floor. On the first floor there was a large semi-circular reception desk behind which sat a guard named Harry.

Harry had a coarse complexion, slicked-back hair, a nose that looked as if it had been broken in a street fight (it had), and a little white scar under one eye.

At first glance you'd take Harry for one of the toughest men you were ever likely to encounter. If you took time to look more closely—much more closely—you'd discover that Harry, whose full name was Harriet Rose O'Connell, was one of the toughest women you were ever likely to encounter.

"Hello, Mr. Scott," Harry said in a low, husky voice. "Is that a gun in your pocket, or are you just glad to see me?"

I laughed at the old Mae West line. I'd forgotten about the pistol I'd taken from Charlie O. I took it out of my jacket pocket and put on Harry's desk.

"You'd better keep it for me," I told her. "I know guns are against the rules here."

"That's right," Harry said. "Are you just visiting, or are you looking for someone special?"

"You're special enough for me, Harry," I said.

"You're always full of the blarney, Mr. Scott. And who's the fella you have with you? He looks familiar."

"Humphrey Bogart," I said, "meet Harry."

They shook hands, and I thought I noticed Bogart wincing just a bit at Harry's grip, though he tried not to show it.

"I'm a big fan," Harry told Bogart. "I really loved *Key Largo*. Your wife, Miss Bacall, she's really something."

I couldn't tell whether Bogart appreciated the compliment or not, but at least he didn't wipe his hand on his pants leg when he got it back. And he was polite enough to say thanks.

"We haven't had any trouble here tonight, Mr. Scott," Harry said. "Not with anyone from Warner Brothers or anywhere else. But I'm sure this isn't a social call. Not unless you've changed a lot since I saw you last."

"It's a business matter," I told her. "We were wondering if you were acquainted with a friend of ours."

"You know I don't talk about our clients, Mr. Scott."

"I know that. And I wouldn't ask you to under ordinary circumstances. You'll have to admit that I've done this place a few favors by keeping its name out of the papers."

Harry nodded. "Yes, you have, but only when it helped out Warner Brothers at the same time."

"OK, that's true. But this is important." I decided to level. After all, Harry was very good at keeping secrets. "Someone's trying to frame Mr. Bogart for murder."

If Harry was surprised, I couldn't tell.

"And you believe that someone might be here? I don't think so,

Mr. Scott. We have a very choice clientele. They don't make trouble for us, and we don't make trouble for them."

"But they might make trouble for someone else," I said.

Harry considered that possibility and admitted that it wasn't out of the question. As for me, I wasn't so sure. We were there because of another of Bogart's hunches. He'd explained it to me as we drove to the Club Sappho.

"I've been thinking about those tarantulas," he said. "You remember the tarantulas, don't you?"

I remembered the tarantulas all to well, and I wished he hadn't mentioned them. I would have preferred not to think about them at all.

"Can't we talk about something else?" I said.

"No. If what I'm thinking is true, then Bob Carroll just might be our guy."

I couldn't see any connection between the spiders and Bob Carroll. Not even the Detective's Handbook had anything about spiders in it. Come to think of it, Bogart had made some joking remark about the Detective's Handbook at the time, but I still couldn't see how the spiders tied into anything that concerned us.

"I'm surprised at you, Junior," Bogart said. "Weren't you wondering why Wendy dumped those spiders on herself?"

"She must be insane," I said. "Or, since most actors are insane, maybe she was trying to catch the director's attention. That's all I could think of."

"You don't really mean that about actors," Bogart said. "Do you?"

"I said *most*, not *all*. I wouldn't include you."

"Thanks. Now think about this. Maybe it wasn't the director's attention that Wendy wanted. Maybe it was Stella Gordon was paying too much attention to someone else. After all, who took little Wendy off into the trees to comfort her in private?"

"Stella Gordon," I said. "But I still don't see what that has..." And then the reason Bogart wanted to go somewhere like the Club Sappho came to me.

"Are you telling me that Stella Gordon is a lesbian? But she's married to Robert Carroll."

"Who's the biggest he-man in Hollywood. Kinda makes you wonder, doesn't it."

Well, yes, it did. If Stella leaned to one side, it wouldn't be surprising at all if Carroll leaned to the other. And it certainly wouldn't be the first time that a studio had arranged a marriage between two of its moneymakers who couldn't stand the sight of each other. The marriage would work to cover up what some people, mainly the ones who bought the cheaper kind of magazines, would consider decidedly unnatural tendencies.

"So I think you should drive us to whatever clubs there are that cater to women like that," Bogart said. "I'll bet you know where they are."

"Only because of my job."

"That goes without saying. So what do you think?"

I told him I thought it was worth a try, and we'd started off. Before getting to the Club Sappho, we'd been to a couple of other places, but nobody at either one of them knew a thing about Wendy Felsen and Stella Gordon. Or so they'd claimed. You could never be sure about the truth in a situation like that.

It seemed as if Harry might be about to make the same claim, but something in her voice made me think that she knew more than she was willing to tell. I hadn't detected anything like that at the other places we'd been.

"Look, Harry, we don't mean any harm to any of your clients. If Stella Gordon is here, we just want to talk to her. This isn't even about her. It's about someone she knows."

I hoped I sounded sincere, because I wasn't at all sure I was telling the truth. If Robert Carroll, Bob to his pals, would kill to keep his secret from getting out, why wouldn't Stella do the same?

I could buy the idea that men were more likely to kill than women. I read the papers, after all. On the other hand, I didn't think you could rule out a woman just because she was a woman.

Harry looked around. Nobody had entered the lobby since Bogart and I had some in, so I don't know what, or who, she was looking for.

"OK You're right. Stella Gordon comes here sometimes. Not that she's ever used that name, but I recognized her the first time she came in."

"Who was she with?" Bogart asked.

"I don't know. Someone very pretty. That's all I can tell you."

Bogart, as good as he was at the private-eye game so far, had asked the wrong question. I asked the right one.

"Is Stella Gordon here now?"

"Yeah. She's upstairs. But you can't go up there, Mr. Scott. You know that."

I'd been upstairs before, so I didn't know that. I reminded Harry of my past trespasses.

"That was different. You were trying to keep somebody's name out of the paper, and I respected that. So did Johnnie."

Johnnie was the owner of the club. She was a pale blonde flower who always wore diaphanous gowns and lots of make-up so that it was hard to judge her age, which I was sure was a lot closer to Bogart's than to mine.

"He's trying to keep somebody's name out of the paper this time, too," Bogart said. "Mine. Attached to a murder rap."

Harriet thought some more and then said, "Oh, all right, then. If it's that important, you can go on up. But you know the rules, Mr. Scott."

I told her I did: no talking, no touching, no nothing. Just get off the elevator, pass right on through the big main room without opening my big yap, and then go down a hall to a room where Stella would meet me. The meeting would be arranged by Harry, who would call Johnnie, who would set it up. But only if Stella would agree.

"Give me five minutes," Harry said.

Bogart and I drifted over to a standing ashtray with a top filled with smooth white sand. There wasn't a butt in it, though Bogart was about to change that.

"I think I have an instinct for this kind of work," he said when he had the Chesterfield going. "Maybe doing all those movies has rubbed off on me."

"Maybe," I said. "But don't forget all those gangster movies you did. They didn't help you with Charlie O."

"You're forgetting how we got in to see him in the first place."

I was, but his reminder brought back to me what had happened. Bogart had been as much like a gangster as any of Charlie O.'s boys. Maybe more like one. That's the way it was in Hollywood. You could never tell what was real and what was fake because the fake was sometimes so much more genuine.

WE'LL ALWAYS HAVE MURDER

I was saved from my philosophical speculations when Harry called out my name and said that Johnnie would meet us on the second floor.

Bogart stuck his cigarette butt into the sand, and we headed for the elevator.

23

Usually Johnnie trusted me to make my own way, but she must have felt that this time was different. Or maybe she just wanted to meet Bogart. At any rate, when the elevator door opened, she was standing there waiting for us.

She was quite a sight in her filmy, floating, shimmery gown. Her hair, which had been blonde the last time I'd seen her, was red, and her skin was pale as a vampire's, thanks to all the powder she'd applied to it.

"Meet Humphrey Bogart," I said to her. "Mr. Bogart, this is Johnnie."

She held out her hand to Bogart, who took it in his, raised it to his lips, and planted a light kiss on it as if he did that sort of thing all the time. Maybe he did, though I sure hadn't seen him.

"Charmed, I'm sure," Johnnie said.

"And I'm equally charmed," Bogart said.

Johnnie simpered at him. Bogart might not have impressed Harry, but Johnnie was a different story. She had little use for men, but a movie star was more than just a man, at least to her.

We were standing in a long hallway. Across from us were doors that appeared to lead to different offices. The doors were half wood and half pebbled glass, and on the glass I could see names like George D. Wood, D.D.S. Having been there before, I knew that all the doors opened into one big room, and we could hear music coming faintly from within it. It sounded like a Marlene Dietrich recording.

"I believe you want to see one of my customers," Johnnie said to me when she'd recovered from Bogart's greeting.

"That's right. Stella Gordon. Didn't Harriet tell you?"

"She told me. I had to ask someone to find Miss Gordon. I don't know her personally, and people seldom use their real names here, as you're well aware."

"Did you ask her if she'd see us?"

"I did, and she agreed. She doesn't know you, Mr. Scott, but I do, and I think you can be trusted. And she knows Mr. Bogart, or so she says. I understand from Harry that he's in some sort of difficulty and believes Stella can help him."

"That's right," Bogart said. "We just need to ask her a few questions. We won't cause any trouble for her or for you."

Johnnie sighed as if she'd heard that line before, as I was sure she had.

"She has a friend with her," Johnnie said.

"Who?" I asked.

Johnnie smiled, but not so wide as to crack her make-up.

"I have no idea. She's using the name Bobbette, but that doesn't mean a thing."

I figured that Bobbette was most likely Wendy Felsen. I found he choice of names interesting, given that Stella was married to a guy that people called Bob.

"Names don't matter," I said. "Is Stella in the usual room?"

"Yes," Johnnie said, "but I'll go with you. Please follow the rules."

She turned away and went to the door of Dr. Wood. When she opened it, the music spilled out into the hallway. Dietrich was getting rowdy, singing "See What the Boys in the Back Room Will Have."

We went through the door. I'd seen it all before, but it was new to Bogart. The big, dimly lit room was full of women, not all of whom looked like women. Some of them were in suits, looking imperially slim, and a couple even wore tuxedos. Some of them looked like dewy-eyed refugees from the set of *Gone with the Wind*. And some of them looked like dockworkers.

Smoke floated in the air near the ceiling, and several of the women were smoking cigarettes in long, thin holders. Others held their smokes the way Bogart usually did, cupping their fingers over their cigarettes.

Johnnie led us right through the middle of the room. The crowd parted in front of us, but nobody looked directly at us. To everyone there, we were as insubstantial as the smoke.

We reached the other side of the room and went to a door that opened onto a short hall. On both sides of that hall were other doors, but these were of solid wood. Now and then some of Johnnie's clients needed a little privacy, and these rooms were available for a small fee. The first room on the right was the one where I'd always talked with people before.

Johnnie went to that door and knocked.

"Come in," someone said from inside, and Johnnie opened the door.

We went in and saw Stella Gordon and Wendy Felsen. They weren't wearing their jungle costumes now. Wendy had on a skirt and bobby-sox. She looked like a sweet-faced high-school student, sort of like Andy Hardy's girlfriend, Polly Benedict. Stella was wearing the pants, which were part of a sharply tailored business suit. Her hair was pulled back tight and wound into a little bun at the back of her head.

What we had here, I thought, was an interesting bit of role reversal, with Stella now taking on the male role in a relationship with someone who was calling herself *Bobbette* for the occasion. I figured a psychologist would have a wonderful time looking into it, but it wasn't my department.

Even with the suit on, Stella Gordon looked like Stella Gordon, which was certainly good enough for me. I had one of those inevitable and involuntary flashes of thought: *if she just met the right man (me, naturally), she might change her mind about Wendy.* I knew better, of course. I just couldn't help myself. A psychologist would probably have a great time with me, too.

The room was furnished with an armchair, which is where Wendy was sitting, a bed, and a small night table. On the table were a clock, a lamp, and an ashtray. Stella sat on the edge of the bed with her legs crossed, swinging her foot. Her arms were at her sides, her hands flat on the bedspread.

Johnnie performed the introductions, and Wendy looked a bit frightened when she heard what I did for Warner Brothers, but Stella wasn't bothered at all. She seemed genuinely interested in helping Bogart.

"What's this problem you have, Bogie?" she asked.

Johnnie appeared satisfied that things were going to be fine and that we weren't going to start any fights, so she excused herself and left the room.

Bogart explained to Stella and Wendy that Frank Burleson had been trying to blackmail him because Burleson owed Charlie O. a lot of money for gambling debts. He told them that the cops had found out about Burleson's shakedown attempt and because of that Bogart found himself a suspect in Burleson's murder.

"I'm sorry to hear it," Stella said. "But what does it have to do with me?"

We'd agreed on the drive to the club that Bogart wouldn't tell the exact truth at this point. There was no need yet to mention that we thought her husband might have killed Burleson.

Or that she might have.

"I was just wondering if Burleson had tried his blackmail gag on anyone else," Bogart said. "I knew you were vulnerable."

"How did you know that?"

"Let's just say I'm an observant guy," Bogart told her, not mentioning that what he'd observed had occurred only that day.

"Don't tell them anything, Stella," Wendy said, her voice unsteady. "Let's leave here. Right now."

Bogart looked at her. "Maybe he didn't try it on Stella, after all. Maybe it was someone else he picked on."

Wendy stood up. "We don't have to listen to him, Stella. He's just trying to cause trouble."

I was beginning to think that Johnnie shouldn't have left so soon, but I needn't have worried.

"Sit down, Wendy," Stella said, and Wendy sat. But there were tears in her eyes.

"Don't mind her," Stella said. "She gets emotional sometimes."

Wendy bit her lip and sank deeper into the chair as if trying to make herself disappear.

"What about it?" Bogart said. "Was Burleson trying to put the squeeze on either of you?" Then he added, as if it was an afterthought, "Or on Bob?"

"What do you know about Bob?"

"We know why the two of you got married," I said, stretching the truth a little. "The cover was as much for him as it was for you. But don't worry. We're not going to tell anybody."

Stella didn't deny that I was right. Instead, she asked Bogart for a cigarette. He got one for her and one for himself, then lit them.

"Bob doesn't think anyone knows about him," Stella said. "He'd be embarrassed if he knew you'd found out."

She didn't mean me. Carroll didn't give a tinker's dam about me. She meant Bogart, who said, "Bob's sex life doesn't matter to me. It's his business. He's still the same Bob. Is he the one Burleson was after?"

"Frank was a turd," Stella said. "He knew about me and Wendy, and he knew about Bob. I suppose he found out in the course of his job, but he never had to do anything that involved any of us. He tried something on me several months ago, right after my marriage. He didn't want money."

I knew what he'd wanted, and I felt a little guilty for my own lecherous thoughts. But at least I hadn't acted on my thoughts, as Frank apparently had. I had a feeling that he hadn't gotten anywhere, however. And I was a little surprised that even Frank would stoop that low, though I shouldn't have been.

"Asshole," Wendy said, to no one in particular. I hoped she was talking about Frank.

"When he didn't get what he wanted from me," Stella said, "he went after Wendy."

Wendy stood up again. "I don't want to talk about this. I don't even want to hear you talking about this. I'm leaving."

"Sit down, Wendy," Stella said, but Wendy didn't sit down. She started for the door.

Stella stood up and grabbed her arm, twisting her around, and practically flung her at the chair. Wendy caromed off the arm of the chair and over to the room's only window. She stood there with her back to us, looking out at the night. Stella went on talking as if nothing had happened.

"Frank didn't try anything more, not then, but a few days ago, he came back. This time, he said, he meant business. He needed money, and if I didn't give it to him, he was going to let the papers in on my little secret. Those were his exact words, your 'little secret.' He went to Bob and told him the same thing."

"And what did you do about it?" Bogart asked.

Stella blew out a plume of smoke and smiled.

"I didn't kill him, if that's what you're getting at."

"What about Wendy?" I asked. "She's getting pretty worked up about all this."

Wendy's back stiffened, but she didn't turn around.

"Wendy wouldn't hurt anyone," Stella said. Then she added thoughtfully, "But Bob might."

Well, that was what we'd come to hear. Bogart walked over to the night table and snuffed his Chesterfield in the ashtray. Stella did the same.

"Tell us about Bob," I said.

"He has a friend. I don't know who. I don't ask. I'm not even sure if he knows about Wendy. We live in the same house, and we get along fine, but we don't often talk about personal things. He has his life, and I have mine."

"You talked about Burleson, though," I said.

"Yes, we talked about him. We decided that we were going to Mr. Wayne and get him fired. But it didn't work out like that."

Wayne had strung me and Bogart along, but we'd known that. We just hadn't known that his stars had been complaining to him about Burleson.

"Wayne didn't do anything," I said, though I thought I already knew the answer. "Did he?"

"No. He told us not to pay Frank, that he'd see to it that Frank didn't bother us again."

"And did he keep his word?"

As if there was any chance of that. This was Hollywood, after all, where a man's word wasn't worth the paper it was printed on.

"No. Frank came back again, to both me and Bob." Stella looked down at the floor. "We told him we'd pay."

Throughout this part of the conversation, Wendy had stood motionless at the window. Now she turned around.

"He came to me, too," she said. "He told me that he was going to ruin Stella if I didn't pay him. He said he wouldn't worry about ruining me, because I didn't amount to anything."

Her shoulders shook as she began to cry, and Stella went to the window and put her arms around her. She did a lot, I thought, first with the spiders and now with the blackmail story.

"She's right," Stella said. "I didn't have the money. But neither did Bob. He's the one who said he was going to get Frank some other way."

"And you think he killed him," Bogart said.

"I don't think anything. It's something we haven't discussed. If he did it, though, I'm proud of him."

I couldn't blame her for feeling that way, and it looked to me as if the word Dawson had scrawled in the dirt must surely have meant Bob Carroll.

"What kind of car does Bob drive?" I asked.

"A pre-War Ford," Stella said.

T here's nothing wrong with pre-War cars," I said as we cruised
down Sunset Boulevard in my old Chevy. I hoped I didn't sound
too defensive.

"I didn't say there was," Bogart told me. "But that wasn't any Ford
that we were chasing tonight. Do we cross Bob Carroll off our list?"

"He could have borrowed a car. What to you know about Wendy
Felsen?"

"Nothing other than what we found out tonight. Why?"

"Bobbette," I said. "Remember?"

Bogart said he hadn't thought about that, but that he didn't think
Wendy, or Bobbette, could afford a Packard.

"Superior isn't known for paying anyone very well," he said.
"There's only one real star there, and that's Barbara Malone." He
paused. "Barbara. Do you think that might be what Dawson was trying
to write?"

I said that I didn't. Unless Dawson was a really poor speller.

Bogart opened the Scotch bottle and took a small swallow.

"Give the guy a break. He was dying. It took guts for him to leave
us any kind of message at all. He couldn't have been very concerned
about spelling."

"You know anybody who can afford a Packard?" I said.

"I can."

"I wasn't talking about you. I was thinking about Charlie O."

"We've already decided he didn't kill Burleson. And there's no way you can get his name into that message."

I wondered if Dawson had left a message at all. What if his hand had simply clawed at the dirt and left something that looked like letters there? I asked Bogart what he thought about it.

"Couldn't be. Those letters were fairly clear. *Bob* or *bab*, one or the other. You couldn't get that by accident."

He was probably right. But if it was a real message, it had left us pretty much in the dark as to what it might mean.

"Besides," Bogart said, "Charlie O. couldn't have killed Dawson. He was at his restaurant. I think it was Babson."

"Does he have a Packard?"

"He's a writer," Bogart said, dismissively.

"Can't writers afford Packards?"

"In Hollywood, a writer is a guy who owns a typewriter and has a big mouth. And Babson has one of the biggest."

"You don't like Babson much, do you."

"No, and it would be just fine with me if he were the guilty party. I hope he does have a Packard, the little son of a bitch."

"Where does he like to be seen at night?"

"Who knows? He's as likely to be one place as another. We could try the Brown Derby."

"Which one?" I asked.

"Not the one that looks like a hat. The one on Vine."

I was getting a tour of all the star hangouts, but I wasn't complaining. Bogart was good company, and besides, Mr. Warner was paying. I took Sunset to Vine and then drove almost to the intersection at Hollywood Boulevard.

It was getting close to midnight, but the streets were still busy. In fact, late at night was when I liked Los Angeles best, at least on nights like this one. There was an air of excitement, almost an audible buzz, as if big things were happening, or going to happen, and that lives could change at any moment for the better or the worse.

Dawson's life had certainly changed for the worse, and the thought of him lying at the edge of the Superior jungle took a little of the edge off the buzz for me.

But the exhilarating feeling in the air came back strong around the Brown Derby. As late as it was, we were lucky to get a parking spot, and the one we got was some distance away. We had to walk a block to get to the front door.

While this version of the famous restaurant didn't look anything like a hat, there was a derby-shaped sign on the roof to let people know they'd come to the right place. Not that the sign was needed. Actors and anyone else who wanted to impress somebody always seemed to know where to come to be seen, and the Brown Derby was one of those places.

The decor seemed to consist mainly of caricatures. I recognized drawings of Bob Hope, Charlie Chaplin, and Bette Davis right off the bat, though I didn't see any of them in the flesh. I didn't see Babson, either, but I saw Stoney Randall sitting with Joey Gallindo and a woman I knew must be Barbara Malone.

Bogart saw them too, and we walked right over to their table without waiting to be seated.

Joey and Stoney didn't seem glad to see Bogart despite the invitation to join them, and they didn't noticeably brighten when I was introduced.

Barbara Malone, however, smiled and showed off her dimples. She was wearing a dark skirt and jacket with a white blouse under the jacket. The collar of the shirt was out over the jacket collar. Her honey-colored hair was smooth on top, with a wave on the side and pincurls at the ends, where it almost touched her shoulders. She was very pretty, maybe even beautiful, but it was Hollywood beauty, not the girl-next-door kind. The camera, it seemed to me, would love her, and I wasn't surprised that she'd finally gotten a break.

Joey Gallindo was a tough-looking little guy, and you wouldn't have any trouble believing him in the role of any kind of villain you could imagine. He'd been in a western or two, but he was most often cast as a mobster of the unsympathetic variety, the sort Bogart had played earlier in his career. He had all of Bogart's edginess with none of his charm. It may well have been that he'd actually killed a couple of men, but he didn't exactly exude a menacing air. He was just unappealing, the kind of guy you didn't warm up to quickly. Or ever.

I thought I'd heard them talking about Dawson when we walked up, so I asked about him. Stoney complained that the shooting hadn't gone too well that evening and that he thought they'd have to do the fight scene again after Elledge saw the rushes.

"Dawson made a wrong move and let his face get into the shot,"

Stoney said. He looked almost as tough as Joey, but whereas Joey just looked tough, I got the feeling that Randall really was. "Even Elledge won't be able to live with something that blatant."

"He'll figure something out," Joey said. "He'll cut that part of the fight if he has to. He never reshoots."

He lit a cigarette, and soon everyone in the booth was smoking except me. I might as well have been. It was sort of like sitting next to a car and inhaling exhaust fumes. But I tried not to let it bother me.

"Dawson's not usually that careless," Bogart said. "Maybe he had something on his mind."

He looked at me and raised an eyebrow to make sure I appreciated what a smooth operator he was.

"He wasn't worried about a thing," Barbara said. "He never worries. He's one of the happiest men I've ever known. Happy as a lark all the time. Always with a little smile, a happy little smile. I like being around him."

I wondered if she hadn't had too much to drink. It was hard to believe anybody was naturally that vivacious.

"Maybe Dawson was worried about Frank Burleson," I said. "He was murdered, you know."

"Yeah," Stoney said. "We heard about that. I didn't know him all that well, myself. I don't know about Dawson."

"Burleson was trying out a little blackmail," Bogart said. "On me, among others."

"Not on any of us," Gallindo said. "But then we don't make as much money as you do. Neither does Dawson. Nobody would blackmail him."

Somebody would kill him, however. Gallindo, Malone, and Randall were going to be mighty surprised when they found out that Dawson was dead, no matter what a wonderful fellow Barbara thought him to be. Elledge was going to have to do what he could with that fight scene or find himself another stunt man if he wanted to shoot it again. Of course I didn't say any of that, and neither did Bogart. We weren't supposed to know Dawson was dead. Besides, it wouldn't have been right to bring the mention of death into such a happy scene.

Not that it was really happy. There was something else going on, some undercurrent of anxiety. They were probably upset at the thought of retakes, or of how angry Elledge was going to be if he had to make them because of Dawson's mistake.

Bogart eventually brought the conversation around to Babson. Nobody knew where he was.

"He might be at your house," Stoney said. "He seemed to want us to go there last night. I think he likes you."

We'd ordered drinks by then. I was drinking only Coke. Everyone had a little laugh at Stoney's comment, though he hadn't said it humorously. At any rate, it seemed that the animosity between Bogart and Babson was common knowledge.

"You must like him, too," Gallindo said to Bogart. "Otherwise you wouldn't have visited him on the set today."

"He tried to get me tossed," Bogart said, taking a drink. "That's how much he likes me. And the *vice* is definitely *versa*."

"He's trying to talk Barbara into letting him write a picture for her," Stoney said. "You think he can handle it?"

"Hell, no," Bogart said. "Don't listen to him, Barbara. If you get that nomination from the Academy that people are talking about, you'll have a little clout for the first time in your career. Don't throw it away on some deal with Babson."

"Clout," Gallindo said. "We should all have some. Like you, Bogie. You have clout to spare."

"And look how long it took me to get it. Barbara's done the same thing, worked her way up. That's the way you have to do it, sometimes, unless you're one of the very lucky ones. And there aren't many of those."

"You don't have to worry about Barbara," Stoney said. "Now that she's finally gotten somewhere, she's not going to make any mistakes. If you say we should steer clear of Babson, we're steering clear. We can't afford any slip-ups. Not now that Barbara's finally gotten her break."

Barbara looked at him admiringly, as if she didn't mind at all his use of we, though she was the one who'd made it nearly to the top and he was still a stunt man. I wondered how long her attitude would last once a few more of the perquisites of stardom started coming her way. She might begin to think of Stoney as a has-been or a never-was who might harm her career if she stayed too closely associated with him.

Or she might not. I'm sure there were some happy relationships in

Hollywood. Bogart seemed to have one with Bacall. But theirs was the exception rather than the rule, in my experience.

We stayed and talked for a while longer, but we weren't getting any closer to Babson or to finding out anything about him that was helpful except that he didn't drive a Packard.

"It's a Chevy," Gallindo said when I asked. "What do you want to know that for?"

"Bogart and I had a bet," I said. "Something about the kind of cars writers can afford."

"Yeah, well a Chevy is about the best one of those guys will ever have."

"Too bad," I said. "Lousy car like that."

"They're not so bad," Gallindo said. "I have one."

"So do I," Stoney said.

Maybe we could have started a club, but it didn't seem like the thing to do. Bogart and I extricated ourselves from the conversation and left.

"This is getting us nowhere," Bogart said when we were back in my lousy car. "Phil Marlowe never has this much trouble finding his man."

"Sure he does. Anyway, if he doesn't, it's because he gets to read the script."

"Yeah. Well, I don't even think there is a script for this movie."

"There's always a script," I said. "Sometimes it's just not easy to follow the lines. I wish there were something we could do about Dawson, though. I have the feeling that all this is tied together somehow."

"But you don't know how, and neither do I. I liked Dawson, but there's nothing we can do for him now except find out who killed him. The cops have taken care of his body."

He was right, but I still felt bad about it.

"We might as well go home, then," I said. "I could use a little sleep."

Bogart said it was early yet, but since we'd already been just about everywhere he could think of, it didn't seem likely that we'd find Babson by continuing to look.

So I drove back to the Garden of Allah, where Congreve and Garton were ready and waiting for us.

25

I wasn't ready for them. I didn't even see them until they stepped out of the darkness at the side of the street and Garton jerked open the car door on my side. Then he grabbed my arm and yanked me out of the car onto the sidewalk.

On the other side of the car, Congreve was much gentler with Bogart. After all, Bogart had clout, something I'd never had and would never have in Hollywood. Even though he was trying to be gentle, however, Congreve was plainly upset.

"What the hell is this?" I said.

"Shut up," Garton told me.

He was holding his pistol. I thought he'd been kidding at least a little bit when he said he wanted to shoot me, but now I wondered if I hadn't been wrong. I realized that it had been a mistake to wink at him. So I shut up.

Bogart didn't. He said, "Yeah, what the hell is this?"

Congreve said, "I told you and Scott not to mess in my case. You didn't listen."

Bogart lit a cigarette as coolly as Philip Marlowe ever did. After taking a couple of drags, he said, "I don't think that's strictly true. You told Scott, but you didn't tell me. Not that it makes any difference, since we haven't been messing in your case, as you put it. We've been out on the town."

As lies went, I thought it was a pretty good one. The good ones are always at least a little bit true, as this one was.

Congreve didn't fall for it.

"Somebody killed a stuntman named Charles Dawson tonight," he said. "At Superior Studios. And it seems to me that two murders of people working for the same studio in a couple of days is a little too much of a coincidence."

Bogart ran the ball of his thumb down his jawline and let smoke trickle up from the cigarette between his lips.

"What's that to us?" he said. "We don't work for Superior."

"You were there, though," Congreve said. "Somebody spotted you."

The man on the gate hadn't been quite as absorbed in his pulp magazine as I'd thought.

"We were looking for some friends," Bogart said. "They weren't there."

"I'll bet they weren't," Congreve said. "But you've said enough in front of your pal here. You and I are going to have a talk in your place."

He gave Bogart a little nudge, but Bogart didn't move. He said, "I'm not leaving Scott with that trained ape of yours."

Garton snorted. He sounded more like a horse than an ape, but that didn't mean I wanted to be alone with him.

"Ray's harmless," Congreve said, and I knew he was lying through his teeth. "We have to talk to you separately to make sure you're not cuing each other. We're not taking you downtown, not yet. It's just a little matter of your telling us a few things, and then it will be all over."

And the moon is made of green cheese, I thought.

"If Ray's so harmless, why does he need a pistol?" Bogart asked.

Congreve clucked his tongue and said, "Why I hadn't noticed it. Put that away, Ray. You won't need it. These two are going to cooperate. Aren't you?"

"I need the pistol," Garton said. "Scott has one."

For just a second I didn't know what he was talking about. Then I remembered.

"Take it out of your pocket, Scott," Garton said. "With two fingers. Be careful. I'd hate to put a bullet hole in that cheap suit of yours."

I lifted the pistol out of my pocket and let it dangle. Congreve walked over and took it from me.

"I suppose you have a permit," he said.

As a matter of fact, I did have a permit, and I told him so. He didn't give me the pistol back, however. He slipped it into his own pocket.

"Did you know he was carrying a gun?" Congreve asked Bogart.

Bogart shrugged and looked bored. He was very good at it.

"I don't notice things like that," he said.

Congreve took Bogart's elbow and steered him into the Garden of Allah, leaving me alone on the street with Garton, who was grinning as if he were about to have the time of his life. He put his pistol back into the holster. He probably didn't think he needed it.

I didn't think he needed it either.

"You and I are gonna have a little talk," he said. "You're gonna tell me about how you killed Dawson."

"I didn't kill anybody."

"Sure you didn't. They all say that. I don't blame you. I'd say the same. But you'll change your mind."

"And you're going to make me."

His grin widened.

"That's right," he said. "I'm gonna make you."

I didn't know how he was going to do it. It was late, but there were still cars passing by every few seconds. Garton didn't seem to care.

"Come with me," he said.

I wasn't planning to go anywhere with him or anybody else. I stayed right where I was.

"You don't have to be afraid," he said. "We're just going over to the car."

I told him I wasn't afraid, and my voice was steady enough. Maybe I really wasn't afraid. After all, it wasn't as if he had spiders in the car.

"We can sit and talk," he said. "Beats standing up."

"All right," I said, and I followed him down the block.

I should have been more suspicious. The car was parked around the corner, and the streetlight was out. That alone should have tipped me. But Garton was walking casually along, whistling something that had a vague resemblance to "The White Cliffs of Dover," as if we were just out for a friendly stroll around the block.

When he got to the car, he opened the back door and leaned into the car. Then he stepped back and said, "You first. Have a seat and make yourself comfortable."

I was about to get inside when he hit me.

He'd gotten a towel from inside the car when he opened the door. It had been there waiting for him, rolled into a tight length and doubled over.

If you think a towel can't do much damage, let somebody roll one up like that, and then club you in the kidneys with it when you're relaxed and bent at a slight angle.

I heard it swishing through the air, so I managed to make about a quarter of a turn before it hit me, not that it helped much.

The towel was thick and soft, and it probably wouldn't leave a mark on me. But it could break a rib or two, maybe bruise a kidney. Give you a concussion if it hit your head just right, and I had a feeling Garton knew the way to do it.

He danced back out of my reach, his grin wider than ever.

"How'd you like that, Scott? Feel good? Ready for another?"

He swung for my side, pivoting like Joe DiMaggio going for the fences. I jumped back and hit the car. The towel passed by about a quarter of an inch in front of my stomach.

"Good reactions," Garton said, puffing a little with the effort. Maybe if I could make him keep missing, he'd keel over with a heart attack.

He swung again, and this time there was nowhere for me to go. The towel hit me squarely in the stomach. All the wind in my lungs whooshed out. I was lucky everything I'd eaten and drunk for the past week didn't follow it.

I bent double. My hat fell off, and the towel smashed across my shoulders. Somehow I managed not to fall to the street. I scuttled along the side of the car for a foot or two, like a crab with the palsy.

"No use to run," Garton said, giving my hat a kick that sent it skipping down the sidewalk.

Run? I thought. I wasn't sure I could even straighten up, much less run.

The towel came at me again, but this time I was able to duck out of the way. Or maybe I was just falling and got lucky, because I found myself on my knees on the sidewalk.

"Home run," Garton said, twirling the towel around as if winding up.

"Dead center field. I'm Babe Ruth, and you're Charlie Root."

He was taking aim at my head, and I had a feeling that I wasn't Charlie Root at all. My head, however, was the ball, and if Garton connected, my head would wind up somewhere in San Jose. Unfortunately, there was nothing I could do to stop him. My knees were as weak as a Baptist highball.

I put out a hand to steady myself against the car, but my fingers met only empty air. I remembered that I'd left the car door open. I threw myself backward into the seat and pulled the door shut just as the towel crashed into it with a heavy thud. There was going to be a dent there. I hope the department billed Garton for having it fixed.

"Come out of there, you asshole," Garton said, his voice muffled.

I scooted over to the other side of the seat and crouched there, feeling as if I'd been run over by an APC. My head throbbed, my stomach was cramping, and my kidneys were twinging.

Garton opened the door. He smiled at me, holding the towel behind his back.

"Come on out, Scott. I don't have the towel any more."

Like hell he didn't. I opened the door on my side and got out, closing it behind me. Now that the car was between us, I felt a little better. I even managed to stand up.

"Maybe you should get the pistol out again, Garton," I said. "Unless you think you can catch me."

He started around the car. So did I, somewhat more slowly than he was moving, but still fast enough to stay ahead of him. We kept going, and we must have looked like a scene from a Three Stooges short as we circled the car, me leaning into it, trying not to fall, him coming as fast as he could, but trying to keep the towel concealed. I didn't know why he didn't just start swinging it. Earlier we'd been mostly hidden from the street by the car. Now someone might see us.

After we'd gone twice around, Garton stopped.

"I've had enough of this shit," he said.

He threw the towel on the hood of the car.

"I was just kidding about the pistol," I told him. "You don't want to shoot me right here on the street. Too much explaining to do."

"You're going to tell me about Dawson," he said, drawing the pistol. "One way or the other."

"Dead or alive? Even you must realize that doesn't make any sense."

"Screw you, Scott. You think you're hot stuff because you have movie-star pals and kiss Jack Warner's ass every day, but you're nothing but a chickenshit leech."

I eased along the side of the car. He slid right along after me, pointing the pistol in the general direction of my chest. It was the second time that night someone had pointed a pistol at me, and I didn't much like it. The funny thing was that Garton, the cop, worried me more than Charlie O., the gangster.

"Don't hold back, Garton," I said. "If you don't like me, just say so. You don't have to be so polite."

And with that I changed directions, moving around the car toward him.

"Come on, Garton," I said. "If you hate me, just shoot me. Ever shot anyone before? I'll bet you have. Did he bleed much? Do you think I'll bleed all over your nice police car?"

"Stand still, you son of a bitch," Garton said, "or by God I *will* shoot you."

"Go ahead. I'm tired of trying to get away from you." I edged along the fenders toward the front of the car. "You don't have to worry about shooting an unarmed man. Congreve has my pistol, and I'm sure he'll be glad to plant it on me. Probably wouldn't be the first time that you and he have done a little deal like that, now would it."

"We don't work that way," Garton said. "But if you come any farther, I'll have to shoot."

"Go ahead. See if I care."

I was around the front of the car now, past the hood ornament and on my way toward Garton. I could see that he was getting nervous, almost as if I had the pistol and he had nothing.

"Well?" I said. "What are you waiting for? Are you too scared to pull the trigger? Look at you. I think your knees are shaking. Congreve would be ashamed of you if he were here to see you."

"All right, Scott," Garton said. "If you want die, then by God I'll take care of it for you."

He would have, too, but I was a little too quick for him.

I snatched the towel off the hood and sent it out like a striking snake, just the way I'd used one in the high school gym. The tip of it popped his hand, and the pistol went flying off to the side. It hit the sidewalk, discharged, and a bullet twanged into the car's front fender not too far from where I was standing.

I didn't look to see where the pistol had landed. Garton did, and I popped the towel again, this time catching him on the cheek, just below his right eye.

He put his hands to his face, and I let him have another pop, this time in a lower and more delicate portion of his anatomy. He moved his hands from his face to his crotch and moaned loudly. It was a nice sound to hear.

While he was sniveling, I tossed the towel back into the car. Then I went over and picked up the pistol.

"You shouldn't throw these things around like you would a toy," I told him. "It's very dangerous. Someone could get hurt."

For some reason he didn't answer me. I took his handcuffs, and jerked one arm behind him. I snapped a cuff on, then yanked the other arm back and cuffed it as well. Garton fell over on the walk and lay there on his side, curled up as if he were a very large baby trying to fall sleep, his hands between his thighs as he clutched himself. He wasn't making quite as much noise as he had been, but he was still whimpering.

"If anyone stops to help, maybe you can tell them where the handcuff key is," I said. "They might find it and turn you loose, so I'd better take your pistol with me, just in case."

I think he called me a very vulgar name then, but I couldn't be sure. He was having trouble with his enunciation. In any case, I didn't care what he had to say, and I left him there while I fetched my hat, then went to find Congreve.

26

Bogart's door wasn't locked, for which I didn't blame him. Who'd want to be locked in a room with Congreve? Not me, and certainly not Bogart, who had a reputation for his inability to suffer fools gladly. Or at all.

Not that Congreve was a fool. He wasn't, though his behavior lately was enough to make a guy underestimate him. He was looking in all the wrong places for Burleson's killer, and now he was wrong about Dawson. I knew for certain that I hadn't killed the stuntman, and I was equally certain that Bogart hadn't. Neither of us had killed Burleson, either, but Congreve couldn't seem to understand that.

Since the door was unlocked, I just walked right in, with Garton's gun in my hand. I wasn't pointing it in any particular direction, but it was up and ready for use.

Bogart and Congreve were talking in the living room. Bogart hadn't cleaned the place since my last visit. He sat on the couch with a drink in his hand. Congreve was leaning against the mantel, looking at the photograph of Bogart's wife as if he might be wondering whether he'd have a chance with her when he got Bogart behind bars. I could have told him that he wouldn't, but I figured he wouldn't care to hear my opinion, and besides, he probably knew it already.

"Hello, Junior," Bogart said as I entered the room, and he raised his glass to me.

him that I don't own a .45 automatic, but he doesn't seem to believe me."

"It's the truth," I said, and it was, more or less.

After all, the automatic was in the hands of the police now, so you could say that they were the owners and not Bogart, who no longer had possession of it. Of course some might complain that was splitting hairs because Bogart still owned the gun, no matter who happened to have it at the time, but I figured a good lawyer could convince them otherwise. And while I couldn't afford a good lawyer, Mr. Warner could.

"I don't know where he got such an idea," Bogart said. "And he won't tell me. He's a very tight-lipped guy, Mr. Congreve is." "That's *Lieutenant* Congreve," I said. "Mustn't be disrespectful."

Bogart said he wouldn't dream of it and handed Congreve Garton's pistol. Congreve pointed it in my direction, and I gave him a wide grin. He dropped the pistol into a jacket pocket.

"That's more like it," I said, putting Charlie O.'s pistol in my own pocket.

"And now you'd better go see about Garton. He might be ready to get back to the station. Unless he's gone to sleep by now."

Congreve's face was almost maroon. I hoped he wasn't going to pop a blood vessel and ruin Bogart's carpet.

"I know what you're thinking," I told Congreve. "It's right out of some bad movie."

"'You'll never get away with this,'" Bogart said, right on cue in his best Duke Mantee voice. "'I'll get you if it's the last thing I do.'"

Even though I knew he was kidding, he managed to send a chill up my spine. It was no wonder Mr. Warner was willing to pay him so well.

"Very clever," Congreve said. "You two should get Jack Warner to star you in a remake of *The Roaring Twenties*."

"Look," Bogart said, "we're not trying to cause you any trouble. I didn't kill anyone, and neither did Scott. You're on the wrong track, Congreve. You need to listen to what I've been telling you, and then maybe you can find who you're looking for."

Congreve might have had something to say about that, but before he could get it out, the door flew open and Garton came into the room. I was gratified to see that he was having a little difficulty walking.

Garton, on the other hand, wasn't in the least gratified to see me. He gave me a look that could have stripped wallpaper.

"You son of a bitch," he said.

"Me?" I said. "Or Bogart? Or your lieutenant?"

"You know who I'm talking to, Scott."

"Well, I thought I knew, but I wanted to make sure. You're walking kind of funny, did you know that?"

"You son of a bitch."

"I've always found that a limited vocabulary is a sign of limited intelligence," I said. "Haven't you found that, Lieutenant? Does the department have any standards at all these days, or can just anyone get in?"

"Let's go, Garton," Congreve said. "We're wasting our time with these blockheads."

"He took my gun," Garton said, still looking at me.

Congreve pulled the pistol from his jacket pocket and held it up.

"I have it. Now let's get out of here."

He put the gun back in his pocket, walked across the room, past me and then Garton, and went out the door. Garton continued to look at me for several more seconds, so I said, "Who took the handcuffs off, Garton? Some passerby? Or are you a direct descendant of Houdini?"

"You'll never know, you son of a bitch," Garton said, and then he turned and followed Congreve.

He didn't bother to close the door, but what can you expect from somebody with his limited vocabulary and undoubtedly limited intelligence?

I went over and closed the door myself. When I turned around, Bogart was back on the couch, sipping his drink as if nothing had happened.

"What did you tell Congreve?" I asked.

"Nothing much."

"You said that he needed to listen to what you'd been telling him, and if he did, he'd find who he was looking for."

"You have a pretty good memory," Bogart said. He set his glass down and lit a cigarette. "Did Garton try to get rough with you?"

"He did more than try."

"You're tougher than you look, Junior."

I wasn't so tough. I was aching all over, and I was afraid that the next time I went to the bathroom I'd find blood in the bowl. I was sorry Garton had gotten loose, and I wondered how he'd explained himself to whoever unlocked the handcuffs. I also wondered how he'd explained himself to Congreve, and that made me feel a little better.

"I'll take that as a compliment," I said.

Bogart smiled. He took a swallow of his drink and a drag off his cigarette.

"Now," I said, "let's get back to whatever it was that you told Congreve."

"You're stubborn, too," Bogart said. "You can take that however you want."

I sat down in a chair and said, "You play your cards too close to the vest, Bogart, and I'm not sure why. Maybe you do have something to hide. Or maybe you were just trying to give me to Congreve. What do you think this is—*The Maltese Falcon*? Do you think because somebody was killed, we have to give the cops a fall guy? Do you figure me for Wilmer? If you do, you're wrong all the way. We don't have to give anybody to the cops, because we didn't kill anybody. And I'm damned sure not Wilmer."

Bogart exhaled a little smoke. "I never said you were."

"But you're not leveling with me about what you told Congreve, are you?"

"I can't help it, kid. It's just the way that I am. There are damned few people I trust in this town."

"And I'm not one of them."

"Look, kid, it's not that I don't trust you. I do. But it's hard for me to get used to the idea."

"Why don't you start by letting me in on your conversation with Congreve?"

Bogart let out a little smoke and then crushed his cigarette in an overflowing ashtray.

"All right," he said. "I admitted to Congreve that we were at the studio when Dawson was killed."

"Oh, swell. That's just great."

"It's not as bad as it sounds since he knew it already. I was trying to get him to tell me something and at the same time get him pointed in some other direction."

That sounded interesting, and I started to calm down a little.

"What did you want him to tell you?"

"I wanted to know who called him and told him we were at the studio."

"The man on the gate," I said. "The one I thought was reading the magazine."

"It wasn't him," Bogart said. "He didn't know who we were when we went in, and he didn't notice us when we left. It was someone else."

"Are you saying it was me? You could have listened in on that phone call I made if you didn't trust me."

"There's that trust thing again. You're too sensitive, kid. I know you didn't call Congreve."

"All right, then. Who was it?"

"I don't know, and neither does Congreve."

"He told you that?"

"Not in so many words, but he doesn't know. You're not the only one who can put a hankie over the telephone receiver."

"Another anonymous caller," I said.

"That's it. Now doesn't that make you wonder just how many anonymous calls the cops have gotten about you and me?"

It was something I should have thought about sooner. Well, I'd thought about it, but not enough. Now that I considered it, and it occurred to me that someone had told Congreve that Bogart had made to Burleson outside Romanoff's.

Someone had also told them that Bogart had a pistol like the one that had killed Burleson.

And someone had told them that we'd been at Superior that evening. Maybe that same someone had told them that Bogart had a .45 automatic.

In other words, someone was keeping up with just about every move Bogart and I made. That brought up two questions: Who? And why?

Bogart said he thought that it was a plot from the beginning, but he didn't know anyone who'd have it in for him.

"OK, maybe I do," he said. "There's Babson. But I can't believe he hates me so much that he'd frame me for murder. It doesn't make sense."

It didn't make sense to me, either. Too many complications, too easy to disprove. My theory was that someone was trying to draw attention away from himself by leaving the pistol behind.

Which brought us back to the big questions.

Who?

Why?

And neither of us had an answer.

27

A re you sure you can't use a drink?" Bogart asked after we'd discussed things for a while longer. "I've found that liquor lubricates the brain cells."

"Not mine. And I thought liquor killed brain cells."

"Who told you that? Somebody who never took a drink, I'll bet. What does a teetotaler know?"

I couldn't answer that one for him, so he got up and poured himself some more Scotch while I tried to remember everything that had been said to me in the last couple of days. I had the feeling that there was something I'd missed, but I couldn't come up with it.

The fact that it was now long past midnight might have had something to do with it, or maybe it was because Garton had pounded me so hard with his towel. Of course I'd lost a few brain cells back when I'd been drinking. That could have been the problem.

I told Bogart that I might as well go on home and try to get some rest. I was tired, and we could start again the next day.

Bogart, who didn't seem tired at all, held his glass of Scotch up to the light and admired the color.

"Before you leave," he said after he'd taken a drink, "we need to talk about one other thing." "What's that?"

"It all goes back to my pistol," he said. "We know that someone took it, and whoever did it was almost certainly here the night before Burleson got killed."

I didn't agree. He might have told others about the pistol. Mayo knew about it, and I was sure Bacall did, too.

"But neither one of them killed Burleson," he said. "Mayo was in no condition to kill anyone, and it couldn't have been her driving that car tonight. She's a lousy driver. And she doesn't have a Packard."

I pointed out that we didn't know that car at Superior had been a Packard.

"Want to bet?" Bogart said. "I'll give you good odds."

I didn't want to bet. I had a feeling the car had been a Packard, all right.

"Forget the Packard," I said. I wasn't feeling so tired now, but I was still feeling beaten up. "Who knew about the pistol. You keep dodging that one."

Bogart went back to sit on the couch. He set his drink on the coffee table and leaned forward, his elbows on his thighs, his hands clasped under his chin.

"If it's not Babson," he said, "and believe me, I'd like it to be, it comes down to whoever's got the most to lose. Who would that be?"

The only one I could think of was Robert Carroll. Bob. If we trusted Dawson's dying message it had to be him or Babson, and we hadn't found either of them that night.

"The way Stella talked," Bogart said, "Bob has a lot to lose, all right. Maybe he's the one we need to talk to."

I was willing, but I didn't know where to look for him.

"You found Stella, didn't you? Aren't there places like that where Bob might go?"

I knew of a couple, but I wasn't as friendly with the people who managed them as I was with Harry and Johnnie. Getting inside wouldn't be quite as easy as it had been at the Club Sappho. And the places I knew weren't as easy to find. One of them was out in the Hollywood hills.

"That's just what we need," Bogart said. "A drive in the hills would be invigorating."

"You'll just fill the car with smoke," I said.

"You can roll down a window." He stood up. "Let's go."

I gave in. What else could I do?

We drove with the windows down in my old Chevy, and the night air did wake me up a little. Bogart had a cigarette going, but the wind carried the smoke away, and, if I wasn't invigorated, at least I wasn't entirely groggy.

It was a good thing I wasn't drowsy because one of the places I knew about where Bob Carroll might be was the Michelangelo, out between Beverly Hills and Bel Air where the highway twisted and turned up into the hills. Driving there at night was always sort of an adventure even if you were completely alert.

Bogart found that the bottle he'd bought earlier–much earlier–was still in the car, so he had a little drink to keep his brain working, or maybe to keep himself awake.

It wasn't until after we'd gotten out of Beverly and into the real hills that he had anything to say.

"You remember that Packard we've been talking about?"

"How could I forget," I said.

"Well, it's back."

I looked into the rearview mirror and saw a pair of headlights, but I couldn't tell what kind of car they belonged to.

"Are you sure?"

"I might not have a copy of that Detective's Handbook you're always talking about, but I know a Packard when I see one."

"How the hell can you see it well enough to tell what it is?"

"I got a pretty good look when we stopped at that stop sign at Beverly Drive, in front of the Beverly Hills Hotel."

"Why didn't you mention it to me?"

I don't know why I was asking. What would I have done? I don't usually get involved in cases that require me to take evasive action.

"I wanted to be sure it was the same car," Bogart said. "I had another look when we passed under the last streetlight, and now I'm sure." Last was the word when it came to streetlights, all right. We were out of the city and into the hills, and there weren't any lights. There weren't many cars, either, not at that hour of the morning.

"Everywhere we go, there it is," Bogart said, still talking about the Packard. "Why do you think that is?"

"Somebody wants to keep tabs on us," I said.

"Right. But why would anybody want to do that?"

"To find out what we know, or at least who we're talking to."

"Maybe it was that way at first," Bogart said, his face illuminated only by the dim dashboard lights. "This time might be different."

I didn't like the way that sounded.

"Different how?" I said.

"They might have decided it's time to get rid of us. This would be a good place."

I couldn't argue with that. Since there was no traffic, the driver could pull up beside my car and let a passenger riddle the body of the old Chevy with bullets. He could riddle *our* bodies with bullets, too, while he was at it, and there wasn't much I could do to prevent it. There was no way I could outrun him all the way to Bel Air. The Chevy had trouble climbing the hills at all, much less making any speed.

While I was thinking about that, the Packard started gaining on me. I shoved the accelerator all the way to the floor, but we were going uphill, and there was no change in our speed. The Chevy was already giving all it could. I thought it might even have slowed down a little, but that was probably only my imagination, which was working overtime as I thought about my bullet-riddled corpse being pulled from the car the next day by some cops I didn't know.

I thought of how much Garton would enjoy hearing about it.

I thought of how much money Mr. Warner would lose if Bogart were killed with me.

I thought about how there was no one who would really miss me.

Bogart didn't seem at all concerned. We might have been out for a Sunday drive in the country for all the anxiety he exhibited. Either he was an even better actor than I thought he was, or he was a lot calmer under pressure than I could ever be.

He took a drag off his cigarette and said, "He's going to try to run us off the road."

"How do you know?" I asked, straining forward as if I could somehow will the Chevy to go faster. It wasn't working.

"I've seen more movies than you have. Not to mention that the top of this hill would be a perfect place. There's no shoulder to speak of, there's no safety barrier, and it's a hell of a long way down."

"You don't sound very worried."

We were reaching the top of the hill now, and I remembered that there was a sharp turn to the left right beyond the crest.

"I'm worried, all right, but I figure you'll think of something," Bogart said, and flipped his cigarette out the window.

Without waiting for it to hit the ground, he lit another one. I don't think his hands were shaking, but then I couldn't see too well in the near darkness.

I looked into the rearview mirror again and saw the Packard. It was nearing my back bumper. If I was ever planning to do anything, I had to make my move.

So I swerved over into the left lane. The Chevy's tires squealed, and the front end shuddered. The car made a couple of fast swerves and then settled down.

There was a hill on our left side now, and I could almost have reached out and touched the bushes that grew beside the road. It gave me a good feeling to think of the solidity of that hill.

"Good move," Bogart said. "I'd like to see him push us off now."

"I wouldn't," I said.

"That was irony, Junior. Very big in the Greek drama. You ever read any of those old plays?"

I didn't think this was the right time for a discussion of Euripides or even Sophocles.

"Dramatic irony," Bogart said, and then, just in case my education was lacking, he gave me the definition. "That's when the audience knows something that the characters don't know."

"Swell," I said, and that's when the Packard rammed my bumper.

I jerked forward, but I didn't lose my grip on the wheel. Bogart was able to get his hands on the dash before his head cracked the windshield.

"Well, he's not going to try to run us off the road," Bogart said.

"I'm glad to hear it."

"He's going to push us off instead."

I wasn't so glad to hear that, but I saw how it could be done. All the driver of the Packard had to do was keep pushing me in a straight line. If he could push hard enough, I wouldn't be able to make the turn. We'd just go straight across the road and over the side.

When we came to the curve, I put on my brake and turned the

wheel to the left as hard as I could. The Packard's driver floored his accelerator. He had more power than I did, and we surged forward.

I took my foot off the break and pressed down on my own accelerator. For just a moment the two cars separated, and I thought I was going to break free and that we'd be headed down the road a little ahead of the Packard.

But the moment didn't last long. The Packard hit me again, and this time it maintained contact. Before I could complete the turn, I felt the front wheels slide as they crunched on gravel, and I knew we were off the road.

We flew over the side of the hill, and for a second there was nothing in front of us but the black night sky speckled with stars.

Then the front of the car dipped, and we were falling.

We didn't fall far because the car hit the ground on all four wheels. We bounced up, hit the ground again, and bounced sideways. This happened over and over, and it was all I could do to hang onto the wheel. There was no question of steering or stopping. I was being shaken like a martini at Chasen's, only more thoroughly.

Bogart didn't have a wheel to grab, and he bounced around like a BB in a beer bottle. If I'd had time to think about it, I'd have worried about our heads banging together.

I didn't, however, have time to think about it because I was much more worried about the car banging into one of the trees that we'd somehow avoided so far, though we'd run right through any number of small bushes.

I was also worried about the car suddenly flipping end over end and not coming to a stop until it crashed into a boulder at the bottom of the hill the way cars always did in a Republic Serials when they went over the side of a hill.

If that happened, I wouldn't be worried about anything. Nobody ever got out of those cars. You couldn't count the hero. It always turned out that he'd gotten out of the car before it went over the side. Neither Bogart nor I had managed to do that. We hadn't even had time to try.

And so, trapped inside the Chevy, we bounced, skidded, and slid along, limbs slapping the sides of the car and reaching inside to swat me in the face now and then.

All this happened very fast, yet to me it seemed almost as if I were watching a slowed-down movie as we approached the big cedar tree that loomed right in front of us, the one we were going to smash into.

We hit it. I distinctly remember hearing the bumper crumple, the tree trunk crack, and the steam hissing and boiling out of the car's wrecked radiator.

After that I didn't hear anything for a while.

The next thing I knew, Bogart was shaking me.

"Wake up, Junior," he said. "It's time we got out of here."

I wasn't sure I could get out. I was wedged between the seat and the steering wheel, and it was a tight fit.

There was something odd about Bogart, too, but I couldn't figure out at first what it was. Then I realized he was outside the car. He had reached in through the window to put a hand on my shoulder and give me a shake.

And there were a couple of other things. He wasn't wearing his hat, and it looked as if there was blood on his forehead. He was pulling on the door handle, but it wasn't doing much good. The door was crumpled and stuck shut.

I looked over at the passenger door. It was dangling open, hanging from one hinge.

"Can you hear me?" Bogart said.

"I can hear you. I just can't do anything."

"Try scooting over to the other side and getting out that door."

I tried, but I couldn't move. I was stuck firmly between the wheel and the seat. I told Bogart that I was pretty much trapped where I was.

"You'd better help me get this door open so I can give you a pull," he said. "I smell gasoline."

Now that he'd mentioned it, I could smell it, too.

"Don't light a cigarette," I told him.

"I won't. Now shove on the door a little."

I leaned over and put my shoulder against the door, but I wasn't able to do much shoving. Bogart kept working at it, and after a while metal squealed and the door moved a little.

"I'm not sure I can get out even if we get it open," I said.

"You're doing fine, Junior. Hit it again."

I hadn't hit it in the first place, but I put my shoulder on the door and gave a little push. There was a louder squeal, and the door moved another inch or two. If I dieted for about thirty years, I might be able to squeeze through the opening. That is, if I could get out from under the wheel.

"Just a little more," Bogart said. "We've almost got it."

This time the squeal sounded like a demon screaming, and the door came open almost all the way. Bogart took my arm and started yanking on it. Pain went all through my body, or so it seemed. I'd hit the steering wheel hard, and I knew there would be a bruise that covered my chest.

"You're not helping," Bogart said.

I twisted around as much as I could, which wasn't much at all, but with Bogart pulling and me twisting, I started to move a little.

"That's the idea. Here we go now."

Bogart put one foot on the side of the car. He pushed with his leg and pulled with his arms, and I popped out of the car and fell onto the hillside. I felt grit and gravel under my cheek and smelled gasoline. I lay there for a while looking at nothing much.

"How badly are you hurt?" Bogart asked from somewhere up above me.

I couldn't tell him because I didn't know. Judging by how I felt, I figured every bone in my body was broken. I'd only thought I'd been hurt when Garton pummeled me with the towel earlier that evening. That had been nothing more than a warm-up for the real thing.

"You're going to have to try to stand up," Bogart said. "I'm afraid the car is going to blow up. Any little spark could set it off."

That reminded me of the gasoline smell again, and it was even stronger now. My face was turned toward the car, and I imagined I could see a pool of gasoline forming on the ground in the darkness beneath it. I heard hissing and popping and creaking sounds, all of them coming from my car.

"I hope my auto insurance is paid up," I said, thinking that it probably wasn't. Dust puffed out in front of my mouth.

"Don't worry about the car," Bogart said. "It's your life insurance you should be thinking about."

Somehow that didn't cheer me up.

Bogart got his hands under my arms and tried to lift me. He didn't have much success.

"You have to help me a little," he said, so I tried.

After about a year, I managed to get up on my knees. Bogart kept tugging and talking, and eventually I was standing, more or less. I was slumped forward and a little to the side, but I was on my feet, and that was what counted.

"Very good, kid," Bogart said. "I knew you could do it."

"Yeah," I said. "Me, too. Never any doubt. Now what?"

"I almost hate to tell you."

"Let me guess, then. We walk back up to the road."

"That's exactly right. Nothing wrong with your brain, kid."

"That's what you think," I said. Now that I was upright, I could feel even more pains, and one of them was right behind my eyes. "What happened to your head?"

Bogart wiped his hand across his forehead and looked at his fingers. Then he wiped his fingers on his pants leg.

"I don't remember exactly," he said. "Is the windshield broken?"

I had no idea, and I wasn't going to look. It would have taken too much effort.

"Doesn't matter," Bogart said. "I hit something when we hit the tree. Might have been the windshield, might not. I was out for a second, but not as long as you. Are you ready?"

"For what?"

"Climbing the hill."

I wasn't ready. I wasn't ever going to be ready. Not only had I been in a severe car accident, but the leg with the shrapnel in it hadn't been in very good shape to begin with. But I didn't see that I had much choice.

So I said, "Sure," and started walking. If you could call it walking.

"Wait a minute," Bogart said. "I forgot about my hat. I want to see if I can find it. That's an expensive hat."

I hadn't walked very far, anyway, about six inches. Maybe seven.

"Take your time," I told him.

He went around to the passenger side of the car and leaned inside.

After a second or two, he leaned back out and held up the Scotch bottle, which was unbroken and still held quite a lot of liquor. He never drank as much as he appeared to be drinking.

He set the bottle down and turned back into the car. When it came to hats and liquor, he wasn't so worried about getting blown to smithereens.

He found the hat and tried to pat it back into shape. He wasn't a hundred percent successful, but he stuck the hat on his head anyhow. Then he picked up the Scotch bottle.

"Now I'm ready," he said.

He looked better with the hat on, and I figured he wanted it as much for vanity as for the cost, since he wasn't wearing his hairpiece. My own hat, unaccountably, had stayed on in spite of everything.

It didn't take Bogart long to get ahead of me. When you're taking six-inch steps, or maybe seven-inch steps, you're not going to win a lot of races.

Bogart looked back at me.

"You look like Boris Karloff in one of those Frankenstein movies," he said after having a slug of Scotch. "But without the elevator shoes."

"It's not how a man looks that matters. It's how he conducts himself with others."

Bogart gave me a hard look.

"Maybe I was wrong. Maybe there *is* something wrong with your head."

I shuffled along for six or seven more inches and said, "I wouldn't be a bit surprised."

Bogart didn't respond to that. He just turned around and started walking up the hill.

I don't know how long it took us to get to the top. I stumbled a lot, but I didn't fall. Some of the time I was able to help myself along by pulling on tree branches. I thought that if Bogart were any kind of friend at all, he'd get behind me and push, or maybe take one of my hands and pull, but he was probably in nearly as bad a shape as I was.

When we finally got to the top of the hill and found ourselves at the roadside, I felt as if I'd circumnavigated the globe. On foot. I thought my leg might fall off if I took another step. I started to ask

Bogart what we did next, but I was afraid he'd tell me we were going to walk back to Beverly Hills.

"I think it's safe to smoke now," he said after taking a look around.

He stuck the Scotch bottle under one arm and got out a crumpled pack of Chesterfields. He looked at it and shook his head. He straightened the pack as best he could and shook out a cigarette. It was too dark for me to see it very well, but it looked crooked and maybe ben broken to me. Bogart didn't care. He stuck it in his mouth and lit it anyway.

"Too bad we can't call a cab," I said.

"Someone will come along eventually. I don't feel like walking much farther."

I was glad to hear him say that. I didn't feel like walking any farther at all. Then I had a disturbing thought. I said, "What if the Packard comes back?"

Bogart blew out a plume of gray smoke. It hung in front of him in the still air and then drifted away.

"That guy won't be back. He thinks we're dead. And God knows we should be. If that tree hadn't stopped us halfway down, we'd be packed inside what's left of that car like a couple of sardines."

He'd hardly finished reassuring me when I heard a car coming from the direction of Bel Air. I looked and saw the glow of its headlights around the curve.

"Speak of the devil," I said.

T hat's not a Packard," Bogart said, puffing casually on the cigarette. "Hear how the motor's lugging? Sounds a little like your car."

My car would never sound that way again. It wouldn't sound any way at all. I was going to miss it.

"Maybe we can get a ride," Bogart said. "You'd better do something about that gun."

I'd forgotten about the pistol, which was causing one side of my jacket to sag badly. I took it out of the pocket and stuck it in my belt at the small of my back.

Bogart stood at the side of the road, and when the car rounded the curve, he waved his arm.

The car, a Ford of about the same age as my Chevy, chugged right on by us, but after it had gone about fifty yards, it stopped and started backing up.

The car came to a stop beside Bogart, and the driver leaned out the window.

"I think you were right, Bernie," he said. "He *does* look a lot like Humphrey Bogart."

"I *am* Humphrey Bogart," Bogart said. "That's why I look like him."

He tossed his cigarette to the ground and stepped on it.

The driver opened the door of the Ford and got out. He was a nice-looking gent in a short-sleeved Hawaiian shirt covered with pineapples of various sizes. His upper arms bulged with muscle and the sleeves fit tightly around them.

His passenger, Bernie, got out as well. He was smaller than the driver, and he was wearing a suit and a tie painted with what must have been a tropical sunset. His hands fluttered when he talked.

"Oh, Mr. Bogart," he said, "I'm *such* a fan of your movies. You were absolutely wonderful in *The Big Sleep*. Wasn't he, Evan? Wasn't he absolutely wonderful? And your wife, Miss Bacall, is simply gorgeous. Isn't she gorgeous, Evan?"

"As gorgeous as anyone ever was," Evan said. "What happened here, Mr. Bogart?"

"We had an accident." Bogart gestured over his shoulder with his thumb.

"The car's down there somewhere."

"You could have been *killed*," Bernie said. "I'm just so happy you weren't."

"I'm awfully happy about that, myself," Bogart said. "By the way, this is my friend Scotty. We're both feeling pretty rocky right now."

Scotty? I thought. What the hell? Then I realized it was just the needle again. Bogart couldn't resist.

"Hi, Bernie," I said. "Pleased to meet you."

"It's such a privilege to meet *both* of you," Bernie said, but he was looking at Bogart and not me. "What can we do to help?"

"You could give us a ride back to L.A. if you don't mind," Bogart said.

"The Garden of Allah, if you know where that is."

"We certainly do, and we don't mind at all, do we, Evan. We know where everything is in L.A., and it would be a privilege to drive you home. You just get in the car, and we'll take you there right now."

"You two look like you need a doctor," Evan said.

"We'll be fine," Bogart said. "A drink and a bath will take care of us."

Bernie looked pretty excited at the idea of the bath, but Evan said, "They won't need any help with that, Bernie. And they already have something to drink."

He looked pointedly at the bottle under Bogart's arm.

"Don't worry," Bogart said. "Scotty was driving, and he's a tee-totaler. Can I offer you gentlemen a swallow of Scotch?"

They turned him down, an we got into the car, Bogart and I in the back seat. Evan started the motor.

"You know what I liked about *The Big Sleep*?" Bernie said as we drove off. He was turned in the seat so he could look at us. "I simply *loved* the part where you went into the bookstore to ask for the copy of *Ben Hur*."

Bogart pushed up the brim of his hat.

"The *Ben Hur* 1860?" Bogart said in the same milquetoast voice he'd used in the movie, and I thought Bernie was going to swoon. "The one with the erratum on page one-sixteen?"

Bernie wriggled with delight. When he'd recovered he said, "If you don't mind my asking, where were you and...Scotty going when you had the accident?"

"We were going to the Michelangelo," Bogart said, still in the same voice. He was amazing. For the gangsters, he was a tough guy. For Bernie and Evan, he was something else entirely. "You know it?"

Bernie sneaked a look at Evan, who kept his eyes straight ahead as if concentrating on the road. Maybe he was. It was tricky even when a Packard wasn't pursuing you.

"We know the Michelangelo," Bernie said after a slight pause. "Don't we, Evan."

I had a feeling they knew it, all right. I had a feeling they were coming from there when they stopped for us.

Evan didn't say anything, but he inclined his head a little as if nodding assent. If Bogart played this right, he might find out something that would help us.

He played it right.

"Then you might know a friend of ours," he said. "Bob Carroll. He's in the movies, too. We were on our way to see him when our car went off the road."

Bernie looked at Evan again. This time Evan didn't give him a cue.

"How well do you know Bob?" Bernie said.

"He was at my house a couple of nights ago. We're old friends."

"Oh. Well, then I suppose you know *all* about him."

"Not all," Bogart said. "I know a lot, though. I know where he likes to go to have a good time."

"He was there tonight," Bernie said. "You would have missed him, though. He left about at least two hours ago. Evan and I closed the place down. We're a couple of real night owls. Isn't that right, Evan?"

Evan inclined his head slightly, and Bernie rattled on.

"Bob was there with his special friend. Do you know him, too?"

I couldn't speak for Bogart, but I didn't have a clue as to who Bob's friend was. I had a feeling I was about to find out, however.

"I thought Bob played the field," Bogart said.

"Oh, no. Not Bob. You don't know him at all if you think that. He's very faithful to Carl."

Bernie made an *O* with his mouth and put a hand over it, as if he'd blurted out the plans for making an A-bomb.

I tried not to show how surprised I was. Bogart, of course, being an actor had no trouble at all. He said, "He and Carl have been an item for a while. They were together at my house, but I wasn't sure they went other places."

"Well, they don't. Not the kind of places where they can be seen by just anyone. Bob has a reputation to keep up, you know, and you've probably met his wife, Stella. She's gorgeous, absolutely gorgeous. Not as gorgeous as Miss Bacall, of course, hardly anyone is, but still a very lovely woman. Anyway, she's the one he goes out with when he's in public."

"I know Stella," Bogart said. "We saw her earlier at the Sappho Club."

"My, my, you do get around, don't you. I wouldn't have guessed it in a million years."

"It's all Scotty's fault. He likes adventure."

Bernie really looked at me for the first time. He didn't appear to be in the least impressed.

"I suppose you never can tell about people," he said, and turned his attention back to Bogart. "At least by looking at them."

I wondered what Bernie would say about me if he knew that a pistol was digging into my backbone at that very moment.

"No, you certainly can't tell by looking," Bogart said. "Scotty here is a real wild man. Isn't that right, Scotty?"

"Never a dull moment when I'm around," I said. "One adventure after another. Dead bodies piling up all over the place."

"Oh, my," Bernie said, shrinking down in the seat a little. But he popped right back up. "You're such a kidder, Mr. Scott. You had me going for a second there, with those dead bodies."

"Call me Scotty," I said.

"And you can call me Bogie," Bogart said, sending Bernie into another near swoon.

It was going to be a long ride back to L.A.

By the time we arrived at the Garden of Allah, it was almost three o'clock. I was feeling worse than I had since my little sojourn on Saipan. It was almost enough to make me want to start drinking again.

Adding to my misery, Bernie had spent the whole trip talking to "Bogie" about the movies, about his leading ladies, about the sexual habits of some famous leading men.

I could have told him a thing or two about Buck Sterling, but I restrained myself. I never talked about my work for Mr. Warner to anyone except Mr. Warner. Bernie probably wouldn't have cared about Buck Sterling, anyway. He was too wrapped up in the fact that he was actually having a conversation with "Bogie" to listen to anything I might have to say.

But when I got out of the car, even Bernie seemed a little concerned about me.

"You don't look very good, Scotty," he said.

"He's fine," Bogart said. "Isn't that right, Scotty."

I was wobbling a little as I stood on the walk.

"Absolutely fine," I said. "Fine as wine. Ready for another adventure."

Bernie gave me a skeptical look, cocking one eyebrow, something I could never do.

"I still think you should go to a hospital," Evan said. "And maybe call the police about that accident."

"Believe me, they wouldn't do a thing," Bogart said.

Except throw us in jail, I thought. Or shoot me if Garton got his way.

"We'll send a wrecker for the car tomorrow," I said, trying to sound chipper. "A good night's sleep, and I'll be as good as new."

Bernie looked at his watch and laughed.

"I think a good night's sleep is out of the question," he said.

"I meant a good day's sleep," I told him.

Evan gunned the motor of the car just a little and Bernie took the hint.

"It was wonderful to meet you," he said, "even though the circumstances could have been better. I do hope we'll meet again."

"You can be sure of it," Bogart said, and when Evan drove away, Bernie was wearing a grin that you couldn't have removed with a case of steel wool.

"You're such a tease," I told Bogart.

"I wasn't teasing." He was using his normal voice again. "I'm sure I'll see Bernie again. I'll send him tickets to a premiere. He'd enjoy that."

I was sure he would, but I wasn't really interested. What I wanted was a ride home.

Bogart said he'd give me one, though I really didn't want him to know what kind of dump I lived in, but first he wanted to talk about what we'd learned.

I didn't think it was a good idea to talk until I'd had some sleep. I wasn't sure I could remember half of what had happened to us, much less half of we'd heard.

"You're a trained detective," Bogart said. "You'll surprise yourself."

I wasn't really trained. I'd become a detective because I wanted to work for myself, and I thought maybe my military experience would give me a little edge on the competition. It hadn't helped much, but it had been enough to persuade Mr. Warner to put me on a retainer. Now I wasn't so sure even that had been such a good idea.

I told Bogart that I needed sleep, but somehow he persuaded me to go with him to his bungalow. My acquiescence had something to do with the fact that he refused to take me anywhere until we'd talked things over. So I found myself sitting in the chair again while Bogart relaxed on the couch with his bottle of Scotch and a Chesterfield.

He looked a lot more comfortable than I felt, and I was sure that if he'd hit the windshield with his head, it was only a glancing blow.

"Here's what we know for sure," he said. "Babson and Carroll couldn't have been driving the car at Superior Studios or out in the hills because they were otherwise occupied."

"Are you surprised about Babson?" I asked.

"Kid, the last time I was surprised by anything that happened in Hollywood was sometime back in the late thirties. I didn't know about

Babson, but then I didn't know about Bob, either. That doesn't mean I'm surprised."

I wasn't surprised, either. After Buck Sterling, it would take a lot more than a couple of homosexuals to surprise me.

"You know what the problem is, don't you," Bogart said.

I wasn't thinking clearly, and I had no idea what the problem was. He looked at me the way my high school math teacher had on those occasions when I had once again proved my inability to comprehend the binomial theorem.

"If Babson and Carroll were both somewhere else, they weren't driving the car," Bogart said. "And if they weren't driving the car, that means..."

He let his voice trail off, and I sat there looking at him. He was obviously waiting for me to finish the sentence, but I couldn't do it.

"Look," he said, waving the hand holding the cigarette. "What's our one big clue?"

I was glad to be able to answer him. I said, "What Dawson wrote in the dirt as he was dying." "Right. *Bab* or *Bob*. We thought he was trying to tell us who'd killed him. But since neither Babson nor Bob was driving that car, where does that leave us?"

"Sleepy?" I said. "Tired? Banged up?"

"All of those, maybe, but it also leaves us without a clue."

That was fine with me. I was used to being without a clue. I'd spent most of my life that way.

"Wake me when it's over," I said.

I leaned back in the chair and went to sleep.

30

R ita Hayworth was sitting at the mirror, brushing that long, lovely hair. She was wearing only a white slip, and it did little to cover the part of her I was most interested in. She smiled at me in the mirror, and I walked over to tell her how beautiful she was. But I never got there because Bogart was shaking my shoulder again.

"I'm going to kill you," I said. "Very slowly, an inch at a time."

"Mr. Warner would fire you," Bogart said. "You'd never work in this town again."

He was right, but then I wasn't really going to kill him. Though I would have liked to.

"How long did I sleep?" I asked, hoping that I'd slept at least a couple of hours.

"About ten minutes. Long enough for me to go to the bathroom and wash my face."

"Ten whole minutes. No wonder I feel so refreshed."

"Come on back in the kitchen. We'll drink some coffee, and you'll feel a lot better."

It was going to take more than coffee to make me feel better. I didn't see how Bogart could be so alert, considering that he'd been through as much as I had. Even at the best of times he looked a little fatigued, as if he hadn't slept well for a while, but that was all part of a pose. Most of the time I'd been around him, he'd been positively perky, in action if not in appearance.

He made lousy coffee, though. I'll have to give him that. He dumped it in the Silex without measuring it, and put it on to boil. When it was ready, it tasted as if it had been filtered through about a quarter mile of Mississippi mud.

"It's a treat to beat your feet on the Mississippi mud," Bogart said when I described the quality of the coffee to him. He lifted his cup at me in a mock toast.

"It tastes like somebody's had his feet in it, all right," I said. I drank some of it anyway, in the hopes that it would make me feel better. It didn't.

The kitchen was a good bit cleaner than the living room, which I attributed to the fact that the party Bogart told me about had never reached the kitchen. I had the feeling that the people who attended weren't interested in drinking Bogart's coffee. I didn't blame them.

"What we have to figure out," Bogart said, "is where we went wrong in our thinking."

I could have pointed out any number of ways. First we'd thought of Orsini. Then we'd thought about everybody else. And so far we'd gotten nowhere. Even worse, we seemed to have gotten Dawson killed.

"We've been wrong from the start," I said. "I'm not even sure now that Burleson was killed because of his blackmailing. Maybe there was some other reason, something entirely unrelated that we don't even know about. We should have left all this to the cops."

"Sure," Bogart said. "Leave it to the cops. That would be swell, since they think I did it. Or maybe that you did it."

"They don't have any reason to think that."

"You're forgetting my pistol," Bogart said. "The one somebody left by Burleson's body. I'm connected to this somehow, and if I am, then the people who were here the other night are, too. One of them must have lifted that pistol."

He had a point, but I wasn't sure it helped us any. I drank a little more of the coffee. It hadn't improved a bit.

"All right," I said, after choking down a swallow of coffee. "Maybe we were on the right track, but somehow we got off it. I don't see how anything we've found out fits in with anything else we know."

"What about the process of elimination? We know who *didn't* kill Dawson, don't we?"

"Nobody did. Gallindo, Randall, and Malone were at the Derby, and they'd been there all evening. Babson and Carroll were at the Michelangelo. Stella and Wendy were at the Club Sappho. So who does that leave?"

"Slappy Coville."

"And we know where he was, too. So there's only one answer. Dawson killed himself, and someone in a big car tried to run over us because we might implicate him in the murder if he hung around. He missed us that time, so later he pushed us over a cliff to make sure we wouldn't get him in trouble."

"He didn't get us that time, either," Bogart said. "And it wasn't a cliff. Just a hill."

"A very high, steep hill."

"It was high, but it wasn't really steep."

It had seemed steep enough to me when we were climbing it, but I wasn't going to argue with him.

"It doesn't matter," I said. "By using the process of elimination, we've just proved that nobody on our list of suspects killed Dawson. So much for that process."

"Thomas Wayne," Bogart said. "We didn't eliminate him."

"Somehow I don't think a studio head would be out at night killing one of his stuntmen."

"Not even if he screwed up the take?"

"Very funny. But, no. The director might kill him for that, maybe, but not the studio head. And from what I've heard about Elledge, he wouldn't do it, either. He's not exactly a perfectionist. So you can forget that."

"There has to be an answer somewhere," Bogart said. "And we're going to find it."

"Not tonight," I told him. "Even this awful coffee isn't going to keep me awake much longer, and my brain's addled. I'm throwing in the towel."

"You're not as durable as Phil Marlowe."

"True. But he hangs out with a better class of people. The Sternwoods, for example. You take that Vivian Sternwood. Now there's a woman I wouldn't mind hanging around with."

"You have good taste," Bogart said. "I'm not so sure about your manners."

"They're pretty bad," I said. "I grieve over them long winter evenings."

"Your memory is good, though. I'd forgotten that line."

"It's a pretty good line, but my memory is in terrible shape. If I don't get some sleep, it will be gone completely. I don't even think I can make it home."

"Can you make it to the couch?"

I thought I might manage that, and I did. But it was close.

I don't remember whether I dreamed about Rita Hayworth, but when I woke up I felt much better. That is, I felt better until I moved. After that, things became a bit more problematic. There might have been an inch or two of my body that didn't hurt, but if there was, I couldn't identify it.

I sat up, very carefully, and looked around. Bogart wasn't in sight, but I could hear him moving around somewhere in the house.

I didn't try to get off the couch. I sat there with my head in my hands for a few minutes, and eventually Bogart showed up. He was wearing his ratty robe and leather slippers, and he looked as if he hadn't slept for a month. The circles under his eyes were so dark they might have been drawn there in charcoal.

But he was chipper. Disgustingly chipper.

"I'm glad to see you survived," he said. He handed me a mug of coffee. "Try a drink of this."

I was almost afraid to, but I took a sip. It was just as bad as I'd feared. Maybe worse.

"Better, huh?" Bogart said. "I remembered to add a pinch of salt this time. That gives it a better flavor."

"Urk," I said, or some sound like that.

"I knew you'd like it. Did anything come to you while you were sleeping?"

"Urk," I said, and drank a little more coffee. The second sip was even worse than the first.

"Good. I knew something would occur to you. Finish the coffee and we'll talk it over."

I didn't finish the coffee. Nobody could have finished that coffee.

But I did drink more than half of it. I don't think anyone could have done more.

Then I used the shower. I stood under the hot water for a long time, letting it draw out some of the soreness.

There was a vivid bruise the size of a dinner plate on my chest, along with other cuts and contusions, but nothing seemed to be broken.

I dried off and shaved with a razor Bogart let me use. Then I knocked the wrinkles out of my suit as well as I could and dressed in my slightly gamy clothing. I still had Orsini's pistol, so I stuck it in my belt at the back again.

I didn't look exactly ready to take a seat on the New York Stock Exchange, but I was as presentable as I could make myself, and I didn't ache quite as much. I winked at my mug in the mirror and then went into the kitchen, where Bogart was scrambling eggs in a big black iron skillet.

"I'll have my own laying hens one of these days," he said. "Nothing like fresh eggs."

I sat at the table in front of a plate that had been set for me.

"I thought you always had breakfast at Romanoff's," I said.

"If I could get fresh eggs at home, I wouldn't. Before long, Baby will be trying to get us into a bigger place, and I'll have some hens there. Hell, maybe I should just get some here."

He came over and scraped eggs out of the skillet and onto my plate.

He went away and returned with a couple of strips of bacon on a saucer, which he set by my plate.

"The toast is almost ready," he said.

"If only Bernie could see us now."

"He'd just be jealous," Bogart said. "Now eat your eggs and bacon."

I ate my too hard eggs and undercooked bacon, along with the toast, which was only slightly burned. When I was finished, Bogart took up the plate, silverware, and saucer. He put them in the sink and ran water in them.

"That should hold them," he said with satisfaction. "Baby doesn't realize how domestic I am."

Something that he'd said started a buzzing in the back of my mind, but I couldn't quite pin it down. I said, "What time is it?"

"Afternoon. Around two o'clock. Did you get enough sleep?"

"No, but I'll live."

"Want another cup of coffee?"

"God, no."

"Well, if you feel that way about it, I won't offer it again. Now tell me what new ideas you've come up with."

"Did I say I'd come up with anything?"

"No, but I can tell by the keen detective's look in your eye that something did occur to you."

"I haven't got it pinned down yet. Did you think of anything?"

"A new angle. That's what we needed all along. A new angle."

"And what new angle have you discovered?"

"We're back to blackmail. Who'd kill Burleson because of something he knew? The one with the most to lose. So who has the most to lose?"

I thought everyone we'd talked to had plenty to lose, but they were all eliminated as suspects. So I didn't see that the new angle was much help.

"Maybe not," Bogart admitted when I told him what I thought, "but it puts a whole new light on things. Let's say, for argument's sake that people found out that Stella Gordon was a lesbian or that her husband liked other men. How bad would that be?"

"They'd be finished in Hollywood," I said, and it was the truth.

"But they've had their time in the sun. Some people never have, people like Stoney Randall and Barbara Malone. Think about what they were saying last night."

I didn't have to think about it. I remembered it all, because their conversation was one of the things that had been bumping around in the back of my head. They'd talked about mistakes and how they weren't going to make any, not now that Barbara had finally gotten her big break. They'd had nothing to lose for a long time. Now they had everything.

And I remembered something else. I remembered that Randall had said he didn't really know Burleson all that well.

That wasn't what Dawson had told us. He'd said that Randall was one of the few people who liked Burleson and that Burleson had once let him borrow a hundred dollars. So somebody had lied to us.

I'd also wondered why Barbara had been so animated. It hadn't seemed natural, and I'd attributed it to alcohol. But what if it had been something more? She might have been covering up her nervousness at knowing the truth about Dawson.

Randall and Malone. They finally had clout, or Malone did. But maybe not for long if she had some terrible secret that Burleson had uncovered. What kind of secret could it be?

"Oh, hell," I said.

"What does that mean?"

"What was it that you were calling your wife a few seconds ago?"

"Baby. I always call her that. Nearly always. Sometimes I call her Betty. Why?"

"What if Dawson was trying to write *baby* in the dirt last night?"

"You're saying Betty killed Dawson? You must be completely nuts."

"I'm saying what if Barbara Malone was pregnant. That's what Dawson was trying to tell us."

"Nothing wrong with being pregnant, except that she's not married. That would be easy enough to cover up. She and Randall are going to get married any day now."

"But they're not married yet. What if she had an abortion? You told Dawson that she and Randall took a vacation. What if they left town so Barbara could have an abortion, and the money Randall borrowed was to pay a doctor?"

Bogart thought it over for a few seconds.

"It fits," he said.

And it did. Randall and Malone wouldn't have gone to Thomas Wayne about the problem. They'd have been afraid of what he might say. If either of them had been a big star already, it might not have been such a problem, but they didn't have any clout, as they'd pointed out. Barbara hadn't won that Oscar yet, and Wayne didn't have anything to gain by helping them. If they were found out, he'd be in as much trouble as they would. With his only legitimate star under a dark cloud, he'd be laughed at by the other studio heads.

Malone and Randall could have gone to Burleson, however, since he was supposed to be discreet. Little did they know.

"All right, maybe I'm right this time," I said. "Maybe they killed Burleson. But they couldn't have killed Dawson."

"I want to get whoever did that. Dawson was my friend, and I don't forget friends. But shouldn't we take this one murder at a time?"

"I suppose you're right. I've never been involved with murder before. Now that we know who did it, we should call Congreve."

"Why? We don't owe him a thing. He'll just mess it up, or his lackey will kill somebody. You, if he gets his way. Besides, we don't even know if you're right about all this."

"How do you propose that we find out?"

"We could just go to the studio and ask them," Bogart said.

So that's what we decided to do.

CHAPTER

31

We had no trouble at the gate, and we drove on back to the backlot jungle. There was no sign that anyone had been killed there the night before. The cops had completed their investigation, and the body had been taken away. Dawson was in the morgue somewhere, sleeping the big sleep.

I'd thought that with Hollywood being such a sentimental town, the murder would put a stop to the filming of *Jan of the Jungle*, but Bogart assured me that I was wrong.

"You don't know this town at all if you think that. Some of the actors might go to the funeral if the press is going to be there taking pictures, but that's about it. Elledge doesn't stop shooting this picture for anything like a little murder. Dawson's death won't even slow him down. They'll have a new stunt man on the set already."

We got out of the Caddy and walked back into the jungle. I could hear people farther back among the trees, and when we got there, they were setting up for a scene with a lion. The lion, which looked older than any of the actors, lay in its cage and looked out at the proceedings with a notable lack of enthusiasm.

I was relieved to see that there were no spiders in sight. Lions I could deal with. Spiders were another matter.

Stella Gordon was there in her jungle girl outfit, but I didn't see Wendy Felsen anywhere around.

Slappy Coville was off to one side, leaning against a tree and cracking jokes with some of the crew, but I didn't notice anyone laughing. I didn't blame them. His jokes were probably even older than the lion.

Timbo the chimp would have been funnier than Coville, but he wasn't there. He was probably in his trailer, having a smoke and reading the *L. A. Times.*

Robert Carroll was talking to Stoney Randall, who was getting ready to fight the lion, though judging from the looks of the lion I didn't think there was going to be much of a fight. On the other hand, the lion was an actor, and sometimes actors didn't want to expend any energy until the cameras were rolling. It could have been that the lion was like that.

Joey Gallindo was talking to Carl Babson, who looked up in our direction, saw Bogart, and flared up immediately. He started walking our way, and by the time he reached us, he was already yelling.

"I don't know what you're doing back here again, but I want you to leave right now," he said.

"You know, Carl," Bogart said, "you're a good example of the reason no one likes to have the writer on the set."

"You son of a bitch, you think you're too good to be in any picture I write, but all you are is—"

"Bernie says hello," Bogart said.

"—a ham actor with...what did you say?"

"Bernie says hello. Evan, too. They said they had a great time with you and Bob last night."

"Y-you...know B-bernie?"

"And Evan. Nice guys. Scott and I went for a drive with them last night."

"Scotty," I said. "Call me Scotty."

Bogart cut his eyes at me, but Babson didn't notice. He was still stuttering. He said, "They t-told you about me and B-bob?"

"Bob? I don't recall that they mentioned Bob. Was he with you? They just said they'd seen you somewhere and asked us to say hello when we saw you."

"G-good. T-that's good. If you see them again, t-tell them I said the same."

Babson turned away and walked back to where he'd been talking to Gallindo, but Joey was no longer there. He must have had a part in the scene, or maybe he'd gone off to look for the chimp.

They let the lion out of the cage, and it walked apathetically toward Carroll, who was posing like a Muscle Beach boy. I thought he'd look right at home there in Venice with all the other strong men, though of course he wasn't going to do any actual wrestling with the lion. That was Randall's job.

The trainer finally persuaded the lion to go into a crouch as if it was about to pounce. Randall moved to the spot where Carroll had been standing, and soon he and the lion were tangled up in a not-so-titanic struggle. It was interesting to watch and see how Randall managed to keep his face hidden behind the lion, and for all anyone would ever know (if they sped up the film a bit), Bob Carroll was engaged in a struggle to the death with a ferocious jungle beast.

Elledge told them to cut and print, and Bogart and I walked over to talk with Randall, who was toweling lion drool off his arms. We'd decided on the drive to the studio how we were going to play it, and I let Bogart take the lead.

"I always thought I could trust you, Stoney," he said, "but you really let me down when you killed Burleson. Especially when you tried to frame me for it. You should have known that I play the sap for nobody."

Randall stopped toweling and looked at us.

"I don't know what the hell you're talking about," he said, but he was a stuntman, not an actor, and his face gave him away. Our reasoning had been right.

"We know about Barbara," I said. "We know that Burleson let you borrow the money for the abortion. It's just a matter of time until we find out the doctor's name."

"You should have gone to the cops to begin with," Bogart said. "They would have protected you. Mr. Wayne would have protected you, too. This way, everybody loses."

"No," Randall said. "Not this time."

He threw the towel in Bogart's face and ran.

I started after him, but Bogart got in my way, and we did a little dance around each other while he clawed the towel away from his eyes.

"Where does he think he's going?" I asked.

"To get help or to warn Barbara. We'd better stop him."

We started after him, and everyone on the set was staring at us as we passed by. They must have thought we were part of some scene they hadn't located in their versions of the script.

Running wasn't easy for me. I'm not a natural athlete in the first place, and all my bruises and abrasions were twinging. I could have pulled Orsini's pistol, I suppose, but I didn't want to scare everyone on the set, and I wasn't going to use it anyway. I hadn't shot anyone since the war, and I didn't want to start with Randall.

Bogart was more a natural athlete than I am, and he was running better, not that it was doing him much good because Randall was a physically gifted guy, something that stood him in good stead in the stunt business and in chases. He was easily outdistancing both of us.

He would have gotten away if he hadn't fallen.

One of the many disadvantages of running in a jungle, even a fake one, is that there are all kinds of vines and roots around. Most of the vines and roots are just as fake as the rest of the place, but they're still there nevertheless, and they can still trip you up if you're not careful. It was a root that tripped up Randall and pitched him headlong on the ground. He pushed himself up on his hands, shook his head, and jumped to his feet.

By that time Bogart had caught up. He reached out and grabbed Randall's shoulder. The stuntman whirled around and hooked a short right that would have connected with Bogart's midsection if Bogart hadn't moved back. It was almost as if Randall had pulled the punch, the way he would have in a movie, though I knew that wasn't the case.

Randall closed with Bogart and swung again. Bogart ducked under the flying fist, bulled forward, and locked his arms around Randall just above the waist. Together they rushed backward until they smashed into a tree.

Bogart moved his hands just in time to keep them from being crushed, and Randall crumpled, the breath knocked out of him. Bogart moved back. The stuntman slid down the tree trunk and lay slumped against it as if unconscious. Bogart moved toward him warily, and Randall snaked out a foot, sweeping Bogart's feet from under him. When Bogart fell, Randall jumped up and swung back a foot to kick him in the face.

He didn't get a chance because I had finally arrived on the scene. I launched myself in a short, shallow dive, the only kind I'm capable of. If I'd been more of an athlete, I'd have flattened Randall and landed on top of him. As it was, I almost missed him, but I threw off his timing enough that he missed Bogart with his kick and staggered awkwardly to his left.

I landed on my side, and Randall took out his frustration by kicking me in the stomach. I was already feeling a little queasy from the run, and the pain was excruciating. It wasn't as bad as it would have been if he'd kicked my bruised chest, but it was bad enough. I had to clamp my teeth together to avoid expelling the breakfast I'd eaten at Bogart's.

Randall was going to kick me again just for the hell of it, but Bogart got up and grabbed him from behind, holding Randall's arms tight against his sides as his feet danced in the air a few inches off the ground.

I got up and braced myself against the tree with one arm while they struggled.

"Don't just stand there, Junior," Bogart said a little breathlessly. "Hit him."

I didn't feel like hitting anyone, so I fumbled under my coat and brought out the pistol.

"Why don't I just shoot him?" I said.

"Fine, if you're sure the bullet won't go through him and hit me, too."

"No guarantees," I said. "Or you could just let him go, and I'll see if I can get him on the run."

"On the count of three," Bogart said. "Don't forget to lead him a little."

"You crazy bastards," Randall said, kicking wildly in an attempt to escape Bogart's grasp.

"Let him go," I said, spreading my feet and gripping the pistol with both hands. "Five dollars says I get him in the head with the first shot."

"Ten bucks," Bogart said.

"All right. Make it ten."

"Goddammit! You can't do this!" Randall said.

"Who says?" Bogart asked, and he let Randall go.

32

I never intended to pull the trigger, as I'm sure Bogart was well aware, so I don't know what I would have done if Randall hadn't simply fallen to the ground, curled up, and covered his head with his hands.

Why he covered his head like that, I have no idea. If I'd actually been planning to shoot him, his hands wouldn't have provided a hell of a lot of protection. Maybe he thought the pistol was loaded with blanks, as if he were in a movie.

Bogart poked at Randall's backside with the toe of his shoe. Randall cringed but otherwise didn't move.

"You can get up now," Bogart said. "We've decided not to kill you right here. It wouldn't look good on the police report. We'll just take you to the station house instead and turn you in."

Randall sat up. I was still pointing the pistol at him, so he didn't get up and run.

"You're making a big mistake," he said.

"That line was old when the Keystone Kops were rookies," Bogart said.

"Try another one."

"I mean it. You're really making a mistake. I didn't kill anybody. Sure, you can cause a lot of trouble for me if you turn me in, but I'm not a killer, no matter what you think."

"You wouldn't have run if you weren't the killer," I said. "We have the whole thing figured out."

"Not quite," Randall said. "You just think you do. Can I stand up now?"

"Go right ahead," Bogart told him. "But don't try to run again. Junior there qualified as a marksman in the Army."

I'd never told him that, even though it was true. But that had been with a rifle, not a pistol. I'd never been too good with a pistol, not that Randall had any way of knowing that. He got up and dusted himself off, keeping a wary eye on me the whole time.

"You can put the pistol away," he said. "I'm not going anywhere."

I stuck the pistol back in my belt. I didn't feel comfortable holding it. I didn't want to shoot anybody by accident.

"I suppose you're going to tell us who killed Burleson," Bogart said to Randall. "Since you say it wasn't you, it stands to reason that you know who did."

It didn't stand to reason at all, but this wasn't the place for me to conduct a seminar in logic. Anyway, this was Hollywood. Logic didn't always apply. And it didn't matter. I'd already figured out who Randall was talking about. Or whom, since I was being pedantic.

And it even made sense.

"You're an accessory to murder, Randall," I said. "You're the one who took the pistol from Bogart's house. Barbara wouldn't have done that."

Randall looked back toward the jungle as if he might be hoping someone would come to rescue him. It was very quiet, but then it usually was on a movie set. They added all the jungle sounds later. They weren't made by real jungle animals but by some sound-effects man who wished he were Mel Blanc.

Nobody came to Randall's aid. That sort of thing only happens in the movies. He turned back to us with a hopeless look in his eyes.

"Yeah, I took the pistol," he said. "I knew you had one. You told me once. Remember?"

Bogart said he didn't remember at all.

"Well, it was a little drunk out at the time. Anyway, I knew you had it. I even knew where it was. So I was going to grab it when I got the chance. Mayo nearly spoiled it by pulling the gun on you."

"If you knew about the pistol, then you were planning to frame me," Bogart said.

"I wasn't planning to frame anybody. The pistol was just for protection. Barbara dropped it when she shot Burleson, and then she was too scared to pick it up. She just ran away."

That might even be true. I'd never been sure there had been an attempt to frame Bogart.

"She went to Burleson's house to kill him?" I said, knowing his answer would make a difference to a jury if not to me.

"No. I was supposed to be the muscle, and I was just going to threaten him, not kill him. But I didn't have the nerve to do anything at all." Randall's shoulders slumped. "I can jump off a cliff or a running horse. I can take a punch with the best of them. But when it came to bullying somebody, even somebody like Burleson, I couldn't do it. Barbara could, or she said she could. She didn't plan to kill him. The gun was just for protection, in case Burleson got nasty."

Burleson didn't have to get nasty. He was that way all the time.

"What happened, then?" I asked.

"He'd told us he needed help to pay off a gambling debt. If we didn't give him money, he was going to the scandal magazines about Barbara. She went to tell him we couldn't afford to help him out right now. To reason with him. We both knew we owed him, but we don't have any money, not yet. We'll get some, sooner or later, as soon as Barbara wins the Oscar, but that's a long way off. So we had to do something to let him know that."

It was farther away then he could imagine, as far as the moon, as far as the sun. Barbara would never be getting an Oscar, or even a nomination, not after what she'd done. The most glamorous event she'd be attending anytime soon would be visitor's day at the state pen.

"She was offering him something other than money, then," Bogart said.

"And you let her."

Randall looked so miserable that I thought he might be going to cry.

"We couldn't let Burleson tell about the abortion," he said. "Barbara knew he wanted to sleep with her. She thought it was a way out. I tried to tell her it wasn't. Oh, Burleson wanted her, all right. He just told her that he could have her and the money, too. He'd been drinking some, and he made a grab for her. The pistol was in her purse, and she got it out. He tried to take it from her, and she shot him. She didn't plan to do it. She didn't even intend to when he attacked her. It was self-defense."

It was a pretty good story, and I was sure Barbara could tell it beautifully on the witness stand. I didn't think it would keep her out of the crossbar hotel, but she might not have to stay there as long as I'd figured at first. If she'd been Fatty Arbuckle, no story would have helped, but she didn't look a thing like Fatty.

"She must have thought that Burleson's death would be the end of it," I said. "And that nobody would find out she'd killed him. But it turned out that Dawson knew about the abortion. When he told people that Bogart and I wanted to talk to them, he figured out about the loan Burleson had made you. It got him killed."

"I don't know anything about that. I didn't kill him, and neither did Barbara. We weren't anywhere around here last night, and you know it."

The hell of it was that I did know it. There was still one piece of the puzzle missing, and I couldn't quite figure out what it was. So I made the mistake of saying, "We won't worry about Dawson right now. We'll go see what Barbara has to say about all this. Come on, Randall."

"I can't leave. I have a scene coming up."

Maybe it was Hollywood that made people like Randall so unrealistic. Or maybe everyone was that way, all over the country, and I just didn't know it.

"You won't be doing any more scenes," Bogart said. "Not unless they shoot a movie in San Quentin. Now do what Scott says."

Randall looked back toward the jungle one more time. Nobody came to his rescue that time, either. Nobody was even looking for him. Not yet, at any rate. Someone would miss him eventually, but by then it would be too late to do him any good. Then he looked down the long street that led to the entrance. I didn't know who he thought might come from that direction, and nobody did.

He gave it up, and I took his elbow to turn him in the right direction. We went to Bogart's Cadillac and got in. Randall sat in the front passenger seat, and I sat behind him to keep an eye on him. I didn't

think he'd try to jump out. He was too dejected to try anything like that. But just in case he did, I was ready to grab him.

Barbara Malone's house was modest, as was to be expected, a little white frame job with a tiny porch and a roof that needed replacing. No doubt she'd had plans to find a much bigger house as soon as she won that Oscar and started getting big roles and plenty of them, a house that fit her image as a star. It was too bad, in a way, but her next accommodations were hardly going to live up to her expectations.

It was a quiet neighborhood, with small green yards, a few tiny flowerbeds, and only a few palm trees. Bogart parked at the curb, and we got out.

We were just about to start up the walk when the dark blue Packard pulled in behind the Caddy and stopped. The front bumper of the Packard was slightly dented from its run-in with my Chevy.

Mike and Herbie got out of the Packard. Herbie looked as if he'd grown another six or seven inches since the last time I'd seen him. Maybe he'd been eating his spinach.

"Jesus, I thought you guys were never going to show up," Randall said.

Well, now I knew who'd killed Dawson.

33

Mike and Herbie had guns, and they were pointed at me and Bogart.

"You've been following me around, Herbie," I said. "And too closely, at that. I hope your bumper's not dented too badly."

Herbie told me to shut up, and they marched us into Barbara Malone's house. Mike didn't say anything, but he was walking a little gingerly. From the way he was looking at Bogart I could tell that he'd welcome the opportunity to use his pistol. He was the kind of guy who held a grudge for a long time.

I was still trying to figure out who had told them what was going on when Randall asked them where Joey was.

"He's still on the set," Herbie said. His voice was oddly wispy and light for such a big man. Maybe somebody had hit him in the throat at one time. "He managed to get away long enough to call Mr. Orsini. That was it."

What was Charlie O. doing mixed up in this? I couldn't figure it. He'd implied that he knew what was going on, but of course he hadn't let us in on anything.

As for Joey Gallindo, I supposed that the rumors tying him to the mob were all too true, at least if Charlie O. was considered part of the mob.

"What are you going to do with these two?" Randall asked, meaning me and Bogart. "They know everything."

I didn't like the way he said it. And I didn't like the ugly grin that spread itself across Mike's face when he heard it.

"They don't know everything," Herbie said. "But they may know too much. Mr. Orsini will let us know what he wants us to do with them. Mike's going to call him. Where's the phone?"

"In the hall," Randall said, and Mike went off to make his call, giving Bogart one last grisly smile over his shoulder.

"You're looking good, Herbie," I said.

Actually he didn't look good at all. His head was about two sizes too small for his body, and with a hat on he looked like a cartoon gangster. His complexion was so pale that he might have just gotten out of prison, but I knew he hadn't. As far as I knew he'd never served time, even though he was guilty of plenty of things, from mopery to murder.

"You can shut up, Scott," he said.

I had no intention of shutting up no matter how many times he told me to. I said, "You nearly got us last night. If there hadn't been a tree in front of us about a third of the way down, you'd wouldn't have had to bother with us today."

"I thought I told you to shut up," Herbie said.

Herbie had eyes that were too small and set too close together even for his too small head, and they made him look mean and a little stupid. He wasn't stupid, but he was definitely mean. Kindness wasn't among his virtues, assuming he had any. In my acquaintance with him, I hadn't discovered any. I was going to ask him why he'd killed Dawson when Mike came back into the room.

"Mr. Orsini says to bring them in. He wants to have a word with them before he disposes of them."

He seemed to enjoy saying *disposes* entirely too much, so I said, "Disposes? Disposes of Humphrey Bogart, the highest-paid star in town? Even Charlie O. wouldn't do anything that stupid."

"I hope he does," Mike said. "But even if he don't, he can dispose of you. Nobody'd miss you."

He was right about that, but I didn't want him to think so.

"Plenty of people would miss me, Mike. Mr. Warner, for one. If

Charlie O. is planning to dispose of me, he'd better think again. He wouldn't want Mr. Warner after him."

"I told you to shut up, Scott," Herbie said. If he was getting tired of repeating himself, there was no indication of it. "Let's all go for a little ride."

"Me, too?" Randall said.

"Not you. You can go back to the movie set."

"I don't have a car."

"Take Bogart's," Mike said, grinning again. "He won't be needing it for a while."

"That wouldn't be smart," Herbie said. "You can call a cab."

Randall looked relieved. He wouldn't care if we were disposed of, but he didn't want to be there when it happened. He didn't have the stomach for it.

Barbara, on the other hand, did have the stomach for it. I wondered where she was, but I didn't figure anyone would tell me. So I didn't bother to ask.

Mike and Herbie took Bogart and me back outside. Randall stayed in the house. He didn't even wave good-bye when we went out the door.

Herbie drove and Bogart sat in front with him. Mike and I sat in the back. That way Mike could cover both me and Bogart with his pistol, and Herbie could concentrate on the road.

As soon as I leaned back in the seat, I was reminded that I had a pistol, too. I'd forgotten all about it, and so had Randall. We'd had other things on our minds, I suppose. Bogart hadn't mentioned it either. I didn't know if he'd forgotten or if he was hoping I could figure out some way to use it. Because of its location, there was no way I could get to it before Mike shot me four or five times. I'd just have to wait and see what developed.

Nobody talked much during the ride to Charlie O.'s club. There didn't seem to be a lot to say. I would have liked to scream at some of the people on the sidewalks to call the cops, but Mike would just have shot me. So I didn't scream.

We'd gone several blocks when Bogart asked if it would be all right if he had a cigarette.

Herbie said all right, and Bogart used the lighter on the Packard's dashboard. After taking a couple of puffs on the cigarette, he turned around in the seat and asked me if I'd like a smoke.

He knew better than that, and he knew I knew, so he had to be up to something.

"No thanks," I said.

"What about you, Mike?"

Mike pointed the pistol at Bogart and shook his head.

"I could light it for you. You wouldn't even need to put the gun down."

"It's just the condemned men that smoke," Mike said.

He laughed as if he'd made a funny joke. I didn't think it was funny at all. I kept my eyes on Bogart, ready for whatever he had in mind.

"Ain't that right, Herbie?" Mike said. "It's just the condemned men that get to smoke."

"Shut up, Mike," Herbie said.

Mike grinned, not looking a bit chastened.

"That's pretty big talk," Bogart said. "Of course you have a gun, and that makes it easier for you. If Scott or I had a gun, things would be different. The way they were in Charlie O.'s office at the club."

We did have a gun, and Bogart was letting me know he was aware of it. But I still had no idea what he was planning to do about it.

"You hit me in the balls, Bogart," Mike said, his tone peevish. "That was a dirty damned trick, but it got you out of trouble. Now you're in trouble again, and this time you won't be hitting anybody in the balls."

"I don't suppose I will," Bogart said. "But do you know what I am going to do?"

"Not a goddamned thing," Mike said.

"That's where you're wrong, Mike. I'm going to do something, all right."

"Little man, big talk. If you're gonna do something, do it."

"Fine," Bogart said. "I will.

He took a drag on his cigarette and flicked the glowing butt into Mike's face.

Mike knew, or would have known if he'd given it any thought, that there was nothing much a cigarette butt could do to him. Sure, it might give him a momentary sting if it hit him on the nose or cheek. It might even burn a hole in his pants if it landed in his lap. But it wasn't going to disable him permanently, even if it burned through to his skin.

However, most people, including Mike, don't think about all that when someone flicks a burning cigarette into their faces. They react, instead.

Mike reacted by jerking his left hand up to keep the cigarette from hitting his face. He was successful at that, but it bounced off his hand and down to his crotch, which got him excited, maybe because the area was still tender from being hit earlier by Bogart or because the idea of having his balls set on fire didn't appeal to him in the least.

He started digging frantically at his crotch with his left hand and waving the pistol around with his right.

Bogart lunged across the top of the seat and grabbed Mike's forearm, forcing his hand up.

I twisted around in the seat, snatching at the pistol at my back.

Mike's pistol went off and blew a hole through the roof of the Packard.

One place you don't ever want to be is in an automobile, even a fine automobile like a Packard, not even if the windows are open, when a pistol goes off. Not if you value your eardrums and your hearing, you don't.

For a second it was as if I'd gone deaf, but I didn't have time to worry about it because Herbie lost control of the car, and it swerved off the street and started down the sidewalk. Pedestrians scattered like frantic chickens, and people in the cars along the street must have been wondering if a bomb had gone off in the Packard.

Herbie fought the wheel, and Bogart fought to hang onto Mike's arm. I struggled to my own pistol past my belt, but the sight was hung on something, maybe my shirt.

Herbie managed to miss a telephone pole, but he couldn't avoid the corner of a newsstand. The stand didn't collapse, but it moved a few feet and made about a quarter turn to the right. Newspapers and magazines flew everywhere, and I bounced into Mike, who was now trying to hit Bogart with his left fist. I just prayed that he wouldn't pull the trigger of that pistol again.

I pushed away from Mike and back to the other side of the car, and as I did the pistol came free. I leveled it at Herbie's head, holding it as steady as I could as the car rocked along with two wheels on the walk and two in the street.

I told Herbie to stop the car, but I was sure he didn't hear me. I was sure because I didn't hear myself.

Mike said something to me, and his lips peeled back from his teeth. I didn't hear him either. All I could hear was a kind of roaring noise, as if I was lying in the surf.

There had to be some way to get my point across, but first I had to relieve Mike of his pistol. Bogart was still hanging on to Mike's arm, so I hit Mike on the wrist bone with the barrel of my pistol. I didn't hit him hard, but then I didn't have to. He winced and dropped his gun, and it fell to the floorboard on my side. That was a good place for it, as far as I was concerned.

I put my foot on it so Mike wouldn't get any ideas. Then I leaned over and tapped Herbie behind the ear with my pistol barrel just under the brim of his hat and yelled for him to stop the car. He might not have heard me, but he got the idea. We came to a halt not far from an Owl drugstore. I thought about going in for a vanilla Coke at the fountain, but it wouldn't have been a good idea. There wasn't really time for an indulgence like that.

The four of us sitting there in a car halfway up on the sidewalk wasn't a good idea, either. The cops were going to come along at almost any time now, and I didn't want to have to deal with the cops, not right at the moment. Earlier, they would have been welcome, but now they'd just be in the way.

Bogart quit struggling with Mike. He gave him a shove and let go of his arm. Mike fell back against the door. He looked as if he might want to make a try for me, but the pistol in my hand discouraged him.

I kicked the back of the seat, and Herbie looked at me in the rearview mirror.

I mouthed "Charlie O.'s," exaggerating the syllables. He got the message and drove the car off the curb and onto the street. We went away from there, and if there were sirens in the distance, I didn't hear them.

34

W hen we got to Charlie O.'s, the parking lot was deserted. There would be a crowd there later on, after dark, but for now we had the place to ourselves.

Herbie parked the car around back, and we got out. I could smell the garbage that overflowed from a can near the wall. There was another new Packard parked back there, Charlie O.'s no doubt, and a Ford. I had a feeling I knew who'd driven it.

Bogart got Mike's pistol from the back floor and put it in his jacket pocket. The jacket sagged to one side, but it didn't look too bad.

My hearing had partially returned, and I told Herbie and Mike to lead the way inside. I had the feeling that I was yelling at them, the way a man who was hard of hearing might do. My voice echoed in my head as if I was speaking on the inside of a large bucket. I was a little punchy from lack of sleep, and the odd sound of my voice added to the surreal atmosphere that the day seemed to be taking on.

Mike opened a door and we found ourselves in the same hallway Bogart and I been in not so many hours before.

"You and Mike go up first," I told Herbie. Loudly.

They looked at one another and then at the gun I was holding. Maybe they were thinking that if they jumped me, I'd get only one of them and the other one would get me. If that was on their minds, Bogart put a stop to that line of thought by bringing the other pistol out of his pocket in one smooth motion. Playing a movie gangster had its benefits.

"You heard him," Bogart said.

It was as if he were talking from the bottom of a deep well somewhere, and I wasn't sure that Mike and Herbie could hear him. But they must have because after looking at one another again, they turned and went up the stairs.

They stopped outside the door to Charlie O.'s office. I knew this was the most dangerous point of the trip so far. For things to look right, Bogart and I had to go in first. If we didn't, Charlie O. would know that something was up. And if we did, Mike and Herbie would be behind us. I didn't trust them to be behind us.

So I decided that it didn't matter one bit if Charlie O. knew something was up. After all, Bogart and I were the ones with the guns. I didn't want to shoot anyone, but I'd shot people before, during my time in the Pacific, and I knew I could do it again if I had to. Bogart claimed to have shot a man, too, so that made us not only armed but dangerous. Mike, Herbie, and Charlie O. were merely dangerous.

"Go on in," I said, and Herbie opened the door.

He went inside, followed by Mike. Bogart went next, and I brought up the rear. I closed the door behind me and looked around the room.

Orsini sat behind his rundown desk, and Barbara Malone was in a chair nearby. The chair had been brought in since my previous visit, and it was brand new. It looked out of place beside the shabby desk, but then Barbara looked out of place as well. Her kind of glamour didn't belong in that room. Tank was nowhere to be seen. I hoped he was somewhere in bed, nursing his wound.

"Well, well, well," Orsini said when we'd all trooped into his office. "It appears that things didn't turn out exactly as I'd been led to believe they had."

I could hardly hear him, but I could hear well enough to get the gist of what he said.

"That's right," I said, or yelled. "You won't have the pleasure of disposing of us after all."

"I don't think I ever said that. You must have gotten the wrong idea."

I looked at Mike, who gave me a brutish grin and shrugged. I didn't really believe Orsini, but then Mike wasn't exactly a font of truth, either. I'd probably never know precisely what had been said, but it didn't really matter.

"You never know who you can trust these days," I said, too loudly.

"Is there something wrong with your hearing?" Orsini sounded solicitous, as if he actually cared, although I knew he didn't. "Have you suddenly gone deaf?"

I told him what the problem was, trying to keep my voice down to a reasonable level.

"I'm sorry about the hole in the roof of the car," I said when I concluded, though I wasn't sorry in the least.

Orsini waved a hand in dismissal. He could afford to replace the car rather than having the hole repaired. I thought this might be a good time to bring up another point.

"The bumper's damaged a little, too," I said. "That's also my fault. Herbie here had to hit my old Chevy pretty hard to push me and Bogart over that cliff last night."

Orsini didn't wave a hand this time. He just looked at me as if wondering what I was talking about.

"Don't worry," I said, though it was clear that he wasn't worried in the least. "I'm not asking you to replace my car. Not that I'd mind having a Packard, even if it has a hole in the roof and a damaged bumper."

"Ah," Orsini said. "And suppose that I'd like to sell you the car for a nominal sum. Five dollars, shall we say. What then?"

"Nothing then. I'll have a car to replace the one Herbie wrecked. A car for a car."

"Old Testament justice," Orsini said. "It seems a fair exchange."

Barbara Malone had been growing increasingly agitated during this little conversation. Now she couldn't stand to keep quiet any longer.

"What are you talking about cars for?" she said. The way she said it twisted her mouth and turned her beauty into something repulsive. She was far from glamorous now. "He doesn't need a car. You have to get rid of him."

"You seem to be forgetting who has the pistol," Orsini told her.

"Fuck the pistol. You promised you wouldn't let people find out about me."

I felt almost sorry for her. She'd wanted to be a star, and now she had almost become one. But as Orsini had pointed out to her, she didn't understand the situation.

"How'd you get into this mess, anyway?" I asked Orsini.

"I was just doing a favor for a friend," he said.

"Thomas Wayne?"

"That's right. Burleson was trying to bleed him, just the way he tried with your friend Bogart here. And Miss Malone. I sent Herbie to have a little talk with him, but Miss Malone got there first. And she did a little more than talk."

"The son of a bitch was going to rape me. What should I have done? Let him?"

"No," I said, "and if you stick to that story and drop the vulgarity, a jury might even believe it."

"Fuck you, Scott. You're just a cheap snoop."

I couldn't argue with that, and I didn't even try.

"At any rate," Orsini said, "Herbie thought he should do what he could to help out one of Mr. Wayne's stars, so he took Miss Malone under his wing, so to speak, and brought her to me."

"I guess he saw me and Bogart at Burleson's place," I said.

"Indeed. You got there almost as soon as he removed Miss Malone from the premises. And he might even have done something about you if the police hadn't arrived when they did."

"So he just followed us around and kept track of us until we started getting in the way. Then he tried to kill us."

Orsini entwined his pudgy fingers and leaned forward to rest his hands on the desk.

"You were a bit inconvenient, I admit," he said. "But Herbie does have a tendency to exceed his instructions."

"You're going to have to give up Herbie, too," Bogart said.

I was beginning to hear much better now, and I supposed he was, too.

"And why is that?" Orsini asked. "You weren't seriously injured in the accident, were you?"

I would have questioned his use of the word *accident*, but Bogart didn't give me a chance.

"The accident has nothing to do with it," he said. "Herbie killed Charlie Dawson. Charlie was a friend of mine."

Orsini nodded. "As I said, Herbie can be a bit of a freelancer at times. Dawson was saying that you wanted to talk to some of the *Jan of the Jungle* cast about Burleson's murder, and he happened to remember Miss Malone's unfortunate medical experience while he was talking to Joey Gallindo. Joey is...an acquaintance, and he called me, knowing my interest in the matter. I sent Herbie to reason with Dawson, but according to Herbie, Dawson wasn't reasonable."

Unfortunate medical experience was good, maybe even better than *accident.* I wondered why Orsini had never gone into politics. But maybe he owned a few politicians and thought that was better than having to run for election.

"Was it Joey or Herbie who called the cops and told them it was us who killed Dawson?" I asked.

"That was Herbie again, on his own. He really needs to learn to ask me before acting. Joey, however, is the one who called when you showed up on the set today."

I remembered that Joey had been outside Romanoff's when Burleson and Bogart had their little run-in.

"That Joey is a regular little snitch, isn't he," I said.

"He has his uses. He was rather surprised to see you today."

"I'll bet he was. But not as surprised as you when you got his phone call."

"I wasn't surprised, Scott. I know a little about your resilience. But Herbie, well, Herbie was another story. He felt like a failure."

I glanced at Herbie, who was glowering at the floor. He didn't like the way things were going.

Neither did Malone, whose face was contorted with anger and fear.

Bogart wasn't angry, but his face was tense with anticipation. So was mine, for that matter.

In fact, the only one in the room who appeared to be relaxed and comfortable was Orsini.

Which meant that he knew something the rest of us didn't know.

I couldn't figure out what it was until I heard the door open behind me.

H ello, Tank," Orsini said, looking past me. "I'm glad you could drop by."

Tank didn't say anything, but I knew he'd be the one who'd opened the door. I looked around and saw that he was standing there taking up most of the doorway. He had a pistol in his right hand. He leaned against the doorframe as if he might be a little uncomfortable, but other than that there was no sign that he'd recently been shot. I thought it was too bad that his wound hadn't been more serious.

"How're you doing, Tank?" I said. "You'd better watch out, or Charlie O. will shoot you again."

"That's not funny, Scott," Tank said. "Why don't you and Mr. Bogart put your guns on the desk, and then we'll sort things out."

"I don't think so," I said. "Bogart?"

He shook his head and moved a little to his left to spread the room out and make it more difficult for Tank to get a shot at both of us. I didn't know if he made the move instinctively or whether it was something he'd learned from making a movie, but in any case I approved.

"You see, Tank," I said, "there's one problem that you haven't thought about."

"Yeah?"

"Yeah. If you shoot either me or Bogart, the other one of us is going to get Orsini."

Thinking about that taxed Tank's abilities to the extreme. He looked at Orsini as if expecting help. Orsini raised his shoulders about a quarter of an inch. Not much of a shrug, but it was all the help Tank was going to get from him.

Barbara Malone jumped out of her chair and said, "Give me the fucking pistol. I'll kill the bastards."

I wondered how I could ever have thought she was beautiful, and the thought distracted me for just a second. It was a second too long. I should have just shot her as soon as she stood because I didn't see Mike when he grabbed at Bogart's arm.

I heard the shot, however, when Bogart pulled the trigger, and as Mike was falling I dropped to the floor and fired at Tank. Part of his face flew off in a haze of blood.

I heard shots from behind me as well, and I knew that Orsini hadn't wasted any time in replacing the pistol I'd taken from him. Lead passed through the empty air where I'd been standing and smacked into the wall near the doorway.

I rolled over and Herbie fired a shot that splintered the floor beside me. I hadn't been the only one with a concealed pistol on his person somewhere. I should have known Herbie would be armed. He just hadn't had a chance to get to his gun yet. I shot him twice in the chest and he went down.

The room was full of powder smoke and the sharp smell of it. My eardrums were never going to be the same.

Tank, Mike, and Herbie lay on the floor. Bogart was backed against the wall with his pistol held straight out in front of him, pointing at Orsini, who had laid his own weapon on his desk in front of him. It seemed to be a habit of his. Barbara Malone was back in her chair with a blank stare on her face as she looked out over the room. Her stomach was more delicate than I'd thought.

Mike wasn't hurt badly and tried to stand up, but he couldn't manage it. Bogart had shot him in the calf. So Mike sat back down on the floor and started ripping his pants leg to make a tourniquet.

Tank squirmed around like a crippled spider. He made unintelligible gobbling sounds with what remained of his mouth, which was more a red, gaping hole than a mouth now. I couldn't really tell, but I thought I'd shot off most of the left side of his jaw.

Orsini was looking at Herbie, who wasn't moving at all. There was a small pool of blood beside him, but not really very much at all.

"We seem to have a difficult situation here," Orsini said.

"Difficult, maybe, but not impossible," Bogart said.

I think he said it. My hearing was messed up again. I stood up, hoping my knees would hold me. They were nowhere near as steady as Bogart's voice.

"How do you see it?" Orsini asked Bogart.

"Like this. Malone killed Burleson. She and Randall have to take the fall for that. Your men, without your knowledge, were protecting her for Wayne, and one of them, Herbie there, was a little over-zealous. He killed Dawson. So far it's all true, except the part about you."

"That's true, too, in a way."

"Yeah. True enough to keep you out of jail, maybe. Malone can use her self-defense story and see how far it gets her. She's a pretty good actress. Maybe she gets off with a slap on the wrist."

"It's possible," Orsini said, glancing at Barbara, who was still staring with horrified fascination at Tank, who continued to make those noises. They were beginning to bother me a little, too, to tell the truth. But Bogart and Orsini ignored him.

"Wayne might be a problem," Bogart said. "It will look as if he was covering up a murder."

I didn't see a problem with that. I was sure Wayne, through Orsini, knew everything that had happened. He'd have to admit it, but he had enough clout to survive. He had access to the best lawyers in town, too. When it was all over, he might even become more acceptable because of his notoriety. Hollywood is a funny town. Some things, like the fact that Stella Gordon liked women, had to be kept hidden, but everybody in Hollywood loves a gangster. A successful one, that is, with a patina, no matter how thin, of respectability.

"I can handle Wayne," Orsini said. I'll just bet he could. "But what about Herbie?"

Bogart switched his pistol to his left hand and ran the ball of his right thumb down his jawline.

"Like this: your other two goons decided they didn't like being part of a murder cover-up," he said. "They turned on Herbie, and there was a little shooting."

A little? That was as good as Orsini's calling the abortion an "unfortunate medical experience." Bogart was good at this sort of thing.

Orsini must have thought so, too. The corners of his mouth twitched in what might have been a smile.

"I think we can make that work," he said. "Tank and Mike will say what I tell them to say. Tank might not be able to say much for quite a while anyway. What about you and Scott?"

"We don't know a thing. We were never here, and this never happened. Not the way it really did."

"Do you think we can trust Miss Malone to go along with that?"

"Maybe not. But who's going to believe her if she starts telling people that Humphrey Bogart was involved in a wild gun battle in your office?"

"No one," Orsini said. "Though it would make a good story for the papers."

"Let them print it. I'll deny it and threaten to sue. You'll back me up."

"I will, indeed. And you're going to trust me to take care of all this?"

"I don't see why not. You're in it up to your neck, but this way you'll come out all right. Call a cop named Congreve. He's your kind of guy."

"I like the way you think," Orsini said. "If you ever decide to retire from making movies, you might consider coming to work for me."

"No thanks," Bogart said. "I couldn't stand the excitement."

After that it was just a matter of working out the details, one of which was the transfer of the Packard to my name. Orsini said there wouldn't be any trouble about it and that he could take care of all the paperwork without even my signature. I believed him.

Barbara Malone was coming out of her trance when we left, and Orsini was going to have his hands full with her, but I thought he'd manage.

I suppose I should have felt bad about Tank. He was going to be messed up even after he got treatment. He'd have trouble eating and talking for the rest of his life. He wasn't going to be very pretty, but then he hadn't been pretty in the first place.

As for Herbie, well, I did feel bad about that. There was a hollow place in the pit of my stomach, and as much as I tried to tell myself that I'd shot him in the same way I'd shot men in the war, I couldn't quite convince myself. But I'd get over it. He'd tried to kill me and Bogart, after all.

"You know what I don't like about this car?" Bogart said as we drove through the streets back toward the Garden of Allah.

"The hole in the roof?" I said.

I didn't like the hole, either. I thought that it would be a problem for someone with normal hearing because the wind might whistle in it when the car was moving, but I could get it fixed. I wasn't worried about rain because it never rains in Los Angeles, or so the Chamber of Commerce would have you believe.

"The hole doesn't bother me," Bogart said. "The trouble is that this car isn't fully equipped, even if it is a Packard."

I couldn't think of a thing that was missing. There was a radio and even a heater. Cruising the streets in a car like that was pure luxury, even with the hole in the roof and the dented bumper. I planned to get the bumper fixed, too, as soon as I could afford it.

"I don't get it," I said. "What's missing?"

"A bottle. Even your old heap had a bottle."

"We can fix that," I said, and we did.

36

T here was still something bothering me when I pulled up at the Garden of Allah. When I told Bogart about my vague misgivings, he held up the Scotch bottle and said, "Have a drink of this, and you won't be so bothered."

It was getting dark, and the fog had rolled in from the Pacific. Maybe it had come all the way from China. It put a chill in the evening air.

"I'm not looking to forget anything," I said. "I'll have some bad dreams about Tank and Herbie, but they won't last forever. They're not what's bothering me."

Bogart had a swallow of Scotch and lit a Chesterfield.

"Then what is bothering you?" he asked, blowing out a stream of smoke as gray as the fog.

"If I knew, it might not be bothering me. Something just wasn't right about the way things played out back there in Charlie O.'s place. I don't know exactly what was wrong, but something was."

"You were good in there, kid. You don't have to worry about that."

"You were no slouch, yourself. And that's not what's worrying me."

"You have a new car, you have the cops off your back, and Mr. Warner is going to be very grateful. The cops will be off my back, too, so I'm also very grateful. What could be wrong?"

"Something," I said.

But for the life of me I couldn't figure out what it was.

I left Bogart and went back to my apartment, which seemed shabbier than ever now that there was a new Packard parked out in front. But I could get used to that.

After I took a shower, I lay down and tried to sleep. For a while I just stared at the brownish water stain on the paper of the ceiling. The stain was shaped vaguely like a longer, thinner version of the state of Texas. I don't know how long I looked at it. It seemed like a long time. And then I finally went to sleep.

Rita Hayworth was dressed in one of her costumes from *Blood and Sand*. She was talking to Tyrone Power, who was mournful because Rita had decided she didn't really care about him any more. As far as Rita was concerned, Linda Darnell could have Tyrone, and she wished them all the best. Rita explained to the forlorn Tyrone that she had found someone better, someone more handsome, more cour-ageous, more manly. She beckoned for me, and I walked to her side. Tyrone looked at me with considerable skepticism, but Rita didn't care. She put her arms around me and smiled, and I drew her me to me for a kiss.

I woke up before the kiss happened, of course. I never got as far with Rita as I would have liked to. You'd think that I could do better than that, at least in my dreams, but I always woke up too soon.

The difference this time was that I didn't mind waking up. While I was asleep and dreaming, I'd somehow figured out what had been bothering me about the deal with Charlie O.

It had all been too easy, that's what. Charlie O. hadn't even bothered to insult me or to tell me never to darken his door again. He'd gone along with everything Bogart had said without making a peep of protest.

Granted, Bogart was smooth. Granted, everything he'd said made sense.

But it wasn't in Orsini's nature to go along so calmly with a plan that wasn't entirely to his advantage. And in fact, several things about the plan were distinctly unfavorable to him. It was his men who'd done the murder, and even if they'd been "over-zealous" as Bogart put it, Orsini was still their boss. He could probably handle Congreve, but it would take some doing, as would handling Barbara Malone.

And then there was the little matter of the car. To say that Orsini didn't like me was to say that most citizens of the United States didn't like Tojo and Hitler during the late war. Why would Orsini give up a new Packard so easily? OK, so it had a hole in the roof, and the bumper wasn't in pristine condition. He still shouldn't let go of it so ungrudgingly.

He could always double-cross me, give the cops a call and tell them I'd stolen it, but I didn't think he'd try that, not with Bogart as my witness that the car had been given to me fair and square.

So there had to be something else going on, and I thought I now knew what it was.

I got out of bed and turned on the light to check the time. It was a couple of minutes after three o'clock. I wondered if Bogart was up. I had his number, so I gave him a call. He answered on the second ring.

"What the hell do you want, Junior?" he asked when I identified myself.

"I was wondering if you were awake."

"The telephone took care of that. What makes you suddenly so concerned about my slumbers?" I told him.

"Christ, kid, are you sure?"

I wasn't sure, and I told him so.

"But it makes sense," I said, and I explained why.

"Let's say you're right about it. What are you going to do?"

I told him that, too.

"And you called because you thought I might like to go along for the ride? Or just for the fun of it?"

"That, and I thought you might enjoy the chance to use your new pistol again."

Bogart had kept Mike's gun, just as I'd kept Orsini's. We'd also collected Tank's pistol, Herbie's, and Orsini's new one before we left. We were nearly as well armed as The Big Red One.

"You don't think there's a chance of that, do you?" Bogart said.

"Not really. If everything goes all right, we'll be in and out without anyone even knowing we're there. Charlie O. will find out later, but by then it'll be too late."

"All right, then. You can count on me."

"I'll pick you up in half an hour," I said.

The Chamber of Commerce was wrong. It did sometimes rain in Los Angeles. It was raining when I got in my new car, and I'd been right about that bullet hole. It was big enough to let in water. Not much, but enough to be aggravating. Luckily, it wasn't raining hard, just a thin drizzle, as if the earlier fog had gotten better organized and decided to improve itself. The moisture gave the pavement a sheen that smeared and reflected the colors of the lights and signs as we drove back to Charlie O.'s.

"Did you clean your pistol before you went to bed?" Bogart asked.

"No. I didn't clean any of them. I was going to do it in the morning."

"The Army didn't teach you much, did it."

"Probably not. Did you clean yours?"

"I'm Navy. Of course I did. Are you sure about this wild idea of yours?"

"You thought it made sense when I called you."

"That's because you woke me up. Now that I've thought about it, I can see the holes in it."

I couldn't. As far as I was concerned, there was only one reason that Charlie O. would have let us off so quickly and with so few objections. And that was because he had something that meant more to him than his car or Barbara Malone or just about anything else we'd discussed. Maybe something that was worth more than the money Burleson owed to Charlie O.

And I thought that something was Frank Burleson's little black book, or whatever records that Burleson had kept. I'd mentioned those records to Thomas Wayne. He'd looked a bit concerned, and it was no wonder. Especially if he knew that Charlie O. already had them. They'd give Charlie O. even more power over Wayne than he already had, a scary thought since Charlie O. wouldn't be anywhere nearly as easy to get rid of as Burleson had been, not for Wayne, not for anybody.

So Bogart and I were going to steal the book back.

"What if you're right about there being a book," Bogart said, "and Orsini has it in a safe? I can shoot a pistol, but I'm no safecracker."

I hadn't thought about a safe, which was a mistake.

"We'll have to deal with that when we get there," I said. "Maybe Charlie O. just stuck the stuff in a desk drawer."

"I'll just bet he did, along with the day's take from the club."

Bogart was right. Charlie O. was certain to have a safe to keep the club's money in, and he'd probably put anything else of value there, too. I should have thought of that. If I'd been smart, I would have turned the Packard around right then, gone back home, and tried to dream myself a kiss from Rita Hayworth. But I wasn't smart. I kept right on driving.

It was raining harder when we got to the club. The parking lot was as deserted as it had been earlier, and water washed across it. The club's neon sign had been turned off, and everyone had gone home. Orsini liked to think he ran a respectable club, as opposed to some of his other operations, and he always closed down around 2:00 A. M. It gave him a chance to think of himself as a legitimate businessman.

I parked around back. There were no cars there, and the whole interior of the building appeared to be dark. The only sound was the rain on the roof of the car and the slight ticking noise that hot metal made as it cooled.

"You should stick a rag in that hole in your roof," Bogart said.

I thought that was a fine idea, and I took out my pocket handkerchief and crammed it into the hole.

"When it gets soaked, it'll still drip onto the seats," Bogart said.

"It's better than nothing. Are you ready to go inside?" "Sure."

We got out of the car. Bogart buckled his raincoat around his waist and pulled his hat down over his eyes while I jimmied the side door of the club in about ten seconds with a thin piece of metal I'd brought with me for that purpose. I'd also brought a flashlight with fresh Ray-O-Vac batteries. Bogart closed the door behind us, and I turned on the light and shined it down the hallway.

It was very quiet inside the club. I couldn't even hear the rain on the roof. I went down the hallway and up the stairs. The door to Orsini's office wasn't locked. I opened it and went inside.

"Don't turn off the flashlight," Mike said. "It makes it a lot easier for me to see you."

"Shit," I said.

37

A nd don't try shining the light in my eyes to blind me," Mike continued, "because if you do, I'll just start shooting. I got you covered, so I'm not likely to miss."

I kept the flashlight pointed at the floor, but I could see the desk well enough. Mike was leaning back with his feet propped up on it. One foot didn't have a shoe on it because it was heavily bandaged.

"Just come on in," Mike said. "And then put your gun on the floor.

I didn't see that I had any choice, so I did both things. There was a bloodstain on the cheap rug by the pistol.

"What are you doing here?" I asked when I'd straightened back up.

"Waiting for you." Mike swung his feet to the floor. "Mr. Orsini thought you might be a little smarter than you looked, so he told me to hang around just in case you showed up here."

"How's the foot?"

"You can shut up about the foot right now. That movie star pal of yours was lucky. All he did was pull the trigger when I hit his arm. Another quarter of an inch to the right, and he might have crippled me. Where is that son of a bitch, anyway?"

"Home," I said. "Asleep, I suppose."

Bogart was, I hoped, wide awake out in the hallway, having been standing to one side when I opened the door. If Mike hadn't spoken so soon, Bogart might have followed me right into Charlie O.'s trap. As it was, I still had a chance to get what I'd come for. I might not be smart, but for once I was lucky. It was about time.

"Kick the pistol over here with your foot," Mike said. "Don't kick it hard. Just slide it."

I did what he told me. The pistol slid across the floor and came to a stop near the desk.

"You can turn the light on now," Mike said. He kept his eyes on me while he picked up my pistol. "Move real slow."

I took a couple of steps back and flipped the wall switch. The room light came on.

"Did Charlie O. tell you why he thought I might show up?" I asked.

"No. He just told me to take care of you."

"I hope he meant by that to give me a good breakfast and send me home happy."

Mike didn't laugh. I didn't blame him. It wasn't very funny. Maybe it wasn't funny at all.

"Slappy Coville don't have a thing to worry about," Mike said. "You'll never be a comedian."

"You know Slappy?"

"No, but I hear him on the radio. He cracks me up."

Well, if I learned nothing else from my experience, I now knew who Slappy Coville's audience was.

Mike started to get up, and I said, "I came here to find something worth a lot of money. Maybe we could work out a deal."

"No way in hell. And I'm tired of talking to you. Mr. Orsini don't like you at all, and neither do I, not after what you done to Herbie and Tank. Taking care of you is going to be a pleasure."

He stood behind the desk and looked around as if trying to decide what to do with my body when he'd finished with me.

"If you kill me here, you'll have to carry me downstairs," I said. "You wouldn't want to have to do that, not with your foot hurt the way it is."

"I told you to shut up about the foot. But you got a good idea there. I don't want to mess the office up any worse than it is. You can walk downstairs."

"Are you sure you can make it?"

"If I start having trouble, I'll shoot you."

He sounded far too pleased with that idea to suit me.

"I figure you'll fall the rest of the way," he said, and I liked that even less.

He hobbled across the room and stopped about three feet from me. "Go," he said.

I turned and walked out the door, careful not to look to either side. Mike followed me, and Bogart clubbed him on the back of the head with his pistol.

I didn't see that, but I heard the cracking of the impact. I heard Mike say, "Ummmp," and I heard him hit the floor.

"I wasn't sure that would work," Bogart said. "I never really hit anybody like that before."

I looked down at Mike. He was breathing but not moving.

"You do good work for an amateur," I said.

"Thanks. Now what?"

"Now we get him back in the office and tie him up."

"I think we should tie him up first," Bogart said.

We found the safe before Mike came around. It was in a little closet, and it looked like a good one. Charlie O. could, after all, afford the best. There was a note to prospective safecrackers painted on the front of the safe: WARNING! POISON GAS INSIDE. I didn't really believe it.

"How could you ever open the safe if that was true?" Bogart asked.

"It doesn't mean inside the safe," I told him. "It means inside the door. That's to discourage you from using explosives."

"I didn't bring any explosives. Did you?"

I hadn't brought any explosives, either. We'd have to find another way to get the safe open, so we'd never know about the poison gas. I hoped.

Mike wasn't coherent for a while, and I thought he was probably concussed. When he was finally able to make sense, he started cursing us. Not very imaginatively, either.

"I hate to interrupt," I said when he stalled for a second, "but do you happen to know the combination to Charlie O.'s safe?"

He started cursing again.

"I didn't think so. Charlie O. would never trust a gunsel like you."

When I called him a gunsel, he strained so hard that he almost broke loose. However, we'd used our neckties to bind his hands and feet, and they were made of silk. He didn't stand a chance.

"You think he knows what *gunsel* means?" Bogart asked.

"Maybe he saw *The Maltese Falcon*," I said. "I'm pretty sure he didn't read the book."

"Hardly anybody who saw the movie or read the book knew, either." Bogart grinned. "I'll bet Bob Carroll would know."

"He might, but would he know the combination to the safe?"

"No, and neither do we. Mike doesn't know or won't tell. Are we just going to go home?"

"We'll find it," I said. "Everybody keeps the combination written down somewhere, just in case. Charlie O.'s memory is no better than anyone else's."

Bogart thought I could be right, so we started looking. There weren't that many places to look, and we didn't find a thing. Mike cursed us the whole time, but by then it was easy to ignore him.

"Orsini must keep that combination on a piece of paper in his wallet," Bogart said. "It's over, kid. We're not going to get in that safe, and it's going to be daylight before long. We'd better get out of here."

I thought it over. We'd looked in the desk drawers. We'd taken them out and looked on the bottoms and backs. No soap. We'd looked on the bottoms of the chairs, too, with no results. The metal wastebasket by the desk didn't hold anything of interest, either. There was nothing else in the office, and the only thing in the closet was the safe, black and heavy, with a silver dial in the middle of the door and the gold-painted warning.

I was ready to give up, too, but then I thought about the safe. It sat about three inches off the floor on short legs that ended in heavy casters.

I went into the closet, knelt down, and reached under the safe. There was a piece of paper taped to the bottom. I brought it out and looked at it. It was the combination.

"Who'd ever look there?" Bogart asked.

"A desperate man," I said.

I got the safe open in under a minute. There were bundles of money, but I hardly glanced at them. I didn't steal, not even from a crook like Orsini.

What interested me more was a couple of small blue notebooks, the kind you can fit into a shirt pocket if you're so inclined. They were held together by a rubber band, and I picked them up and removed it. I flipped open the cover of the top notebook, and on the first page was Thomas Wayne's name. Under it were scrawled notes about Wayne's relationship with Orsini and some bigger names from the underworld, along with some dates and telephone numbers. I flipped through the pages until I came to Barbara Malone. The details I'd suspected I'd find where there, including a doctor's name and address. I was tempted to see if there was anything about Buck Sterling, but I didn't really want to know.

"These are what we came for," I said.

"What do you plan to do with them?" Bogart asked.

"Build a little fire," I said.

I tore some pages out of the notebooks and dropped the books and the loose pages into the metal wastebasket.

"Got a match?" I said.

Of course Bogart had a match. He used it to light a cigarette and then dropped it into the wastebasket. One of the loose pages caught fire, and then the others started to burn.

When the smoke started curling up out of the wastebasket, Mike stopped cursing and said, "You two are crazy. Mr. Orsini will kill you for that."

"No, he won't," I said. "He'll just add it to the list of things he hates me for. He hasn't really lost anything by it, not anything that was really his to begin with." I looked at Bogart. "Are you ready to go?"

"Sure. Do you think it's safe?"

The fire was already almost out, the notebooks already nicely charred.

"It's safe," I said.

"Untie me," Mike said.

"Not a chance."

"I gotta take a leak."

"I'll leave a note downstairs for Leo. He'll untie you when he gets here."

"That'll be an hour or two."

"You can hold it," I said.

The rain had stopped by the time Bogart and I got back to the Garden of Allah. I felt as if some of the grime had been washed out of the air and I could breathe more easily. The sky was reddening in the east. The sun would be up soon, and the streets would fill up with cars and pedestrians, and things would go on pretty much as they always did. Charlie O. would be angry for a while, but he hated me already. I didn't expect any reprisals. What I wanted to do was finish my dream about Rita Hayworth.

"Want to come in for a cup of coffee?" Bogart said as he was getting out of the car.

I thought about the coffee he'd made for me earlier.

"No thanks," I said.

"I don't blame you." Bogart gave me a confident, self-mocking grin. "You forgot to leave that note for Leo, didn't you?"

"Darn," I said.

Bogart grinned again.

"I'll see you around, kid," he said.

He turned and walked away. With his raincoat and hat on, he looked just as he had at the end of *Casablanca* when he and Claude Raines had walked away from the camera. I wondered what had happened to Rick and Louis Renault after that night, whether they'd really had that beautiful friendship.

Probably not, I thought, and I drove my new, slightly damaged, Packard down the rain-washed street.